CROSSOVER SPY II

First Edition

Published by The Nazca Plains Corporation
Las Vegas, Nevada
2012

ISBN: 978-1-61098-290-0
E-book: 978-1-61098-291-7

Published by

The Nazca Plains Corporation ®
4640 Paradise Rd, Suite 141
Las Vegas NV 89109-8000

PUBLISHER'S NOTE
Crossover Spy II is a work of fiction created wholly by Buck Roberts's imagination. All characters are fictional and any resemblance to any persons living or deceased is purely by accident. No portion of this book reflects any real person or events.

Cover Photos, Konrad Bak and Matthew Carroll
Art Director, Blake Stephens

In Memory of Barton Wimble

CROSSOVER SPY II

First Edition

Buck Roberts

CONTENTS

CONTENTS CONTINUED...

PROLOGUE

In the 200 year old Vladimir Prison, 100 miles northwest of Moscow, Igor Petrov and Uri Koslov share a small cell. Petrov, a former soviet scientist, conspired with triple agent Koslov and others to engage in the illegal arms trade. An American agent, Cliff Bradshaw, after being schooled in the art of gay sex, was dispatched by Homeland Security to Moscow to help bring down the illegal arms network. Bradshaw, a former SEAL, was trained to pass for gay so as to infiltrate the secret organization through Igor Petrol, who was a closeted homosexual. Cliff submitted himself to Igor's depraved sexual acts to gain his confidence and unearth the secret cell which operated under the radar in Russia.

Igor and Uri were assigned to the same cell in this maximum security prison which houses mostly political radicals and dangerous criminals. They were placed in the same cell for their own safety. Vladimir Prison is a dangerous place to do time.

Igor, an S and M top, has enjoyed the pleasures in humiliating the many young men unfortunate enough to have gotten caught in his web. Now the tables have turned and Igor finds himself the slave of Uri who got his training in dominance from experts in the KGB of the former Soviet Union.

"You've enjoyed your many years of prestige and privilege being a much praised Russian scientist, Igor. There were many young men who fell before your spell and submitted to your aberrant pleasures. Now we will see how the shoe fits on the other foot," said Uri. "You will now learn to be obedient to me and do exactly what I tell you for you are now my slave. Cross me and you will get in touch with what suffering can really be like!"

"What are you talking about, Uri! You know I've always been a dominant top. I can't possibly function in the way that you demand."

"You will learn soon enough, Igor. Since we have to share this cell together, I intend to be the recipient of the favors you've demanded of your legions of butt boys. Taking his big cock out of his pants, Uri grabs Igor by the hair and forces him to his knees. "Open your mouth, whore, and suck my cock!"

The 46 year old Russian scientist, long a dignified member of the establishment, thrusts his aristocratic nose into Uri's pubic hair as he swallows down Uri's giant prick. Uri, a roughhewn, former soldier, packs a solidly muscular body into his boxy frame. Grabbing the back of Igor's head, Uri plows the open-mouthed scientist, hitting the back of his throat unmercifully before spewing a powerful orgasm down his gullet. "Ah yes, Igor, when I'm not fucking you up the ass, I shall enjoy penetrating your obviously talented mouth."

Igor turns out to be quite the opposite of his former self and submits to all of Uri's demands. "You know, Igor, as much as I enjoy your favors, I don't intend to spend long years in this godforsaken prison. We need to figure a way out of here now or the incentive to escape will elude us. We need a way to make a little money so we can bribe a couple of guards who will aid in our escape."

"How do you propose we do that, Uri? Working in the bakery hardly gives us an opportunity to make any money on the side. Are you thinking we can deal in drugs?"

"That's not the only means to an end, Igor. No, we need to sell your favors for whatever we can get so we'll have something with which to negotiate with the guards who are greedy enough to be compromised."

"Surely you can't be serious. I'm too old to be passed around for cigarettes or other contraband.

There are younger, more desirable men out there than me."

"That's the beauty of this scheme, Igor. No one will be on the look-out for you or suspect you of selling your body for lucre. But you know you have learned to be a good fuck and a hell of a cocksucker. So we can use your talents to our advantage."

"What about you, Uri, when I'm servicing all takers, what will you do to advance our cause?!"

"Well obviously I'll set up your liaisons and collect the booty. With your earnings I'll have something with which to tempt the guards. I've identified who will be most susceptible to our offers. You only have to open your mouth and spread your legs. I'll have to do the heavy lifting. You'll need to spend some time in the gym first to tighten up your tits and that soft butt."

"If you can really line up guys horny enough to take me on, then I guess I'm willing to do my part. I just think it's an insane scheme, destined for failure."

Uri forces Igor to get in shape. Igor takes to exercise with a vengeance even when he's in their cell. In short order, he bulks up into a very tasty piece indeed. Uri has no trouble in lining up sex starved inmates willing to barter to get their rocks off. Their war chest keeps rising until they are in a position to seek out the guards with whom they can forge a deal to exit the prison.

The guards also proved useful in contacting outside assistance in conceiving a way to foil strict security measures that have withstood the test of time. The truck that delivers all the required ingredients for the bakery makes weekly visits to the prison and had become much a part of the routine. Uri's comrades on the outside managed to divert the usual delivery truck and replace it with their own which had a significant modification. Bribing the drivers presented no problem for they planned to flee as well, having been generously compensated for their betrayal.

The substitute truck has a hidden compartment in the back that would only just conceal two men. When the emptied delivery boxes were returned to the truck, the compartment virtually disappeared, making detection almost impossible during inspection.

Uri and Igor flee the prison, ditch the truck, and are removed by a hijacked helicopter to a landing strip where a private jet awaits to whisk them away to a remote dacha in Zvenigorod. Considerably enriched by their former dealings in the illegal arms trade, Uri and Igor have the wherewithal to resume activities in concert with the Russian mafia and pose a new threat to the US and the rest of the world.

CHAPTER 1

Cliff Bradshaw, who was so instrumental in bringing Igor and the illegal arms network down, is no longer a full time special operative for Homeland Security and is now engaged in a private security business with his lover, Brad Ames. Brad was a SEAL instructor, who because of his bi-sexuality, was enlisted by the Director of Homeland Security, Jason Stone, to train Cliff in how to function as a gay man so as to entice the gay Russian scientist, Igor Petrov, into a relationship that would expose the illegal network of mercenaries. The plan was successful in more ways than one in as much as Brad and Cliff fell in love during the training exercise and are now a couple.

Word of Igor and Uri's escape and their subsequent reentry into the lucrative illegal arms network reached the head of Homeland Security, Jason Stone. It became imperative again that they be stopped. Jason felt compelled to ask Cliff to step out of semi-retirement to return to duty. Since Cliff was involved both with Uri, when he was acting as an American agent, and Igor, when he was pretending to be responsive to Igor's depravities, Jason felt he'd be the ideal operative to send to Moscow to seek them out and destroy their activities once and for all.

When Jason sent Cliff on his original mission, he didn't concern himself with the enormity of the task he put before Cliff in performing as a gay man. Upon completion of his assignment, Cliff took vengeance out on Jason by forcing him to experience all the carnal acts he was required to perform with Igor and others. Jason, also an apt pupil, is now an avowed bi-sexual, enjoying the favors of both women (except for his celibate wife) and men.

While Jason apologizes yet again for asking Cliff to assume the role of a gay man on the make, he none-the-less dispatches him to Moscow to uncover the whereabouts of Igor and Uri so as to stop this new and even more dangerous network of illegal arms dealers from endangering world peace.

Cliff, fluent in Russian, returns to Moscow and assumes the role of a Russian construction manager working in Moscow under the assumed name of Anatoly Nevesky. He returns to the gay club where he met Igor Petrov and reconnects with club members, unaware of events surrounding Igor's disappearance. Coming up with a plausible excuse for his absence, no one suspects the fate of either Uri or Igor since their activities were hushed up by Russian authorities.

His former lay in the club, Vasily Borodin, who still carries the torch for Cliff, gives him a tip which helps him begin tracking down Igor and Uri. Vasily hopes by helping Cliff that he can maneuver him into bed for another session of hot sex. Cliff continues to be a magnet for the attentions of other men, being a 6'-1", blonde, blue-eyed, ruggedly handsome stud. Vasily puts Cliff on to looking up Alexi Volkov, who was caretaker at the dacha to which Cliff escaped from his Russian prison before being airlifted home. Cliff will follow this lead, not knowing where it will take him.

In his effort to get in touch with Alexi, Cliff learns that Alexi is not at the dacha but in Moscow at the lavish apartment of his employer, the industrialist Grigory Vasiliev, who is away on a business trip. Before Cliff was airlifted from the grounds of the dacha, Alexi had exacted a price for his help in facilitating Cliff's escape. Cliff was devoured by Alexi in the dacha's mud room while awaiting his plane to freedom. Alexi was obviously aware of Cliff's status as an American operative assigned to Moscow and was willing to take on the attendant risks in aiding a fugitive.

"Hello, Alexi?" This is Cliff Bradshaw, your overnight guest at the dacha in Zvenigorod with my friends Eric Sidorov and Eric Holtz."

"Why yes, Cliff, I certainly remember you. How could I forget! Where are you calling from?"

"Well actually I'm here in Moscow and am anxious to meet with you to talk over — old times."

"That would be delightful, Cliff. Our brief encounter left me wanting more. Let me tell you how to get to the apartment that my employer keeps here in Moscow. He's not due back until — next week!"

Cliff negotiates his way through Moscow streets to find the luxury apartment building and finds himself knocking on the door of the penthouse. "Ah, Cliff, you are a welcome sight! Hope you had no trouble finding this building with my rough directions. Come in!" He wraps Cliff in a big bear hug. "I've been awaiting your arrival with great anticipation. Our last encounter was ever so brief."

"Thanks, Alexi, good seeing you too. You look amazing! I owe you a lot for helping me, along with Eric and Viktor, to leave Russia when it was critical. I want to thank you again."

"You showed your appreciation is spades last time, Cliff. Now I'd like to enjoy a reprise of that memorable fuck you tossed me in the dacha's mud room." Alexi truly does look amazing. Given that his job running his employer's household doesn't occupy his full time, he has plenty of time to work out in the employer's well-appointed gym. Alexi pulls Cliff over to an enormous white leather Italian modern sofa. Wasting no time, Alexi slips off Cliff's shoes and socks followed by his slacks and undershorts. Cliff is left with only his button down, oxford dress shirt and T-shirt on.

"Man, Alexi, you are one horny dude! I thought maybe you'd offer me a drink first. You must think I'm an easy mark," Cliff said as Alexi is removing his own clothes.

"I've no doubt you're selective, Cliff, and so am I. That's why I'm going for what I want for I have no doubt that you came here for reasons other than to renew our acquaintance. Am I right? Before we get to that, I want to get into your pants for a full helping of the treasures to be had there." Cliff's traitorous dick is already responding. Alexi takes hold of Cliff's stiff cock, raising it up so he can feast on the ball sac below. Sucking each orb, Alexi then swallows both, enjoying an appetizer before the main feast.

"Oh, Alexi, that, that feels — fantastic. Being away from home, I've been doing without. Oh yeah, eat my balls!"

"Your balls are a treat, Cliff, but now I feel like filling my mouth with some SEAL cock. Popping Cliff's balls out of his mouth, Alexi goes down on Cliff's jumping prick in one hungry gulp, using his tongue to great effect, laving the 9" long stiff shaft. "Umm good, Cliff, that's grade A meat." Moistening his fingers, Alexi digitally penetrated Cliff's ass to loosen his sphincter for the impending assault. Alexi's practiced fingers make short work of loosening Cliff's tight opening.

"Shit, Alexi, you're making me horny as hell to feel that big cock shoved up my ass, as much as I'm getting off on being finger fucked."

"First, Cliff, I'm going to raise you gorgeous legs so I can jam my tongue up your pussy as far as I can drive it." Raising Cliff's legs from behind the knees, Alexi makes good on his promise and dives into Cliff's gaping opening to eat out his asshole. With his face crushed against the inside of Cliff's ass cheeks, Alexi furiously laps Cliff's pussy.

"Uhhoo, croons Cliff," reduced to a quivering bottom, wanting only to be deeply fucked. "I want you in me, Alexi. Plow my ass! Don't hold back. Take me!!"

"Slipping on a condom, Alexi butts the knob of his cock head at Cliff's hole, savoring the moment that he'll drive his turgid shaft to the hilt. Unable to restrain himself for long, Alexi bucks his ass so as to drive into Cliff's wet cavern forcefully. "You feel so good, Cliff, just like I remember. Umm, I really do get off on American butt. Your hole feels awesome."

"Yes, oh yes, Alexi, screw me. You feel amazing inside me. Don't stop!" Alexi's body slams repeatedly into Cliff's upturned ass, grinding him into the soft leather sofa.

"Aaahhhggg," screams Alexi as he drives his prick down hard into Cliff's hot hole for the last time, lodged deep into his quarry, spewing volleys of cum into Cliff's bowels.

Simultaneously, Cliff gives up his load, his throbbing prick spurting cum all over Alexi's heaving chest. "Hell, Alexi, you've drained me dry and filled me up. Man, I needed that."

"So did I, Cliff, but now it's time you confessed to what your real purpose was in coming here. No doubt you want recompense for sacrificing your favors to a friend who once did you a service."

"Well actually, Alexi, there is something you may be able to help me with. You'll remember when I was here last that I had run into trouble with Russian authorities because of spying I had done on a scientist here in

Moscow. As you will recall, his name was Igor Petrov and he was suspected of involvement in an illegal arms network. Unbeknownst to me, my Russian contact and supposed US agent, Uri Koslov, was actually a triple agent. Of course, thanks to him, I was apprehended and taken to the interrogation facility where I met Viktor Sidorov and Eric Holtz, my interrogators."

"Against all odds, we became friends with the shared agenda of escaping from Russia. With your help, we managed our escape. I returned to the US. Viktor and Eric returned to Bavaria where they run Eric's family's auto parts factory. I know you helped us because you had been Viktor's assistant before Eric and remained loyal to him. Well, to get back to the point of my story, I have been charged with finding Igor and Uri. It was felt by my superiors that with my knowledge of the Russian language and each of these fugitives that I could use my Russian contacts to trace them. All of the above would give me an edge in tracking them down."

"What's the urgency in tracking them down? Surely they don't now represent any threat. You were instrumental in smashing their network of illegal arms dealers."

"That's the thing, Alexi, they are dangerous criminals and do represent a very real threat since they've become involved with the Russian mafia who have the resources to present a severe threat to world peace."

"Hmm, the connection to the Russian mafia, Cliff, is truly disturbing. While I'm no patriot, I do love my country and don't like the rampant corruption that's occurred since the break-up of the old Soviet Union. I've had some suspicions of the involvement of what could be a key player."

"Alexi, I hope you will trust me enough to share that information with me. It could be critical in stemming an even greater threat that this new illegal arms network represents."

"It's not that easy, Cliff. My life and my livelihood could very well be at stake. There's the possibility that I could be mistaken."

"Please, just tell me your suspicions so we can evaluate together what, if anything, needs to be done. This is too heavy a burden for you to handle by yourself. Let me help you sort through it."

"Very well, Cliff, but how did you know to come to me in the first place. What did you suppose I knew to bring you here and let me ravish you only to secure from me the information you needed. Don't suppose I'm foolish enough to imagine you really desire me."

"Of course you're right, Alexi, I was willing to — prostitute — myself to insure that you'd be forthcoming with the vital information I need in tracking down Igor and Uri, as well as their new network. I'm sorry for my deceit."

"To say that I'm sorry would only make me a hypocrite, Cliff, because I savored every minute of your defilement. So perhaps it's I that owe you an apology. But I'd be insincere in making it. I wanted you and took what I wanted, despite my misgivings about a shared interest."

"Let's call it even with our crossed purposes, Alexi, and get on with the task at hand. What are you holding back that might be of importance to me in my investigation?"

"Come, Cliff, down to my room." Sitting together in his room, Alexi opens up. "You see, Cliff, it's — my employer, Grigory Vasiliev. I've long suspected that he is an important figure in the Russian mafia hierarchy. I've closed my eyes to it because I feared losing my job and even my life if it became known that I was aware of the nefarious activities in this household. I've heard him on the telephone referring to Uri and Igor and the need to secure their release from prison by whatever means necessary. What became apparent was that Uri and Igor were significant players in the illegal arms network."

"Are you sure, Alexi, Grigory Vasiliev is a respected member of Russia's wealthy business class. His complicity in such a conspiracy would be stunning."

"Sadly, I really have no doubt. Grigory made one of the planes from his fleet available to pluck Uri and Igor up after they were helicoptered away from the getaway bakery truck. Shortly after their rescue, Uri and Igor disappeared. Initially, they had been flown to Grigory's dacha in Zvenigorod long enough for a change of clothes before being spirited into Moscow to a secret hiding place. But Uri and Igor had their own plans, disappearing into oblivion. It's been reported that they now have set up a parallel organization, competing for the lucrative illegal arms trade. Grigory wants to find them as badly as you do to both punish them for their treachery but also to get rid of them for the threat they've become to his ill-gotten profits."

"Uri and Igor have balls I must say, taking on the Russian mafia. Prison must have made them crazy and even thirstier for riches."

While they were talking in Alexi's room, they had no idea that their whole conversation was being monitored and recorded by two of Grigory's henchmen in a concealed room in the building's basement. Cliff and Alexi finish their conversation before Cliff leaves to meet with his handlers at a safe house. Grigory had become suspicious of Alexi's prying into his business and decided it would be prudent to keep an eye on him.

Cliff, with the lead provided by Alexi, knows that Uri and Igor are probably hiding out somewhere in Moscow. He's in the midst of following up with that and other promising leads that he hopes will lead to their whereabouts when he gets a mysterious call from one of Grigory Vasiliev's associates. He's summoned to return to Vasiliev's apartment for a meeting with the man himself. Cliff becomes alarmed that Alexi may be in trouble and has no choice but to go, despite his fears that he's being set up.

Arriving at the apartment door, it is opened by one of Grigory's muscled associates and he is ushered into the living room where Grigory can be seen standing in front of the apartment's massive fireplace, faced with black carrara marble in the modernist style. Grigory motions Cliff over to the bar and dismisses the associate. Grigory pours them each a glass of vodka on the rocks. "So it's Cliff Bradshaw is it, an agent for the US government operating here in Moscow. It seems we've never met although our paths were bound to cross eventually."

"True enough, Vasiliev, although I don't understand the timing of this interview. What is it that you want?"

"Well, Cliff, it seems you've been meddling in my affairs and could become a nuisance for my business interests. This simply can't be tolerated. It has become known to me that your paramour, Alexi Volkov, has shared with you some privileged information. That was very foolish of him."

"You've been misinformed, Vasiliev. I know nothing of which you speak."

"Please don't insult my intelligence, Cliff. We have your clandestine meeting, here in this apartment with Alexi, on tape. You see I suspected he was nosing around into matters that didn't concern him. Thus the bug in his room. So please, cut the crap!"

"What have you done with Alexi? Surely you don't hold him responsible for my activities in doing my duty to my government."

"He has been disloyal to me, his employer of many years. He deserves what punishment I decide to give him! You, Cliff, are in a position to mitigate his suffering by cooperating with me."

"What is it you expect me to do, Vasiliev?" Your activities are not unknown to Russian authorities. You can't expect to continue your activities unchecked."

"Please don't be naïve, Cliff. There's no one among Russian authorities I can't buy. No, it's Uri and Igor I must concern myself with, making incursions into my business."

"So how does that concern me or Alexi for that matter? We know nothing about Uri or Igor's whereabouts."

"Perhaps not at this moment but you will, Cliff. Your government puts great faith in your abilities in tracking them down. I too have the same trust that you will prevail. I just need to know what you know."

"What makes you think I'd ever share any such information with you, an acknowledged criminal?"

"It's your natural decency, Cliff. Surely you couldn't countenance any harm coming to Alexi. Because I can guarantee to you that his suffering will be profound if you don't supply me with what I want. By the way, under intense questioning, he's admitted to the dalliances he's had with you here and at my dacha. It seems you're a delightful whore, Cliff."

"As a very rich businessman, I've enjoyed the company of high class whores for years, mostly women. But I enjoy men too on occasion. Since my wife died, I've preferred playing the field. Alexi was most complimentary on the joys to be had getting it on with a former SEAL who is now an American agent."

"Alexi spends too much time alone and is too easily impressed," said Cliff fearing that Vasiliev was about to make a move on him.

"You're much too modest, Cliff. You are indeed a hump and please call me Grigory because we're about to become intimate. We should therefore be on a first name basis, don't you think?"

Cliff surveys Grigory from head to foot, seeing him for the first time. What he sees is a Sean Connery look alike, aging but still virile, and a potent force. He realizes he's toast and isn't altogether sure he objects. "So you're saying Grigory, that I put out or Alexi will be the recipient of your wrath?"

"Well put, Cliff, and true. Shall we repair to my bedroom where we can be more comfortable? It's not that often that I'm taken with a man sufficiently that I'd forgo the pleasures to be had with my many female playmates."

Arriving at a grand pair of double doors with mirrors set into its panels, they enter into the lavish Master suite. An oversized bed is featured on the long wall with a headboard of white leather upholstered panels extending up to the high ceiling. The bed sits on oceans of plush gray carpeting and is covered with a billowy white silk coverlet with crimson colored sheets peeking out from beneath.

"Show time, Cliff! Strip off your clothes and slip on those white silk shorts I've laid out for you on the loveseat at the foot of the bed. I shall return momentarily."

Returning from his dressing room wearing only a white terrycloth bathrobe, Grigory views Cliff standing at the sliding glass doors overlooking a private terrace and the magnificent view of the Moskva River beyond. The silk see-through shorts Cliff wears features his round butt cheeks in the most alluring manner. Grigory moves up behind Cliff and unfastening his robe, rubs his cock against Cliff's ass crack. Grigory's cock springs up to its full 10".

"You are all that Alexi described, Cliff." Reaching under Cliff's arms, Grigory tweaks Cliff's nipples, causing Cliff's cock to tent the front of the shorts. Releasing him, Grigory moves Cliff around to face him. Now kissing Cliff, Grigory moves to deepen the kiss into erotic territory, probing the depths of his mouth with his tongue.

"Umm, you taste good; Cliff, but now I want your beautiful mouth on my cock." Grasping Cliff's shoulders, Grigory maneuvers him down on his knees. "Suck it, Cliff. Show me what you can do."

Looking up at Grigory, Cliff laps at his piss slit, teasing the stiff cock to its ripe fullness. "Oh yeah, Cliff, open up your mouth and make love to the head of my dick." Cliff obliges, taking in only the big knob and twirling his tongue around its purple head. "Ooo, murmurs Grigory, yeah that's it. Now take down the rest!" Opening his mouth wider, Cliff goes down on the throbbing 10" boner until he reaches the pubes, laving the shaft all the way along the trip.

"Christ, Cliff, I'm going to lose my load down your throat with the talent you've shown in sucking my dick but it's your ass I'll have. No one else has done justice to those shorts as you have. I want into your crack." Grigory helps Cliff up and draws him over to the white leather loveseat at the foot of the bed. Sitting down, Grigory flips open his robe to expose his towering prick. He takes a condom and some lube out of the pocket of the robe and prepares himself.

Reaching around the back of Cliff's silky, see-through shorts, Grigory rips them open. "Come, Cliff, step up on the sofa and straddle me. Before you lower your gorgeous ass on my dick, let me lube up your hole." Stuffing a finger into Cliff's ass, Grigory lubes his hole using first one, then two and finally three fingers until Cliff's sphincter is loosened up enough to accommodate the enormous, thick headed cock.

Slowly lowering himself down with Grigory's assistance grasping his buns, Cliff impales himself on Grigory's dick. "Oh yes, Cliff, just sit on my lap until you get used to being stretched open before I fuck you in earnest." Grigory enjoys the brief interlude to reacquaint himself with Cliff's mouth while kneading his buns which have bubbled appealingly around the thick shaft.

"Alexi was too restrained in his praise of you, Cliff. I've rarely enjoyed a fuck this much and we haven't even begun to get serious. Ok, time to cut to the chase, babe. Raise and lower your butt cheeks in concert with my hands. I want to savor fucking you for as long as possible."

With his hands braced on Grigory's shoulders, Cliff slowly levers himself up and down while he works the muscles in his ass to massage Grigory's engorged phallus. Ripping off what's left of Cliff's shorts, Grigory begins working his dick with one hand while pinching his tits with the other. "Aaahhhoo, Cliff, you've got the sweetest asshole. I'm going to begin jerking you off now and I want you to increase your speed, sitting on my cock." Cliff rides Grigory's prick intensely, his ass cheeks being pounded into great round orbs with each grinding descent.

As Cliff's joy spot is repeatedly battered with Grigory's great cock head, his prick erupts into a shattering orgasm, coating Grigory's massive muscled torso. Cliff's orgasm starts a chain reaction when his ass muscles contract around Grigory's giant dick, pushing the Mafioso over the edge with a powerful orgasm exploding up Cliff's stuffed pussy.

"Uugggaaa," cried Grigory as his balls were emptying of their seed in wave after wave of ecstasy. The condom was no match for the ferocity of the semen blasts and was in tatters as Grigory's heavy cream oozed out of Cliff's ravaged asshole. Wrapping his arms around his conquest, Grigory's chest heaved in testament to a transcendent experience. "Wow, oh wow," murmured a spent Grigory.

After each had showered and dressed, they found themselves back in the living room sitting at the bar, each sipping a vodka. "So what happens now, Grigory? I think you owe me and Alexi some special consideration."

"You've certainly caught my attention, Cliff, I'll admit that. Against my better judgment, I'm going to cut you some slack. You will join Alexi in his confinement down in the basement. You will find the suite down there quite comfortable for your brief stay. What I require is that you and Alexi put your heads together and pool your considerable resources in a way that will most likely lead to the whereabouts of Uri and Igor."

"My business has gone international and I'll not have these upstarts create hurdles for me becoming number one. I do hope I won't have to subject Alexi to any — 'indignities' — if you refuse to cooperate fully with me. I could just eliminate both of you now but I'm willing to give this approach a try but my patience will not last long."

"Very well, Grigory, I'll meet with Alexi and see where pooling our knowledge and resources can lead us."

"You will remain here as my 'guests' until I'm satisfied that you are cooperating with me fully. Is that understood?"

"Understood. Please take me to Alexi so I can begin the process." Pushing a button at the bar, Grigory summons his associate. Upon entering the room, the associate is charged with taking Cliff to the basement confinement suite. A second associate accompanies them for the trip to the bowels of the building.

As Cliff enters the suite, the associates close and lock the heavy steel door behind him. "Alexi, are you all right? What have they done to you?!"

"They've only roughed me up slightly, Cliff. It's always good to see you but not under these circumstances."

"It is as it is, Alexi. Have you thought of any avenue of escape from this place?"

"One slim chance, Cliff. As it happens, I'm friendly with Grigory's chauffeur, Lev, with whom I've had occasion to share — 'intimacies'. He has a wife in Reutov but sees her rarely so we manage an ongoing — 'relationship'. There's a lot of down time in each of our jobs, you see. Grigory has no clue. We've been very discreet. He's not really in a position to help us directly but he may be able to contact someone who can."

"As you know, I spend a great deal of my time at Grigory's dacha in Zvenigorod especially during summers. He has a college age son, Ivan, who spent his summers there as well as holidays. He came out while in his freshman year and became sexually active. Summers were a bit lonely for him until he discovered that he had a kindred spirit in me. We'd fucked like rabbits summers and holidays for years. We enjoyed a mutually agreeable association that suited us. He also had a boyfriend at his college who was a year ahead of him and is now in graduate school in the US at Duke University. Ivan plans to follow him this year to study at the same university."

"The thing is he's due home this evening, after graduating college, for a rare visit to the Moscow apartment. He hates the opulence of it which he finds embarrassing. Lev has been charged with bringing meals to me in this elegant dungeon. I can ask him to approach Ivan about our predicament. I feel sure Ivan can figure a way to help us. He's a very clever boy and doesn't approve of his father. While Ivan has had his suspicions about his father's business, he really has no idea his father is a criminal."

That evening Ivan is allowed into the basement lock-up by Lev who is on duty for his 4 hour shift, guarding the prisoners. "Oh, Ivan, it's so good to see you!" said Alexi, embracing him. Ivan is a 5'-10" tall, athletic looking man who has light brown hair and brown eyes. His square jaw and angular Slavic features gives him a uniquely Russian look.

"And you too, Alexi. What has caused father to treat you in this way!"

"First, let me introduce you to Cliff Bradshaw, an old friend, who has also incurred your father's wrath."

"Good to meet you Cliff although I wish it could be under different circumstances," Ivan said, obviously impressed with Cliff's studly appearance. So tell me you two, what the hell is going on?!"

"Ivan, I'm sorry but I have to be the one to tell you that your father is not what he purports to be. In fact, he's — he's a criminal — and a dangerous man. While I've had my suspicions in the past, it's only recently that I became aware that your father is — well a kingpin in the Russian mafia."

"My, god, I've never really allowed myself to accept the fact but I guess I've really known for a long time that something like this had to be true. But the mafia! I didn't think it was anything that evil."

"That's why Cliff is here in Russia. He's an American agent charged with destroying an illegal arms network operating out of Russia and suspected of being controlled by the mafia. He was instrumental in bringing down an earlier network, not involved with the mafia, in a previous visit to our country. Two of the conspirators were then put in Vladimir Prison but have only now just escaped. Cliff, knowing these men and their habits, has returned to Moscow to track them down. Through a tip from a friend, he was directed to me. This friend somehow knew that I might have some knowledge that connected the escaped prisoners, Uri Koslov and Igor Petrov, to your father. When Cliff came to me, I was just in the midst of working out how your father was involved."

"What did you conclude, Alexi? What could my father possibly have had to do with such men? They are traitors to their country!"

"Sadly, Ivan, your father, in his role as a mafia kingpin, has gotten heavily involved in the international, illegal arms trade. It was he who conspired to free Uri and Igor from prison so he could use their expertise in expanding his business. But they've had a falling out and it seems Uri and Igor have set up a competing organization, robbing your father of some of the huge profits he's been accustomed to getting."

"How is it that you and Cliff were found out and have become embroiled in this fiasco?"

"As I've just told you, Cliff came here to me to see if I had some pertinent information he could use in finding Uri and Igor. Things finally gelled in my mind, things I've managed to ignore. I decided to confide in Cliff and took him to my room and laid it all out for him. Unfortunately, your father, a very perceptive man, could see that my suspicions had been aroused and thought I bore watching. He had a bug put in my room. When he listened to the tape of our conversation, he interrogated me and got me to admit everything including an — indiscretion — with Cliff on the living room sofa. He summoned Cliff back here and threatened to wreak serious harm on me if Cliff and I didn't pool our resources to find Uri and Igor for him. I have no doubt your father will have them killed, once they are found. And in all likelihood, Cliff and I will be taken care of in the bargain. That's why we must get out of here immediately. Can you help us, Ivan?!"

"Yes of course, Alexi. There's no way I'd standby and see you come to any harm. We need to move quickly while Lev is the one on duty here in the basement. Lev has agreed to help me get you out of here. But we must do it in such a way as to protect Lev from reprisals from father. It has to look like you were rescued by outside forces."

"How do you propose to do that, Ivan? Your father is no fool," said Alexi.

"You see, father owns this building and put in this make-shift lock-up facility for reasons unknown to me but now in view of what you've told me, I'm beginning to see the light. He won't be surprised that it could be breached. He thinks that since no one is supposed to know it's here that he didn't have to go overboard with security measures. We can use that lapse to our advantage."

"What is it you're proposing to do?" Asked Cliff.

"First, Lev will be back shortly to let me out of here. That's when you'll be able to leave with me through the rear service entrance to the back of this building where I've parked my car. We'll then go to my apartment not far from here in the Patriarchy Ponds neighborhood. Father is aware that I maintain my own apartment in Moscow but has never been there. He thinks my place is here in that opulent palace he has upstairs, but I digress. Once I've secured you in my apartment, I'll return here and place a drug in Lev's coffee that he takes with his dinner. When he's to be relieved on his shift, they'll find him unconscious and they'll discover the break-in that allowed you to escape."

"The plan, in its simplicity, has a good chance of being successful," said Cliff. "But we must hurry if we're to pull it off." Just then the door to the suite can be heard opening as Lev enters.

Ivan explains the plan to Lev who reluctantly agrees to participate in the scheme. They leave immediately so that there will be plenty of time for Ivan to return, drug Lev, fake a brake-in and return upstairs to his father's apartment where his arrival is expected.

Entering into the upscale neighborhood of Patriarchy Ponds, Ivan parks his car in the garage beneath his apartment house and spirits his guest upstairs to his 2 bedroom, 2 bath luxury apartment. Ivan hasn't been tainted by his father's blood money. When his mother died of cancer at a young age, Ivan inherited her fortune, making him independent ever since. She was the only daughter of a rich industrialist who never approved of her husband. When her father died in a plane crash, she inherited everything and willed it all to her only child.

Concerned for Alexi's physical condition, Ivan took him immediately to the guest suite where he had him take a shower, put balms on his wounds and tucked him into bed, insisting that he take a strong sleeping pill mostly to insure a sound, healing sleep but also to give Ivan free reign in seducing Cliff. Returning to the living room Ivan, wearing an enigmatic smile, invited Cliff into the master bedroom suite where he could shower in the master bath after his ordeal at the hands of his father.

"Wrapped in a towel, Cliff returned to the bedroom to find Ivan stretched out, buck naked, on the king bed which had been turned down to showcase Ivan's magnificent physique, displayed to advantage on the ice blue, silk sheets. On his stomach with a pillow under his groin, Ivan's face was buried in a billowy blue, silk pillow. Raising his head and turning towards Cliff, he slowly spread his legs and said, "There's little time to waste, Cliff. I want you in me now!"

Being a semi-pro in tennis, Ivan's ass mounds were a sight to behold, great muscled orbs with flattering hollows on each side. His broad shouldered back tapered down to meet the bun feast, followed by long sculpted legs. Propped up on a pillow, his buns beckoned to Cliff and weren't to be denied. Dropping the towel and crawling up on the bed, Cliff pounced on the parted ass crack, savagely pulling the cheeks apart and diving in to mount an all-out assault. Cliff's tongue tore through the pink pucker and pressed up the love chute, laving furiously. "Uuooohhh!!" squealed Ivan," driven to the first plateau of an intense high.

Pulling his tongue out of the well moistened hole, Cliff kneaded the hard butt muscles while running the head of his prick up and down in Ivan's parted crack, teasing the pink portal and dripping precum into the pouting pucker. Snapping up a condom and some lube Ivan had laid out on the sheets, Cliff lubed the loosening hole and finger fucked the writhing Ivan. "There's no time to be gentle with you, Ivan, so I'm going to screw you like a long lost lover."

"I've never been stud fucked before, Cliff. Show me the difference form the college boys I've had to make do with!"

With that lusty invocation, Cliff felt free to slake his lust with a no holds barred invasion of Ivan's hot rectum. Raising his own powerful SEAL ass in the air, Cliff swung his hips in a series of punishing arcs to pile drive his 9" cock deep into the silken shaft repeatedly. A mewling Ivan cried out, "Oh, yes, yes, yes!!!"

Smashing his groin into the flattened globes, Cliff fired volleys of searing cum into his newest conquest, now reduced to a fawning sycophant. Falling on Ivan's back, Cliff sucks on his earlobe and whispers, "You are a truly great piece of ass, Ivan. Now turn over so when I take you again on your back we'll see how much ball juice you've got stored up in your nuts."

After a short reprise, the plowing of Ivan's pussy continues unabated until Ivan's cock erupts in concert with Cliff's second explosive orgasm, showering geysers of cum all over himself. "Ok, kid, you need to shower and get the fuck out of here!" Pushing him out of bed, Cliff slaps him roughly on the ass and directs him to shower before leaving.

After showering quickly, Ivan returns to the bedroom. "That was so awesome! It felt as if it were my first time!" Embracing Cliff, he kisses him on the mouth while Cliff cups his ass-cheeks. Then Ivan hurries away to return to his father's lock-up and carry out the remainder of the plan.

CHAPTER 2

A violent explosion rips through a large warehouse in the Istra district of Moscow. Remarkably, no one was killed when the explosives ripped through the building in the dead of the night. Unbeknownst to authorities, what was destroyed was a huge weapons cash. The warehouse belongs to Vasiliev Enterprises International. Learning of the disaster, Grigory Vasiliev is incensed, suspecting who the perpetrators are. Two men were seen loitering around the warehouse shortly before the blast by one of his guards. Their description, although inconclusive, suggested that these men were indeed Uri Koslov and Igor Petrov.

Cliff made irregular visits to the gay club where he reconnected with Vasily Borodin with whom he'd had a brief affair as part of a scheme to move on to the targeted affair with Igor Petrov, who was at that time a club member too. Vasily was a good source of information because he had a wide circle of friends who weren't loath to share secrets. A bit tipsy this particular night, he enjoyed a sexual banter with Cliff. But when the conversation turned to Cliff's encounter with Grigory Vasiliev, Vasily revealed that he works at a sports club as the in house doctor. The club, called "Global Fitness", is owned by Grigory Vasiliev.

Cliff, feeling that more is to be learned from Vasily, buys him another drink to see what other revelations might be forthcoming. Vasily, well into his cups, admits he has a special relationship with Grigory. It seems Vasily is one of Grigory's favorite butt boys when he's in the mood for man on man sex. His compensation as sports doctor pays well so Vasily doesn't mind accommodating Grigory. Quite suddenly Vasily allows as how Grigory has been extremely agitated because two former associates, who have become rivals, blew up a property of his, costing him a great deal of money.

"Are you aware, Vasily, that Uri Koslov and Igor Petrov are the former associates to whom he referred?"

"No! The thought hadn't occurred to me but now — something else I've heard makes sense. It seems that Uri and Igor were known to be somewhere in Moscow recently and were working on some questionable project with Grigory. They had reason to mistrust Grigory who they concluded was about to cut them out once he secured what information he wanted from them. They even feared for their lives and went into hiding. So you see it must have been Uri and Igor who retaliated against Grigory."

"Yes, I'm sure you're right, Vasily. Have you any idea where they may be in hiding because I think they really are in danger."

"It can't be that you think that Grigory would actually consider harming them?!"

"The possibility exists, Vasily. You have to be aware that Vasiliev is a dangerous man and not to be trifled with. Please tell me if you have some idea where I might find Uri and Igor. It could well save their lives."

"I've only just learned where they are hiding from a doctor friend of mine who tended to them after they were injured in an accident which now I assume was connected with the warehouse explosion. My god!"

After securing the general whereabouts where the two fugitives were hiding, Cliff took a rain check on Vasily's invitation to have another go in the sack. Accompanying him outside, he thanked him, gave him a hug and put him in a taxi to insure that he got home safely. Armed with this information, Cliff was confident that he would be able to locate Uri and Igor even without the specific address.

Cliff meets with the US operatives with whom he's coordinating his investigation. In reviewing the status of progress so far, it becomes clear that Cliff will require assistance if he's to be successful in bringing down this new illegal arms ring. The US operatives have been in constant contact with their counterparts in the Russian military. They agree that Cliff needs help and propose that they contact Viktor Sidorov, a former KGB officer and special interrogator, now retired and living in Germany.

Viktor originally had contact with Cliff in his former role as special interrogator in Moscow for spies and dissidents. Under unusual circumstances, Viktor and Cliff, adversaries in a secret Moscow prison, bonded and became friends. Viktor and Eric Holtz, his lover as well as assistant, escaped along with Cliff. Cliff was airlifted home from a dacha in Zvenigorod while Viktor and Eric escaped to Bavaria where they run the Holtz family auto parts business. As it happens the dacha belonged to one Grigory Vasiliev, but it was his caretaker, Alexi Volkov, Viktor Sidorov's former assistant who made their escape possible.

The Russian military put aside Viktor and Eric's transgressions when their liaison with Cliff proved instrumental in bringing down the illegal arms network in which Igor had been a key player. The Russian military felt they could prevail upon Viktor in this present crisis to help them overcome this serious threat, given that they were generous in cutting him slack with his unauthorized departure.

Cliff is prevailed upon to call Viktor at his home in Regensburg, Germany to persuade him to return to Moscow to aid in the destruction of this renewed threat posed by the rekindled illegal arms network. Hesitant at first, Viktor quickly sees that it's in his best interests to respond to the call of duty. As a friend of Cliff's, he also wants to support him in his pursuit of these criminals. The question of where Viktor was to stay, while in Moscow, was solved after Cliff consulted with Ivan. Ivan had the keys to his boyfriend Maxim's flat in the Poklonnaya Hill section of Moscow. Maxim wasn't expected home any time soon. Viktor agreed to come on immediately, leaving his partner, Eric Holtz, behind.

Ivan met Viktor's plane and drove him to Maxim's apartment and helped him settle in. Ivan was beside himself with lust, unprepared for such a super stud. When Viktor removed his jacket, his shirt couldn't hide the massive, muscled shoulders and arms nor the pillowed pecs tapering to an impossibly thin waist that gave way to rising muscle mounds forming his butt cheeks, supported by a pair of magnificent long legs, straining to be contained in his trousers. Since Viktor was anxious to accompany Ivan back to his own apartment to meet with Cliff and plan strategy, there was no time to 'linger'. Ivan vowed that he'd make time soon.

Arriving back at Ivan's apartment, Cliff and Viktor greet each other in a great bear hug with Alexi joining in, happy to see his former superior. "God, am I glad to see you, Viktor," said Cliff.

"Likewise, Cliff, only I wish it weren't because of urgent business. You've got to bring me up to speed. There's no time to waste." Cliff quickly brings him up to date on the progress of the investigation. Viktor thanks Cliff for safeguarding his friend Alexi. They agree that it is imperative that they apprehend Uri and Igor before Vasiliev's men find them. It's decided that Cliff and Viktor would best handle capturing them alone so that the fewer people knowing their whereabouts the better. They agree that the safest place for the fugitives, when they find them, would be to hide them out in Ivan's apartment. His father would never look for them there. Ivan would then vacate, temporarily, and stay in Maxim's apartment.

With the tip from Vasily Borodin's doctor friend, they found it remarkably easy to gain access to Uri and Igor's room at the Sretenskaya Hotel. Viktor's former contacts prove crucial in circumventing hotel security. Impressing upon Uri and Igor the danger they are in, they reluctantly agree to accompany Viktor and Cliff to Ivan's apartment. Viktor explained that if they can supply useful information in bringing down Grigory Vasiliev's mafia operation that he could almost guarantee that they wouldn't have to return to prison and would be given safe passage out of the country to pursue their lives elsewhere. The time they'd already served in prison would be considered their just punishment.

Feeling vengeful and double crossed by the greedy Grigory, Uri and Igor divulge much critical information under Viktor's intense questioning, his expertise garnered when a Russian interrogator for the military. What also becomes apparent is that Grigory is planning to take his operation overseas to the US and pose an international threat. Viktor and Cliff now must pursue uncovering the links to a network in the US, probably with the American mafia. The task just got bigger and more complex.

Calling it a day, Viktor returns to Maxim's apartment. He expects Ivan to temporarily move in while Uri and Igor remain in his apartment. After showering, he wraps himself in a towel to stretch out on the living room sofa to take a much needed nap. Sometime later, still half asleep, he hears the door to the apartment being unlocked and someone entering. He supposes it's Ivan arriving earlier than expected. Turning towards the person entering the living room, Viktor sees a young man who, while not Ivan, could be his twin.

"Who the hell are you? What are you doing in my apartment," said the young man.

"You must be Ivan's friend, Maxim Bondar. What in the world are you doing home? You're supposed to be in North Carolina studying law at Duke University."

"Well yes but I decided to come home for an extended weekend during a break in my classes. Did Ivan let you in here?"

Viktor explains the situation to Maxim's satisfaction and they decide to relax and break open a bottle of vodka to relieve the tension. Three rounds later, Ivan shows up wondering at the scene he encounters. "What the fuck, Maxim! What are you doing home entertaining a half-naked man?"

"Ivan, babe, come here and give me a big kiss," said Maxim slurring his words slightly.

"You're shit face, Maxim, and Viktor is not far behind!"

"Relax, babe, time for you to catch up. I was just about to slip into something more comfortable. I feel way overdressed beside this — what shall I say — Greek God?"

Viktor pours Ivan a stiff vodka while Maxim retreats to the bedroom to change. "It was a pleasant surprise when Maxim walked in on me napping. I thought it was you at first, you look so much alike."

"Yes, they used to call us the twins at school. Little did they know that the twins were banging each other big time at every opportunity? We'll join up again soon when I go to Durham, North Carolina to secure an off campus residence for when I attend Duke."

Maxim comes back into the living room wearing only a filmy pair of white silk shorts, displaying a truly spectacular set of buns. Downing his vodka, Ivan passes Maxim, giving him a lecherous smile, and retreats into the bedroom, returning quickly wearing a matching outfit. "Voila, the twins!!" said Ivan. Viktor was overwhelmed with what only could only be described as a magnificent bun feast.

"Come, Viktor, get up. Maxim and I would entertain our guest in the way that comes most naturally to us." Ivan helps Viktor up from the sofa while removing his towel, exposing his rising cock. "Go on Maxim, sit up on the back of the sofa and spread your legs. That's it sweet cheeks. Let's have a look at that package you're hiding, babe." Kneeling on the sofa, Ivan rips open the front of Maxim's shorts, exposing his hard shaft. "What do you think, Viktor, does my baby have a nice cock or what?"

"His cock is nice but so is your ass, Ivan." Viktor rips open Ivan's shorts, revealing a bubble butt that demands every attention.

"When I first met you, Viktor, I knew the clock was ticking, marking the time when your prick would find my asshole. Well, the time has come and I can't wait. Yours is the biggest dick I've ever seen and I want every inch stuffed up my rectum. While I worship my lover's cock, worship my pussy."

Ivan wraps his lips around Maxims throbbing cock head, sucking, laving and inserting his tongue into the piss slit. Maxim throws his head back and moans. Falling to his knees, Viktor inserts his tongue into Ivan's hole to begin feasting on and suctioning his orifice. Hungry for Maxim's cock, Ivan swallowed down the whole member, stretching his mouth wide open while Maxim's dick pressed the back of his throat.

Viktor slapped Ivan's glutes with his massive dick, stopping only to slip on a condom. Moistening his fingers with saliva, he worked Ivan's hole until he had 4 fingers reaming his crevice. Squeezing the great globes of creamy flesh, Viktor brought his big purple knob to the gateway and shoved in until his pubes met the widening crack. "Uuhhoo," uttered Ivan, knowing he'd just been impaled by the biggest cock he's ever seen and loving it.

Viktor grabs hold of Ivan's hips to steady him before getting into an increasingly fast rhythm, plowing and gyrating into his bent over slave. Viktor's prick spirals around in the silken shaft, stretching it to the limit and driving Ivan to work his lover's prick in a frenzy of lust. Knowing Maxim is close, Ivan shoves a finger up his ass to target the prostate, resulting in Maxim's massive orgasm pulsing down Ivan's throat in wave after wave.

Viktor's rock hard rod is flat out jackhammering the inflamed nates until with one final buck of his hips; he's lodged deep into Ivan's love canal when he unleashes ropes of molten cum into the hot hole. "Oh, Viktor, Yes, yes, you've branded me with your hot poker!!"

Not to be denied equal treatment, Maxim switches places with Ivan and knowingly sucks him off from years of experience they've had with each other. Viktor rips off what remains of Maxim's silk shorts and proceeds to give him the same pounding he gave Ivan. The twins' assholes would be tingling for days, trying to return to their former smaller diameters.

Maxim and Ivan retire to the master bedroom while Viktor retreats to the guest room. The following morning, Viktor leaves early to hook up with Cliff to develop their next strategies. Cliff and Viktor think they have put together enough evidence from what they'd learned from Uri and Igor to squash Grigory's operations in Russia and Europe but there's still the question of how to uncover the American conspiracy.

Returning to Maxim's apartment that afternoon, Viktor rounds a corner coming up on the apartment house just as Maxim can be seen stepping into a black Maybach limousine which swiftly whisks him away, but not before Viktor memorizes the license plate number. Somehow the scene struck him as odd and left him unsettled. Going upstairs, he found that Ivan was out. He decided to call one of his contacts in the Russian military to find out who the outrageously expensive car belonged to. A short time later, he received a call back from his contact who identified the car as belonging to one Grigory Vasiliev. Thanking his contact, Viktor wondered what in hell was going on. Acting on a hunch, he decided to track down who paid for the lease on Maxim's apartment. He wasn't surprised to find that it was, indeed, leased to Grigory Vasiliev. He decided he'd have to confront Maxim.

When Maxim returned a couple of hours later, Viktor seized the opportunity to demand an explanation from him before Ivan returned. Disintegrating into tears, Maxim blurted out the whole long standing relationship that he had with Ivan's father. The truth was that Maxim didn't come from a wealthy family as had been thought. In actuality Maxim's father worked in a weapons factory in Izhevsk that Grigory Vasiliev owns. In visits to the factory, Grigory became aware of the young son of one of the foremen in his factory. The foreman's son, who occasionally worked in the factory, looked remarkably like Grigory's own son. The boy, Maxim Bondar, was a gifted student and Grigory decided to sponsor him. Maxim's widowed father was delighted. There were just a couple of strings attached, of which the father was unaware.

After Grigory brought Maxim to Moscow, he enrolled him in his son Ivan's school, "The Institute of State and Law". The apartment in the exclusive Poklonnaya Hill neighborhood was secured. Once all of this had been accomplished, Grigory explained to Maxim some conditions attached to his largess. First, he was to keep tabs on Grigory's son Ivan and insinuate himself into his company so as to be fully aware of most of his activities.

These activities were to be faithfully reported to Grigory. Secondly, Maxim was to make his body available to Grigory for assignations arranged several times a week when Grigory was in town. The boy had once been found in a compromising situation in the locker room with his tennis coach in Izhevsk. Maxim was given a pass but the coach was held responsible and was fired. Learning of this, Grigory decided to exploit the boy's potential as a butt boy.

What Maxim failed to report to Grigory was that his relationship with Ivan had become one of great intimacy. They'd become lovers and were insatiable in their carnal appetites for each other. Maxim managed both relationships but not without a sense of shame, feeling like a whore, knowing that Ivan would be devastated if he knew of Maxim's duplicity. But Maxim felt he had no choice. He never wanted to return to Izhevsk and wanted to join the professional class, maybe become a lawyer. He admitted to feeling almost relieved that Viktor found him out.

"So what happens now, Viktor? Are you going to expose me and ruin my life?"

"No, Maxim. I have something else entirely in mind. Ivan mentioned to me that you sometimes courier envelopes to the US for his father in the course of your traveling to and from Duke University. What's involved in your doing that?"

"It's no big deal. He has business competitors who would interfere with his business ventures in the US if they could intercept correspondence with his associates there. I merely act as a secure conduit when I travel back and forth so Grigory can avoid lapses in security."

"To whom do you give these envelopes, Maxim? When and where do you connect with these individuals?"

"As I said, I now go to Duke University in Durham, North Carolina. Ivan will soon be going to college there too. A business associate of Grigory's usually calls when I'm there and I meet him at the 'Blue Coffee Cafe' in Durham. I slip the envelope to him under the table or in the men's room."

"What is the name of this individual, Maxim?"

"Let me think. It was — Vince! Yes Vince — Angotti."

"Are you sure? Did you happen to notice the car he was driving?"

"That's the name he gave me. On one visit I happened to notice that he was driving a rental car from Hertz so I assumed he wasn't from around that area. What's this all about, Viktor? Has Grigory involved me in something of questionable legality? I'm studying to be a lawyer you know. This could be a disaster for me."

"Well I'm afraid he's done just that, Maxim, but I think I can offer you an avenue out of your predicament. You must cooperate in bringing Grigory Vasiliev down for he's engaged in serious criminal activity."

"Oh my god, what are you telling me?! It's not possible. Grigory is an important industrialist."

"While that is certainly true, it is not the full story. He is a Russian mafia kingpin and a very dangerous man." Viktor goes on to explain about the investigation into the illegal arms trade and the suspected connection to the American mafia.

Reeling from these revelations, Maxim asks Viktor what he meant by suggesting that there was a way to extricate himself from any culpability he may have in this conspiracy.

"It's as I said, Maxim, you can help us knock out Grigory's operation from starting up in the US."

"How am I to do that and not be found out? If Grigory is as dangerous as you say he is, he will surely see through me before I can accomplish what you want."

"What you'll need to do, Maxim, is carry on as if nothing's happened. We will keep you under surveillance when you return to Durham and be in constant contact with you so we can monitor your next meeting with this Vince Angotti, if that's his real name, and put a tail on him. There's little more you will be required to do for us and no one need ever know that you were ever involved with this whole affair."

"But what about my obvious connection to Grigory? He's paying for this apartment and my ongoing education. This is bound to get out if he's exposed."

"We can doctor the paper trail so that it will show that Ivan Vasiliev, through his charitable foundation, has been sponsoring you, not his father. The only potential hitch is that I must persuade Ivan to go along with us on that point."

"How can I ask Ivan to do this when he finds out about my betrayal? He'll despise me for what I am!"

"Don't be so hard on yourself, Maxim; circumstances conspired against you to put you in these circumstances. You couldn't help being born poor and susceptible to this sort of exploitive arrangement. I think I can convince Ivan that you were as much used and betrayed as he was. Look, Maxim, why don't you go take a nap. I can see that these revelations have drained you. When you wake up, take a long bath. I guarantee you'll feel better."

"You're right, Viktor, I feel wiped out." He goes off to the bedroom and closes the door.

Seizing the opportunity, Viktor phones Cliff to apprize him of the conversation he'd just had with Maxim. Viktor suggests to Cliff how to break the news to Ivan in such a way that Ivan would empathize with the dilemma that Maxim found himself in. It was important that the status quo be preserved between Ivan and Maxim so that Viktor and Cliff could make use of Maxim's relationship with Grigory to uncover the American connection in the sale of illegal arms.

Convincing Ivan that Maxim was an innocent victim of Grigory proved to be no obstacle. Ivan could easily believe that his father was capable of such an unconscionable act. His reaction was one of gratitude towards Viktor and Cliff for wanting to protect Maxim from permanent damage to his life and future career.

"I want to go to him now, Cliff!"

"Let me take you there, Ivan. You're too upset to drive."

Back at Maxim's apartment, Viktor said, "Cliff, Ivan, I didn't expect you to come right over."

"Ivan wanted to come right over to assure Maxim that this was not something he'd allow to come between them."

"Maxim is taking a therapeutic bath, Ivan, at my suggestion. He's been carrying around the guilt of this duplicitous relationship with you and your father, making him anxious and depressed."

"It may be that I have an antidote for what ails him. I'll administer it to him straight away." Ivan opens the bedroom door, enters and closes the door behind him.

"Ivan seems to have the situation well in hand, Viktor, so let's plan where we go from here. Maxim's connection to Grigory provides us with a golden opportunity to find out what contacts Grigory has in the US."

"Yes, Cliff, just when we're winding down our operation here, thanks to Uri and Igor, we can now go to the US and nail those bastards on your side of the pond."

Deep in the throes of planning the logistics to the US phase of their investigation, they failed to hear the door of the bedroom open. Suddenly appearing in front of them were the towel clad 'twins'. "So how are you doing," asks Cliff? "Did you kiss and make up?"

"You could say that, Cliff, although we took matters a little beyond the kissing stage."

"Glad to hear it because we need you boys to help us out."

"That's what Maxim and I have been discussing, the fact that you both have needs that aren't being addressed, what with both of you being separated from your lovers. We'd like to do something about that. We're also grateful that you've saved our relationship from falling apart. But you're both overdressed for what we have in mind." They begin stripping Viktor and Cliff.

"Guys! This really isn't necessary. You must already be exhausted after that 'bath' you took together."

"Well no, Cliff, the 'bath' only whet our appetites to service an ex SEAL and an ex KGB officer, two studs who never need to do without for very long."

Cliff and Viktor are both naked, slouched back in the sofa with their legs spread apart. Despite their protestations, their pricks, at full attention, tell a different story. "Our playmates in college are not nearly so well endowed," said Maxim. "It's time we graduated to large and extra-large."

Dropping their towels and falling to their knees, Ivan buries his face in Viktor's crotch, inhaling the musk scent before sucking into his mouth one of Viktor's big balls. Working in concert, Maxim does the same to Cliff. Showing immense talent for such young men, they have managed to get both sets of balls of their quarries into their mouths. Slowly sucking the ripe fruit, savoring the flavor, they pop the balls out of their mouths only briefly to moisten their fingers before attacking the sphincter muscles. Holding hands, Cliff and Viktor are cooing with contentment.

"We suspect your big cocks' taste as good as your hanging fruit so here goes. We want to deep throat some stud meat." In one deft plunge, the twins have swallowed every inch of the immense pricks. Withdrawing, then laving, they suckle the boners lovingly almost to the point of no return.

"You're spoiling us for lesser mortals, guys. Now we have new standards against which to measure everyone else. But first, Maxim and I must experience other attributes which you both possess in abundance.

When it comes to bubble butts, no one in our experience comes close to either one of you. Lift up those combat ready legs, guys, it's booty call time." Cliff and Viktor lock their hands behind their knees and raise their legs up and back, framing their faces. Two sets of great hanging love mounds were presented for the taking.

"Show us what you can do, boys. We don't lift our legs for amateurs," Viktor challenges.

Overcome with the surfeit of riches being offered, Ivan and Maxim dive in to partake of the feast. The muscled young tongues rapidly lap their way in to the love channels, opening up the gateways to heaven. "Oh, yeah, croons Cliff, eat us out!!"

Producing condoms and lube from a drawer in the coffee table, the boys sheath and lube up while stuffing three fingers up the gaping holes and twisting their digits for maximum expansion. Cliff and Viktor are ready.

"Ready, Maxim? Let's go for it!!" Falling on Cliff and Viktor, they aim their dicks deftly at the half dollar sized holes and plunge in deep to their groins, smacking hard against butt cheeks.

"Aaaooohh!!" squeal Cliff and Viktor in unison. "Come on you horny little fucks, start cranking" said Cliff. Youth has its advantages as Ivan and Maxim bump and grind their hips to savagely pound the stud pussies. Pulling out completely and then jamming their dicks back in, the boys are lost in a delirium of frenzied fucking, pounding Viktor and Cliff to higher and higher peaks of rapture.

A chain reaction of exploding dicks began when the boys arched their backs and stuffed their pricks deep up the quaking assholes, emptying their balls of hot cum. Next Cliff and Viktor's cocks rocketed into the air multiple jets of spraying cum. Falling on their conquests, the boys lapped cum off the men's chests and proceeded to explore the men's mouths with their cum as lubricant.

After extricating themselves from this mélange, they showered in pairs and wound up back on the sofa. "Well that should hold you boys for a while, at least until we meet back up in the US. We have some friends we'd like you to meet. You'll find that you have a lot in common," said Cliff. Cliff and Viktor then outline the plan for all of them to go to the US and carry out the plan to prevent Grigory from connecting up with the American mafia to engage in the illegal sale of arms.

CHAPTER 3

Back in Washington, Cliff is called into a meeting at the Russell Senate Office Building with his boss, Jason Stone, and Lane Cockerall, a Senator from North Carolina who is on the "Committee on Homeland Security and Government Affairs". Entering the Senator's office, Lane Cockerall said, "Good to see you again Jason. Please come in."

"Thank you, Senator. I'd like you to meet my associate, Cliff Bradshaw."

"How do you do, Cliff. Please have a seat."

"After reading your report, Jason, on the prospect of an illegal arms network operating out of Russia coming to our shores, I was obviously greatly concerned." Lane, although a Democrat, is from an old patrician Southern family. He's 39 years old, 6'-2" tall, athletic with prematurely gray hair which only adds to his good looks. In his free time, he's an avid tennis player and belongs to the exclusive Chevy Chase Club, thus accounting for his unusual physical fitness.

"Yes, Senator, that's why I've asked Cliff to join us so you could meet him and be assured of the progress we've made in Moscow to stem the flow of arms to radical Muslims in the Middle East."

"Please, Cliff, proceed to bring me up to date on the situation in Moscow." Cliff goes on to explain that the source of the arms flow has been identified and neutralized, at least temporarily.

"The larger issue for us now is to insure that this illegal weapons network doesn't find its way into the United States. We have become aware, through our assets in Moscow, that that is very much the plan that these criminals have embarked upon. We're in the process of trying to get a handle on it."

"You can count on any support I'm able to offer you, Cliff. This threat must not only be contained but eliminated."

"Yes, Senator, Jason and I are aggressively pursuing accomplishing just that." After the usual niceties, Jason and Cliff depart to validate their assertion that they have the problem under control.

————————————————

Eric Holtz and Viktor Sidorov are in Washington, DC having meetings with local vendors that they use in supplying their auto parts factory located in Fletcher, North Carolina. They're headed home to their condo in Bethesda, MD, which they bought from Cliff Bradshaw after Cliff moved into the Washington townhouse of his lover, Brad Ames.

"Maxim Bondar should be landing at the Raleigh-Durham airport in North Carolina tomorrow afternoon, Eric. This will give you time to arrive in Durham ahead of him and check into the Ritz-Carlton. While I don't like the idea of you being the one we're relying on to be Maxim's contact, you have the best cover. Since you're there regularly on legitimate business connected to our auto parts factory in Fletcher, no one should question why you're in the area."

"It makes the most sense for me to do this, Viktor. From what you've told me of your experience with Maxim in Moscow, I'm looking forward to connecting up with him. When he visits me at the Ritz, I'll give him the GPS device for his car and the tiny tracking unit he can conceal somewhere on his person. Since he is carrying an envelope given to him by Grigory Vasiliev, he should be hearing from this Vince Angotti person soon."

The next afternoon, Eric had only just gotten settled into his room at the Ritz when he received the call from Maxim who was on his way from the airport to his dormitory at Duke University. They agree to meet at the Ritz that night so Eric could hand over the tracking devices and work out ways in which to communicate with each other. Several Homeland Security agents would be monitoring the devices given to Maxim from area hotels.

Eric left word at the reception desk that he was expecting a guest so that when Maxim arrived he was allowed to go right up. When Eric opened the door to allow Maxim to enter, he was unprepared for the vision in front of him. It seemed Viktor was holding out on him. "Come — come in, Maxim, I'm Eric Holtz."

"How do you do, Eric, I'm pleased to meet you! Viktor has told me so many wonderful things about you and your experiences with the Russian military." Maxim was immediately taken with the stunning German who possessed the qualities so often associated with that race. He's a 5'-10" tall, blonde, blue-eyed, square jawed stud with an aggressive edge.

"You must be tired from your long flight, Maxim. It's a bit early for dinner. Perhaps you'd like to take a refreshing swim in the hotel's pool. We can conduct our business after dinner."

"That would suit me just fine but I didn't bring anything to wear for the pool."

"No problem, I have an extra bathing suit and sandals that will fit you and there's an extra terrycloth robe in the bathroom." Eric tosses Maxim a racing Speedo bathing suit from his suitcase. "Here, try these on."

Maxim unabashedly peels off his clothes, tossing them on the bed. Eric can hardly believe his eyes. Obviously being a semi-pro at tennis had done wonders in honing Maxim's body to perfection. Pulling up the skimpy Speedo over his ample basket and perky ass cheeks, Maxim declares, "These fit perfectly, like a second skin."

With his back to Maxim to conceal his swollen cock, Eric strips and slips on his Speedo. "Help yourself to the robe in the bathroom, Maxim." Eric slips on his robe that was thrown over the back of the desk chair and covers up evidence of his attraction to Maxim.

They take the elevator to the pool, encountering no one on the elevator or at the pool. "There's a big wedding reception going on in the ballroom with the guests occupying most of the hotel for a few days. Guess that's why we've lucked out to have the pool to ourselves."

"Suits me," said Maxim as he slips off the robe and sandals to approach the diving board. Poised on the diving board, he flexes his legs to achieve the necessary spring, Maxim thrusts out his ass, barely contained in the Speedo, to bound up and into the water.

Eric is next to dive in and when coming up to the surface of the water, he discovers that Maxim's Speedo was forced off of him and floated in the water. Maxim, in the meantime, was swimming to the end of the pool. Eric pulled the suit over his head and let it hang from his neck. He then followed Maxim and swam to the end of the pool.

With a sly smirk, Eric comes upon Maxim and said, "They don't allow nude swimming in this pool especially if one possesses such a provocative set of buns."

"What, ooh, I didn't feel them come off!" It's good everyone is elsewhere getting sloshed at that wedding. Umm, it feels good not being confined. It's only fair that I be in like company." said Maxim as he plunged under the water and removed Eric's suit. He how wears Eric's suit around his neck.

"What a frisky water nymph I find myself in the company of." Eric wraps his arms around Maxim and kisses him on the mouth. Eric can feel Maxim's prick bounce up to meet his hard dick. Sliding his hands down Maxim's back, Eric cups his ass cheeks before slipping a finger up his asshole.

"Ohh, Eric, seems like you'd like a little hors d'oeuvre before dinner!"

"Actually, Maxim, I'm in the mood for a considerable helping." Eric has two fingers deep into Maxim's ass. Rubbing cocks, Eric and Maxim are fully exploring each other's mouths when they hear footsteps and laughter approaching. They quickly submerge themselves to slip back into their bathing suits. Rising back up to the surface, they are in time to see the tuxedo clad young man and his begowned companion topple drunkenly into the water.

"Time to make a hasty retreat, Maxim." Climbing out of the water, they put on their robes and sandals, amidst giggles emanating from the pool, to retreat back upstairs to Eric's room. Entering the room, Eric closes the door and coming up behind Maxim; he removes his robe and pulls his suit down to his knees, allowing the young man's high cheeks to bounce up to their complete fullness. Kneading the ripe cheeks, Eric said, "Those drunks didn't come a minute too soon for I was about to lose it and ravish you in the pool, whatever the consequences."

"What's stopping you now, Eric? I like my men to take what they want. Am I wrong or are you a bit of a booty hound?"

"Get over to that ottoman and get on your knees, butt boy. I want to get a taste of what Grigory Vasiliev pays so dearly for."

As Eric drops into the chair, Maxim kneels with his back to Eric on the ottoman in front of him, resting his chest on his thighs and clasping his knees with his hands. Maxim's ass is raised up in the air on a level with Eric's face. "I never imagined my room at the Ritz was to have such a wonderful view," said Eric, before nose diving and lapping into Maxim's crack. Lacing his hands through Maxim's Speedo which had settled just below his knees, Eric yanked them off and moved Maxim's legs as far apart as the ottoman allowed. With the greater access, he was now permitted; Eric clamped his hands on the love mounds and twirled his busy tongue into the accommodating hole.

"Uhhooo! Grigory never eats my pussy; he thinks that would make him gay. Man you're good, Eric! Uhhoo! Eating out Viktor regularly would make anyone an expert. He's a booty hound's wet dream."

Eric's loudly slurping tongue comes to a sudden halt. "Your succulent pussy takes my breath away, Maxim. But now I want to shove my prick deep inside you." Scooting back into the chair, he slips on a condom and demands, "Move back on to the chair and place your feet on the arms so you're straddling me. Yes, like that. Now lower yourself down onto my cock." With his knees raised high, Maxim lowered himself down on Eric's cock until he was sitting on his lap.

Pulling Maxim against him. Eric nuzzles and kisses him while tweaking a tit with one hand and playing with his balls with the other. "What a delightful whore you are, Maxim. Grigory's cock has trained your asshole to service an invading prick with the utmost care."

"Let's see what kind of a load I can coax out of your dick, Eric." Now levering himself up and down, Maxim demonstrates further how his ass muscles can massage a boner.

With each penetration up into Maxim's plunging asshole, Eric's prick is engorged to the breaking point. "Uhh, uhh, aaaahhhh!!!" shouted Eric as Maxim grinds his sumptuous butt into Eric's groin, teasing out an explosive orgasm.

"Oohhaaa!!" cries Maxim, as his dancing prick rockets jets of cum into the air, showering them both with a creamy coating.

Slumped in each other's arms, gasping for breath, they nuzzle their heads together, thoroughly sated. Eric's prick remains firmly lodged up his guest's young ass. It isn't long before Maxim works his hips, thrusting his body forward and back to demand another pounding from Eric.

"You insatiable cock hound, Maxim. Yes, shake that booty. I want to pop your pussy again."

Slapping his buns against Eric's groin, Maxim's hot hole caresses the German stud meat to a new plateau of pleasure. Gripping Maxim's pulsating cock, Eric works the cum from their first orgasm to lubricate his butt boy's cock, jerking it and drawing out still another seismic eruption of cum. As Maxim's prick spews great long ropes of cum, his ass muscles clench around Eric's iron hard cock, causing a second massive detonation.

"Yes indeed, Maxim, Grigory need have no complaints about getting his money's worth. You certainly can deliver."

"Oh I rather think I do a bit better when it's by choice. You Aryan German types are hard to resist, especially if you've had a military background. You and Viktor make a winning combination. I'd like to take you on together sometime."

"You'll have to come to our country retreat in West Virginia some weekend. We have neighbors you'll enjoy meeting as well. You won't lack for good 'company'. But now we must get down to business. While you shower, I'll order up our dinner and we can have our meal while I outline what the plan is to nail Vince Angotti. We don't want you involved except to deliver Grigory's envelope. We'll take it from there. We're only providing you with these tracking devices so that we'll be prepared if something unforeseen should develop. While there's little chance of that happening, we want to cover all bases."

"It's much appreciated, Eric. I'm only glad to be trusted to be part of this and I'm grateful for the chance to clear my name in connection with this illegal arms network. To think that Grigory held me in such little regard that he'd place me in such a vulnerable position."

"Men like Grigory care nothing for relationships or loyalties to anyone. It's always only about money and there's never enough to satisfy their limitless greed. Just a lesson in life, Maxim. Grigory is a prime example of the kind of person you don't want to become."

Transferring the envelope to Vince Angotti proved to be no problem. Maxim slipped the envelope to Angotti at the "Blue Coffee Cafe" and the Homeland Security agents put Angotti, now known to be a Mafioso, under surveillance. Little did they know where the trail would ultimately lead.

Maxim returned to college life, trying to put out of his mind the difficulties that could still lie ahead. He had no illusions that he was out of the woods with problems associated with his connection to Grigory Vasiliev. Playing tennis provided a good distraction from his ongoing concerns. His favorite tennis partner was Grayson Hillstead. Gray came from landed gentry in Charleston, South Carolina. He's 5'-11" tall, possessing chiseled features, sandy colored hair and green eyes. While he's a Phi Beta Kappa student, he's also extremely friendly and outgoing. With all those qualities, he's also a knockout and very popular among both the male and female students.

What isn't generally known is that he's gay. He and Maxim have shared sexual favors given that their significant others are far away and generally unavailable. Maxim and Gray enjoy challenging each other to very competitive tennis matches. Besides enjoying the matches, they like their arrangement which allows the winner to take all. They defined this to mean that the winner could demand whatever sexual favors that suited him. Being so equally matched, they each have had to put out regularly, requiring each to be very versatile.

"It won't be long, Gray, before my lover Ivan will be arriving from Moscow to look for an off campus apartment in Durham. Before he comes I thought I'd take advantage of a friend's invitation to spend the weekend at his cabin in West Virginia. It seems his cabin is one of three in what could be described as a private compound consisting of 3 houses surrounded by many wooded acres. I thought you might like to join me. If so I'll contact my friend, Eric Holtz, to see if his invitation still stands and whether I may bring a friend."

"Oh I'd very much like a weekend away in the country. Would it be too forward of me to ask if my lover could join us? You see he's — in government and he's — well — closeted. The country retreat, as you've described it, would give us a welcome opportunity to be together where no one will know us. When he's at his Washington apartment, I can't see him at all. It's only when he goes out to his home in Chevy Chase that I can pass under the radar screen and spend a little time with him. He bought the house in Chevy Chase for that reason. It's a large Georgian colonial overlooking Rock Creek Park. He belongs to the Chevy Chase Country Club so we can sometimes play a round of golf together."

"Is he the one you meet at the Hollow Rock Racquet and Swim Club here in Durham?"

"Yes, I joined so we'd have an opportunity to meet in what is both a public while at the same time private place. He's been a long standing member because his main home is here in Durham, a great pile of a place he inherited when his parents died in an avalanche in Switzerland."

When Maxim phoned Eric to ask if he could bring additional guests for the weekend visit, Eric was genuinely delighted. Arrangements were made and the agreed upon weekend arrived at last. Maxim and Gray drove up for the rendezvous on a Friday morning. Gray's lover was due to arrive in the early evening, in time for dinner.

Arriving at the retreat late in the morning, Maxim and Gray are greeted at the front door by Eric Holtz. "Welcome to West Virginia, guys, come in, come in! I'd like you to meet my lover, Viktor Sidorov." Both Eric and Viktor all but salivated at the delectable eye candy at their disposal.

"Great meeting you guys!" said Viktor. Glad you could make it. Come along, we're just about to have some lunch out on the deck."

"Terrific! As it happens, we're starved," Maxim declares. "All this country air must have stimulated our appetites." *The sight of you guys certainly has stimulated ours, Viktor reflects.*

"Let me show you to your rooms," said Viktor. "While you're freshening up, we'll set lunch out on the deck. Don't be long!"

Maxim and Gray emerge from the house to join their hosts on the deck. "You guys look like you're dressed for the beaches at Cannes. Although tank tops and thongs are appropriate anywhere if you have the requisite body type." Viktor remarks.

"We thought we'd avail ourselves of your Jacuzzi after lunch if that's ok," said Maxim.

"Make yourselves at home. We expect you to take every advantage of what our household has to offer," said Eric with a sly grin.

The lobster salad was a gourmet delight and everyone indulged liberally in glasses of wine. Maxim and Gray began to relax and enjoy the country. They removed their tank tops to drink in the warming sun and to work on their tans. The sight of their ripped torsos only further inflamed their hosts. "We'd better take ourselves down to the Jacuzzi under the deck before we become as red as the lobsters we ate for lunch," remarked Gray.

"You bet, babe, I'm ready for the refreshing waterworks. How about you, Eric and Viktor, care to join us?" asks Maxim.

"We'll be down shortly after we clean up the lunch dishes," said Eric. The hosts watch as Maxim and Gray retreat to the lower deck, revealing two sets of voluptuous buns enhanced by being deliciously presented in miniscule, brightly colored thongs. From the kitchen, Eric and Viktor could hear all the playful horsing around wafting up from the lower deck and Jacuzzi. "Our guests cut a fine figure in those thongs," Eric.

"Indeed, but I think they're a bit over dressed for what I have in mind for them. Don't you think?"

"You have a point, my love. After all, we'd be lacking as hosts if we didn't see to their needs."

"Perhaps you'd like to have a go with Maxim, Viktor. I've already sampled the goods and can attest to his generous endowments."

"Gray is also a tasty little piece who requires more attention than he's getting from his absentee lover. I'm sure you'll be only too happy to fill the void," said Viktor.

Dressed in light cotton bathrobes, Eric and Viktor descend to the Jacuzzi deck and take up positions on two chaise lounges. Eric brought a tray containing a bottle of wine and four stemmed glasses. Viktor carried a tray with a bowl of fresh fruit. Setting down their trays on a coffee table, they shake off their robes and throw them over their chaises before stretching out, naked, with the beginnings of hard-ons.

"Hey guys, come join us in the Jacuzzi! It's time to chill out!"

"No, boys, come on out of the Jacuzzi and join us on the deck for some wine and fruit." said Eric.

"Great idea, we could use a break before our skin gets all pruney," Maxim allows.

Climbing out of the Jacuzzi, the boys flop on the chaises at Eric and Viktor's feet. "Wow, guys, that's the best way to tan avoiding getting any tan lines," Gray observes.

Eric hands everyone a glass of wine. While they all sip the wine, Eric said, "It's good to have some new blood visit our little hide-away. We don't want to run the risk of getting out of touch."

"Looking the way you do, guys, there's no danger of that. You must be hit on all the time even if they didn't get to see you like this — with your pants off," said Maxim.

"Do you like what you see, Maxim? Maybe it's time you ate some fruit." Viktor picks up a bunch of grapes and wraps them around his rising cock. Maxim didn't need to be asked twice. He dove into Viktor crotch and ate grapes and sucked on Viktor balls alternately.

Eric prepared the same fruit offering with the same result. Gray was buried in Eric's crotch, laving his balls and popping grapes into his mouth.

"Enough with the grapes boys, how about taking our bananas into your mouths," Viktor said. "Show us what you college boys can do with ripe fruit."

 Viktor and Eric acknowledged the boys' talents with deep moans while writhing in the chaises. "Ok, boys, you've proved your point with your mouths, now let's see what you can do with your pretty little asses." Drawing the boys up so they were now laying on top of them, Viktor and Eric began exploring their mouths while kneading their ripe butt cheeks. Pulling their thongs down to their knees, the hosts dicks were pressed up against the boys' hard cocks.

"We're glad to see that college life hasn't made you boys stand-offish." Pulling condoms and lube from their robes, the guys sheath up and begin lubricating the loosening assholes. "Ok, boys, flip yourselves over so you're lying with your backs on our chests and throw your legs over the arms of the chaises." Viktor and Eric slip their cocks past the pulsating puckers to be deeply lodged into their guests love canals.

"Ooohhh," cried the boys. "You really fill us up," remarks Gray.

They continue sipping wine while the boys' assholes open wider and massage the invading pricks. "You boys are far from being young virgins," observes Eric. "You spread your legs like old pros."

"You guys inspire us to new sluttish heights!" Maxim declares.

Viktor and Eric fondle the boys' balls and torture their tits before beginning to jack them off. All the while, they methodically plow their young asses and bump their big pricks against the boys tender joy spots. The boys writhe in ecstasy, loving to receive a deep screwing from career booty hounds.

Lifting the boys' legs off the arms of the chaises, Viktor and Eric raise their legs high and jackhammer their dicks into the grasping pussies before unleashing tumultuous orgasms into their young guests. True to their claims of heightened sexuality, the young sluts clenched their assholes, suctioning additional spurts from their captors and produced their own prodigious streams of steamy cum in a drenching spray. Still impaled on their hosts, the boys slowly come down from their high as the guys allow their legs to drop back over the arms of the chaises.

"Lunch was good but dessert was better," suggests Maxim.

"You got that right, Maxim," Gray agrees.

"Well boys, it's been fun but you'd better cleanup and get yourselves put back together before Gray's lover arrives. Also, we've all been invited to our neighbors Cliff and Brad's cabin for dinner. We don't want to present our hosts with two alcoholic college boys looking like major tarts."

"You guys! You're just trying to lavish us with compliments so you can bang us whenever you want," said Gray.

"You're on to us, Gray. Now get those pretty little, well fucked fannies in the house and into the shower," demands Viktor.

Early evening arrived and Gray Hillstead's lover drove up the driveway to Eric and Viktor cabin. Stepping out of his Cadillac SRX, the tall, handsome, distinguished looking gentleman approached the house. Before he could knock on the door, it was opened by Viktor Sidorov. "Hello, may I help you?" asked Viktor, a bit nonplussed as to whom this fine looking gray haired gentleman was when he was expecting Gray's lover.

"Ah — my name is Lane Cockerall and I believe — I've been invited to your home to join your other guests, Maxim Bondar and Grayson Hillstead?"

"Why yes of course, Lane, forgive me — you weren't — exactly what I was expecting."

"Please don't be embarrassed, I know I'm a bit older than Gray but well — you know — it works for us."

"Indeed! Please come in. We'll settle you in your room with Gray before whisking you away to our neighbors for dinner. This is my lover Eric Holtz. Eric please meet Lane Cockerall." They shake hands. "Hope you don't mind stepping out when you've only just arrived."

"No, not at all. Gray and I don't get much chance to socialize, living apart as we do."

Viktor shows Lane to his room and leaves him to spend a few minutes alone with his lover, announcing that they must leave within the hour. Back out in the living room, he exclaims to Eric, "Man, can you believe Gray's lover! Wow, tall dark and handsome would only be for openers. Drop dead gorgeous would be closer to the mark. What a stunning couple they make!"

"Calm down Viktor, surely you're not lusting after Lane already when you only just finished banging his lover a few hours ago."

"Are you telling me you don't share my infatuation, Eric? Pleeease, I know you better than that. You want him too."

"Cool it, lover, he only just got here. Give it a rest. He and Gray have some catching up to do without intrusive come-ons from their horny hosts."

"Well of course you're right, as always, Eric. But he's not leaving this house before we get a little taste of Gray's honey."

Maxim, Gray and Lane emerge from their rooms in brightly colored T-shirts and coordinating shorts, all looking good enough to eat. "Hope our dress code is ok with our hosts," Maxim inquires.

"No problem, guys. They're very informal here in the country. Less is more is a good watchword when it come to a dress code out here."

Arriving at Cliff and Brad's, they are greeted at the door by Brad. Introductions are made all around. Cliff has yet to leave the kitchen since he has been the designated cook for tonight's dinner with help from their caretaker, Hector Rios.

Sailing into the living room with a tray of hot hors d'oeuvres, Cliff almost drops the tray when he notices Lane Cockerall standing in his living room. "Lane! Lane Cockerall what — what the hell!"

"My god, Cliff! This — is your house?! I never imagined I'd meet anyone I know way out here in the sticks."

"You're the last one I expected to be among our guests tonight, Lane. Please introduce me to your — companions."

"Well this is Maxim Bondar and this is Gray Hillstead — my — my lover."

"It's my great pleasure to meet you both! Come let's dive into these hors d'oeuvres before they get too cold. Give Brad your drink orders. Hector has everything under control in the kitchen and we'll eat in just under an hour."

It's a lively group, enjoying their cocktails and tasty appetizers. Everyone mingles well with much gaiety and laughter. Viktor happens to mention the Holsteiner horses he and Eric brought from Germany and board with Hector and his lover, Cole Strong, at the next-door ranch, part of this three house enclave in the West Virginia Mountains.

"You know I've always been an avid horseman," Lane remarks. "Perhaps you'd allow Gray and me to take your horses out for a ride while we're here?"

"You're welcome to ride them, Lane. They love all the exercise we can give them," said Viktor.

Finally Hector rings the dinner gong and serves Cliff's "Noisettes de Chevreuil Saint Hubert", served with a homemade potato salad. A favorite southern dish, "peach ambrosia" was served for dessert. Cognac and Armagnac was served out on the deck after the meal was finished. Cliff found himself in a private corner of the deck with Lane Cockerall.

"You about bowled me over, Lane, when I came upon you in my living room. I had no idea you were a member of the 'club'."

"Same goes for me, Cliff, but you know it might have been fortuitous because you may be able to help me sort through a — personal problem. Being so — well closeted — I've had no — gay friends — with whom I could confide. Sorry, I guess all this wine and cognac has loosened my tongue."

"You know, Lane, I have a great deal of respect for you and what you do as Senator for your constituents. Anything I can do for you would be my pleasure. Let's take a stroll. I'll tell the others that I'm going to show you Viktor and Eric's Holsteiner horses over in their barn."

Strolling on the path over to the barn, Lane opens up, seizing on a rare opportunity to be himself. "You've no doubt surmised that I lead a double life, one as a Washington insider and the other as a closeted gay man with a secret. The honorable Lane Cockerall has a lover 12 years his junior who hasn't even finished law school. My dear friend, Ann Shelby is a divorced Washington hostess and fund raiser who kindly accompanies me to functions where I need to have a woman on my arm. She knows my story and is happy with our arrangement since she has no significant other nor does she plan to marry again. Whenever she requires an escort, I'm happy to be it."

"It's unfortunate that such a charade is still necessary in Washington but it would be foolish to deny that homophobia is alive and well," Cliff responds.

"Being so cautious all the time has a terrible downside since my real private life is so clandestine and — unfulfilling as presently constituted."

"How can I be of any help to you, Lane? Being in public life does rob you of the privacy you could expect as a private citizen."

"It's not so much to do with that as uncomfortable as it is. It's — it's — well my personal life with Gray. I — love him so much and I'm afraid of losing him because of my — hangups," Lane said, his voice breaking.

"Spit it out, Lane, what's the problem. You need to share it with someone before it eats you up."

"The subject is just so hard to talk about. Well ok — it's about what we do — in bed. Gray has been out since he was a teenager and is — very versatile. As opposed to — me."

Arriving at the barn, Cliff slides open the big door and they enter the large space. "Surely you've figured out, Lane, that such a problem isn't unique with you."

"While that's true, I haven't been able to get past it, as much as I've tried to analyze it."

"Maybe that's where you went wrong. A better approach might have been to give sway to your feelings. So tell me, Lane, what is it you can't bring yourself to do?"

"Gray wants to, how shall I say it, — fuck me up the ass! I'm afraid I won't like it and ruin everything so I've put him off and off. This obviously can't go on. Either we're able to satisfy each other fully or we're destined for failure."

"Can I ask you if you — fuck him? Some relationships are a top and bottom combination and many others are more fluid. You just have to find what suits you."

"No, I've never fucked him but I really want to but again I'm afraid that I'll displease him with my inexperience. You see, I came out so late. It wasn't until I became a Senator 4 years ago that I finally came out and had my first experience. I've had very few partners before meeting Gray 2 years ago."

"Yes, I can understand your dilemma, Lane, so what do you propose to do about it?"

"That's where I thought you might be willing to step in — as it were — to help me out."

"Do you mean what I think you mean? That is you want to give up your cherry to me?"

"In a word, yes, Cliff I do. Would I be guilty of wanting to use you so as to disrespect you? For I sincerely hope that we'll become good friends."

"You happen to be a very handsome and desirable man, Lane. Don't think for a minute that there isn't one person in our little compound here in West Virginia who wouldn't like to get into your pants and fuck your ass off."

"What about you, Cliff, do you want me? You're the only man I've met that I could trust with breaking down the barrier that keeps me from complete happiness with Gray."

"Well, not to tell stories out of school but I actually performed a similar function for Eric and Viktor and they are now happily getting it on without barriers. We're all versatile in these three households and we — share the wealth among ourselves."

"Will I ever be so liberated I wonder?"

Pushing Lane against one of the barn's supporting posts; Cliff begins exploring his mouth while he cups his ass with both hands. "Umm you taste good, Senator, what say we take our act up to the hay loft where we can be more comfortable. Hope you're not too inebriated to climb up the ladder."

"No way I'd miss being taken in a hay loft, Cliff." Half way up the ladder, Cliff stops Lane from continuing and pulls down his shorts, exposing two well-toned butt cheeks, showcased in a spanking white jock strap.

"With an ass as pretty as yours, you should never lack for admirers. Let's see if it tastes as good as it looks." Slapping his hands on the perky butt mounds, Cliff pries the cheeks apart to expose the luscious crack and little pink target of his lust. Placing his tongue on the tight sphincter, Cliff indulges himself in a slow lapping of the winking portal and the entire area around it.

"Uhhaaoo," exclaims Lane. "That's incredible. Oh yes, eat me!"

Cliff plunges his tongue past the loosening barrier to enjoy laving Lane's colon. Lane thrusts out his ass to allow Cliff deeper access. "You seem to have a natural affinity for this, Lane. Now climb up the rest of the way. We need to get those shorts and jock strap off you."

Climbing off the ladder and onto the loft, Cliff strips off Lane's shorts and jock strap and shoves him over to a hay bale. "Get on your hands and knees, Senator, because I'm about to own your ass!"

Poised on the hay bale as directed, Lane spreads his knees apart and grabs hold of his buns and spreads them. "Please, Cliff, suck on my asshole! It's so good."

Now stripped naked himself, Cliff gets on his knees behind Lane and feasts furiously on the virgin pussy, driving Lane to heights of pleasure he's never before experienced.

"Oh, baby, your ass needs cock badly and you're about to have that love canal stretched to the limit with my big dick. Do you want it?!"

"Yes, yes, pleeease, Cliff, take me like I was your favorite butt boy. Don't spare me. I want to know what it's like to be powerfully plowed by a butch man who can't get enough."

"Lane, honey, that's not a problem. The fact is I want to jam my cock into you so hard and so far that you'll be branded for life with your first dynamite fucking."

Cliff's groin, slapping against Lane's butt cheeks reverberates around the cavernous barn, causing the horses to stir and whinny below. In a bruising grip of Lane's glutes, Cliff pounds into his newest conquest, reddening the ripe cheeks and forever opening the portal to his new circle of friends and booty hounds.

"AAAgggrrr," shouts Cliff, as with one last deep thrust his big cock explodes into Lane's spasming colon to send a tidal wave of cum deep into his bowels.

Lane, overcome with a sense of completeness, jerks his cock furiously to experience the most thrilling orgasm of his life. Great spurts of his cum wash over the hay bale beneath him. "Oh Christ, Cliff, I never want you to pull out."

"You're not done yet, babe. You're obviously white hot but your beautiful ass has sucked me dry. I need to bring in reinforcements." Pulling out of Lane's well serviced asshole, Cliff flips open his cell phone from his discarded jeans and calls Brad. "What's going on over there, honey? Are you keeping our guests occupied?"

"Viktor and Eric are watching a porn flick with Gray. Hector and Maxim are playing 8-ball pool and I'm just putting the dishes back in the cupboards. Where are you?"

"In Hector and Cole's hay loft. Forget the dishes and get your ass over here. Your services are needed." Cliff flips the cell phone closed and lies down on the hay bale next to Lane. "You, Lane, toss a great fuck. It's good that Gray is a young man because you'd wear him out otherwise. Come here and show the man who took your cherry some appreciation." Wrapping an arm around Lane's neck, Cliff moves in to French kiss him, sucking on his tongue. With his fee hand, Cliff stuffs 3 fingers up Lane's ass, massaging his prostate.

"Uuooo, Cliff, I need it again!" pleads Lane, as he grabs Cliff's prick and runs his thumb over the precum oozing out of the head.

"Oh you're going to get it again, love, but this time you're going to take a 10" cock that's both longer and thicker than mine. You're going to love it as much as I do."

Just then Brad's head pops up over the top of the access ladder. "What gives, guys? Christ, Cliff, are you forcing yourself on one of our guests again?"

"Our guest is more than willing, babe, even if it is his first time experiencing stud meat up his virgin asshole. I've only given him a taste. He wants more and you're going to give it to him."

"What do you say, Lane? Now that my lover has opened you to the pleasures of getting screwed, do you want me to take up where he left off?"

"Please, Brad, show me your big dick that Cliff is so proud of. Dropping his jeans and briefs, Brad kicks them aside as his prick rises to full mast. "Shit! I couldn't possibly — take that!"

Cliff maneuvers Lane to the edge of the hay bale and slides in behind and under him so he's able to both support him and raise his long muscular legs. Lane's freshly fucked hole is stretched open, welcoming Brad's advancing prick.

"Hold on tight, boys, the SEALs have landed and are on the attack!" Pressing his big purple cock head against Lane's ravaged sphincter, Brad swings his studly ass back and swings his hips forward to jam his dick to the hilt deep inside a moaning Lane.

"Christ, yeah, I want it, I want all of it!" cries Lane. "Bang me, Brad! Bang me like you screw Cliff and as Cliff screws you. I want to feel like your whore."

Replacing Cliff's hands on the back of Lane's knees, Brad begins a slow and steady rhythm in sodomizing a mewling Senator Cockerall.

Having waited such a long time to open himself to this form of pleasure, he now cannot get enough. Since Brad freed Cliff's hands, Cliff is now able to fondle Lane's roiling balls while working his prick with his other hand. Lane is in a hyper intense state, experiencing an unprecedented sexual high.

Brad, an experienced top, prefers to be a submissive bottom most of the time with Cliff but he's really getting off on servicing Lane's all but virgin pussy. His long experience allows Brad to bank his fires so as to prolong the excruciating pleasure he's giving Lane.

Lane is moaning and reaches out with his long arms to grab handfuls of Brad's sumptuous ass to pull him in tighter with each thrust to receive every inch of his magnificent cock. Screaming at the top of his lungs, Lane's cock erupts in an explosive orgasm, hurtling wave after wave of molten cum.

The orgasm causes Lane's stuffed hole to clench down on Brad's fully engorged prick to force out a shattering climax. "Aaagggrrr," Brad yells, as his rioting prick fires volleys of cum up Lane's already cum drenched colon. The three men collapse in a pile.

CHAPTER 4

Back at the house party, the game of pool is coming to an end with the hunky Hector Rios losing to Maxim who's on a roll. Maxim sinks his black 8-ball to seal his victory. Hector knows his ass now belongs to Maxim for that is the house rule. Maxim is literally smacking his lips in anticipation. Maxim knows that Hector's lover, Cole, is on the rodeo circuit this time of year and isn't expected home for weeks, leaving Hector behind as needy prey. Hector is 5'-8" tall with smooth olive skin and beautiful brown eyes. A fine example of Latin stud meat, ripe for the picking.

"Well Hector I've been wondering how your full Spanish mouth was going to feel wrapped around my prick." said Maxim, as he comes around the pool table to stand before Hector and drops his shorts. Hector knew he was going to enjoy Maxim's cock in his mouth and up his ass no matter who won the game. Just then Gray pops his head into the pool room to ask where Lane and the hosts were. Hector tells him they went to his barn to look at the Holsteiners and gives Gray directions.

On his knees, Hector hungrily feeds on the college boy's young dick. While not comparing in size to Cole's huge dick, it is none-the-less choice. "You're good, Hector, you're very good but I've a hankering to experience getting into your round little ass. Stand up, babe; I want to see what you're concealing behind that western drag."

Now standing nude against the pool table with his arms folded, Hector asks Maxim what he'd like him to do. "Get up on the pool table, Hector, on your belly and spread your legs far apart." Hector is happy to comply.

Climbing up after him, Maxim can't believe the beauty of Hector's round bubble butt, featuring a winking pink pucker, nestled in his crack. "All through dinner, I could think of nothing but what it would be like to mount the Spanish stallion parading himself in front of me. What a cock tease you were, Hector."

"That was no cock tease, babe, I was just letting you know that you weren't going to sleep alone tonight. Cut the small talk, kid, mount up and take us for a ride."

Nibbling and kissing the butt mounds, beautifully presented by being framed by the pool table's deep green surface, Maxim wasted little time before arriving at his real target, Hector's deep cleft. Laving the inner surfaces of the luscious crack, Maxim's tongue reached the gateway to heaven.

"You're killing me, Maxim, go for it. I want your tongue deep up my hole."

Maxim's tongue darts past the tight gateway and smacks his face against the surrounding butt cheeks which puff up to almost smother him. *What a way to go he thinks.*

Hector, a frequently plowed bottom, knows to raise his butt cheeks to enhance the pleasure of the man rimming him. "Yeah, eat it. Show me how hungry you are!"

Delirious with the delights offered in tonguing Hector's hole, Maxim knows to stop before he shoots his load prematurely. Raising himself up with his hands tucked under Hector's arms, Maxim runs his turgid cock up and down the gaping crack, allowing his precum to pool around the winking asshole.

"Shit, man, stick it in! End my torture. I want your prick to fill me up now!"

Almost simultaneously with that demand, Maxim's cock slides up Hector's shaftway, ending with a loud smack when the law student's tight groin encounters Hector's quivering butt cheeks. "That what you want, butt boy!"

"My cowboy lover knows how to ride me deep and fast. So, college boy, see what you can do to rival what I'm used to."

"So it's a challenge you're giving me, bitch. Well I didn't sleep my way through our football team not to know how to service stud butt. Hang on for the pummeling you asked for."

Maxim demonstrates how youth has its advantages as he mounts Hector in a punishing, penetrating dance. With his legs tight along the inside of Hector's legs, Maxim forces Hector's legs still farther apart to accommodate deeper penetration. Hector's head is bobbing around with the intense assault but he has a smile on his face, reflecting his deep pleasure.

Grabbing Hector's right leg, Maxim swings their bodies so they're lying on their sides. Raising Hector's right leg in the air, Maxim begins his final pistoning of Hector's savaged hole.

Coming together in a tumultuous rolling orgasm, the two men sing a duet in the language of ecstasy. As fast as Maxim pumps Hector's pussy full of cum, Hector's dick riots with ropes of darting cum. "Fuck, man, I think you just joined my stable of lovers," Hector coos.

Back in Hector's barn which Gray had just entered, he calls out, "Where is everybody — hello!"

"Climb the ladder, we're up in the hay loft," Lane calls out.

Having made the climb, Gray steps off into the hay loft to see the tableau before him. "What — what is this! Lane! Have you been deceiving me all this time pretending to be uninitiated in the ways of gay sex?"

"Hold on, Gray, what you're witnessing is a bit of psychological counseling on the part of your hosts as requested by your lover. We owe Cliff and Brad a debt of gratitude for helping me overcome my considerable hang-up in not being able to please you — while on my back."

"Are you telling me you're no longer a virgin and these two studs have taken you?"

"Surely I've made my meaning clear and now I want to complete my studies in the art of gay sex by enjoying the pleasures to be had in penetrating my lover."

Cliff and Brad help Lane to a sitting position, each with an arm around him. Remarkably, after two spectacular orgasms, Lane's 8.5" prick is at full attention. "Slip off your shorts and jock strap, Gray, and get up on these hay bales. I want you to sit on my cock and ride me as you have your many lovers. Show me what I've been missing and what you'd have me do to service you now and forever."

Clad only in his tight, red tank top, Gray hops up on the hay bales and straddles his lover, looking into his eyes with lust and longing. As his anus nears Lane's towering shaft, Cliff and Brad each insert a middle finger into his hole to stretch the opening to receive his lover's first entry.

Unable to restrain himself, Lane bucks his hips to press his prick into the stretched opening as Gray slowly lowers himself down to sit on Lane's groin. "Lane, oh Lane, yes I've wanted this so badly. Your dick feels — beyond my imaginings."

"Ride me, baby, I want to feel your pussy convulse around my dick as you scream out in ecstasy, joined by my shouts of joy."

Gray squats and raises himself up on his powerful legs to take Lane for the ride of his life. Lane takes Gray's cock in his hand and jerks him in concert with the increasing intensity of Gray's lowered and raised butt cheeks. Not being able to stem the tide of the mounting need for release, they reach climax in unison. A shouted chorus of inarticulate exclamations of sheer pleasure accompanies their synchronized climax.

Cliff straddles himself over Lane and stands in front of Gray and feeds his cock past the parted lips, open in the aftermath of his first fucking by his lover. Gray becomes alert immediately and sucks in the big boner to its thick base.

Kneeling next to Lane, Brad turns Lane's head towards him and inserts his prick into the Senator's mouth. Sucking cock is what Lane preferred until now and excels at it. Lane and Gray suck off their hosts, greedy to extend their sexual peak as well as to pleasure two hunks.

The slurping doesn't last long before the butch hosts are about to have massive loads suctioned out of their rioting pricks into the mouths of two practiced cocksuckers. Grabbing each of their tormentors' heads, Cliff and Brad thrust like unbroken stallions to ravage their guests welcoming orifices. Lane and Gray all but choke on the blasting jets of fiery cum.

Withdrawing and flopping on the hay bales, the foursome is satiated at last. "Well the sex therapy class is over, guys. Whenever you're ready for another installment, just sing out. We'll be happy to take you wherever you want to go, positions open to suit preferences," said Cliff.

The next morning everyone was back in their respective homes. Maxim and Gray got up early, still tingling with the previous night's experiences. They enjoy a light breakfast before leaving to explore the glorious mountain property surrounding them. Encountering Viktor as they were leaving, they tell him they'll be back for lunch after hiking the trails. Gray said that Lane was sleeping in. Viktor bids them adieu. Eric is up a little while later and after breakfasting, leaves to do some food shopping for the household as well as other Saturday errands.

Still later that morning, Viktor hears stirring in Gray and Lane's room, indicating that Lane has finally gotten up. Viktor can feel the lust stirring in his loins and listens for the shower being turned on. When he hears the unmistakable noises coming from the shower, he steals down to Lane's room, enters and closes the door behind him. Stripping off his T-shirt, cargo shorts and sandals, Viktor slips into the bathroom and steps into the shower behind Lane who has his eyes closed while letting the shower head rain its spray over his head, face and body.

Wrapping his hands around a startled Lane, Viktor kisses the back of Lane's neck and whispers, "Relax, babe, since you were dispensing favors last night to our dinner hosts, I thought you'd be open to pleasuring the host with whom you're staying."

"When you greeted me upon my arrival, I saw the bulge in your pants. I've been expecting you to make your move. You're in luck too because after last night I no longer have restrictions when it comes to sex. Take what you want."

Feeling up each high and shapely butt cheek, Viktor said, "Bend over, handsome, if your pussy isn't too raw from last night, I want to fuck you!"

"The boys said you've got a big one and yes I'm ready to take it."

"If it proves too painful, let me know and I'll withdraw. It's not my attention to cripple a guest especially one as cute as you."

"You won't hear any complaints from me, stud. Fuck me like you fucked Maxim. I won't be upstaged by that young buck."

Lathering his immense cock with shampoo, already sheathed in a condom, Viktor guides his jumping dick to the swollen sphincter and shoves in to lodge the big head just inside the hole.

Lane winces with pain, inevitable from taking in something so immense, but doesn't otherwise complain. "Shove it in all the way. Fill me up!"

Viktor hesitates but decides to comply with Lane's wishes. With a forward thrust, he spears his prick inside until his big balls bounce against Lane's crack. While Lane is quietly moaning, Viktor bends over, digging his fingers into Lane's muscular shoulders to begin bumping and grinding his powerful butt to batter Lane's burning shaftway.

"Faster, harder, deeper, Viktor. Screw me; screw me as if I were your first lover!"

Viktor's lust for Lane is real so he has no problem giving Lane what he wants. Viktor is now pulling his battering ram of a cock fully out of Lane's ass before smashing it back in and driving it to the hilt, over and over again. New to the pleasure of receiving dick up his pussy, Lane is being brought up to speed fast by a master.

Viktor balls pump great masses of sperm into his cock and into his bent over conquest. "Ooohhhaaa," yells Viktor, as he unleashes his load into his grateful guest. Pulling out, Viktor backs Lane up to the side wall of the large shower enclosure, kneels down and lifts Lane up behind the knees and drops his legs down and over his shoulders.

With his back against the tiled wall, Lane's cock is lined up with Viktor mouth. Viktor bends his head forward to begin sucking on Lane's rioting prick. Gorging himself on the succulent boner, Viktor deep throats Lane.

Threading his hands through Viktor hair, Lane holds on until Viktor sucks his cock dry, swallowing every spurt of cum juice that Lane could produce. "How does Eric ever keep you satisfied, Viktor? You're insatiable!"

"You noticed, Lane. Since no one will be home for a while, I could do with a bit more of your pussy. Let's get out of the shower and on to the bed." Lane lies on the bed with a pillow under his head. Viktor joins him and places the other pillow under his buns. Clamping his hands on Lane's ankles, Viktor raises his legs and spreads them apart as far as possible. Unerringly, Viktor's dick finds the plundered hole and plunges in. "Now, my dear, you're going to enjoy a long slow fuck so you'll know when you're being taken by a man who wants you desperately."

"Oh, Viktor, yes, show me please." Lane's dick is improbably hard again after spewing so much cum already. Victor's huge prick continues an inexorable and relentlessly slow plowing of Lane's pussy.

Lane can't believe the unbelievable sensations in receiving such an unrelieved screwing from such a powerfully built stud who has the staying power of an Olympian.

"Ok, my divine piece of tail, I'm going to fill you up again." Drawing Lane's legs in from their outstretched position, Viktor drops them over his shoulders, releasing and freeing his hands. Propping himself up in a position used in doing push-ups, Viktor now goes for the kill and bangs Lane's pussy, showing no mercy.

Lane shocks himself with how much he likes bottoming for this statuesque stud. Now with a violent thrust, Lane is deeply impaled with Viktor's massive cock just as Lane's mouth is filled with Viktor twirling tongue. Viktor's body shutters uncontrollably on top of Lane as his shattering orgasm bursts into Lane in darting jets of cum.

Lane's prostate took a pummeling with his latest fucking and caused Lane to give up still another excruciatingly wonderful orgasm. They remain wrapped in each other's arms for many minutes until their heart rates simmer down.

Cupping his face with both his hands, Viktor kisses Lane and said, "Whew, you took me by surprise, Lane. I expected you to be much more — restrained. I'm delightfully surprised."

"Perhaps you'll allow me to experience the pleasure of bedding you again this weekend, Viktor. But next time I want to be on top," Lane said while fingering Viktor's hole.

"Definitely, babe, I look forward to giving you my ass. It's always my goal to give as good as I get."

Later that day after Viktor and Eric served their guests lunch; Lane excused himself to take himself over to Cliff and Brad's cabin, saying he needed to talk to Cliff about something related to national security.

Lane finds Cliff outside his cabin doing a bit of weeding in his garden. "Hey, Cliff, could you spare me a few minutes? There's something — something I'd like to run by you."

"Sure, no problem, Lane. If you want a little privacy, we can go into the greenhouse."

"Yeah, privacy would be a good idea, Cliff. Can I drag you away from what's obviously a labor of love?"

Taking themselves into the greenhouse, Cliff said, "So what's on your mind, Lane. You seem troubled."

"Well, I have a situation on my hands, Cliff that may well have national security implications."

"That sounds ominous, Lane. What seems to be the problem? How can I help?"

"The problem only just arose two weeks ago when my need to live a double life finally caught up with me when someone I hardly know approached me and threatened to out me if I didn't do something for him in my capacity on the 'Committee on Homeland Security and Government Affairs'."

"That's very serious, Lane. You've been put in an untenable situation. What does this individual expect you to do in exchange for his silence?"

"Nothing short of betraying my country. He wants me to use my influence to help secure him a berth for his Russian tankers, sailing under a Liberian flag, coming into the Port of Wilmington, North Carolina. Ostensibly his cargo is low-sulfur diesel. While I don't know what his real cargo is, I'm certain it's not low-sulfur diesel. Whatever it is, I'm sure it's not something we'd knowingly accept into our country."

"How do you know this man, Lane? Where did he contact you?"

"While I'm in Washington, I have an apartment there but I also maintain a home in Chevy Chase where I belong to the Chevy Chase Club. Sometimes Gray stays at the house with me and we occasionally take in a round of golf at the club. It was a club member who approached me. He had occasion to observe Gray and me together at the club and had a private detective put us under surveillance. It wasn't terribly difficult for the truth of my relationship with Gray to become apparent."

"So I take it you were approached at the club by this individual who made this proposition to you that either you complied with his wishes or he'd see that you were outed."

"Yes, Cliff, and my life has been hell ever since. I'm seriously considering resigning but that doesn't resolve the problem of who this man is and what he's up to."

"Of course you're right, Lane. The problem has to be confronted. Your being out of the picture doesn't really mitigate the threat. Obviously, this person will seek some other avenue to accomplish his ends."

"That's what concerns me, Cliff. I can't just stick my head in the sand and hope it will all go away, but what do I do?"

"First of all, Lane, does this man have a name?"

"He goes by the name of Vince Angotti but I have no idea if that's his real name."

"My god, Lane, Vince Angotti! You'll be surprised to know that his name has come up quite recently in our investigation of the Russian mafia's attempt to smuggle illegal arms into this country, working in concert with the American mafia."

"While I was suspicious of what his cargo might contain, I never imagined it had anything to do with an illegal arms network. This is so much worse than I thought!"

"Maybe not, Lane, maybe not. As you know after reading Jason Stone's report Homeland Security provided you, we've been hot on the trail of the Russian mafia connection trying to export illegal arms into this country. As it happens, the trail leads to Duke University and Maxim Bondar."

"Maxim? But how can that be true!? He's just a foreign college student."

"This is true but he has a benefactor in Russia who is anything but clean." Cliff goes on to explain the background of how it was that Maxim carried an envelope to the US which he handed over to none other than Vince Angotti.

"What happens now, Cliff? Where do we go from here?"

"Actually, Lane, we're on the verge of apprehending Angotti and shutting down his whole operation. What you need to do is sit tight for now. Your problem should be over very soon."

"Cliff, I can't tell you what a relief that is. It seemed my whole life was crumbling around me."

"You might want to give serious consideration to outing yourself, Lane. You really can't afford to be put in a position like this again. The public has demonstrated its willingness to accept gay people in public office if they are up front about who they are."

"You mean just face up to it and take the consequences. That's an attractive idea especially now when I can see myself building a life with Gray. The prospect of not having to hide anymore is intoxicating."

Greatly relieved, Lane returns to Eric and Viktor's cabin to find an unexpected visitor. "Lane, we've been waiting for your return so we could introduce Maxim's lover, Ivan Vasiliev, who just arrived from Moscow!" said Gray excitedly.

"This is indeed a wonderful surprise. Nice to meet you Ivan. Maxim and Gray have been anxiously anticipating your arrival in Durham. I didn't expect to see you out here in the country."

"Maxim and I stay in touch by cell phone. When I phoned to say I'd be coming early, I prevailed upon him to ask Eric and Viktor to invite yet another guest into their home. They were kind enough to welcome me with open arms."

"There was no point in Maxim sleeping alone when his lover just arrived in the country and could come here to join the group rather than traveling to Durham only to be alone," Eric explained.

"We're going to be serving a light supper on the deck tonight," said Eric. "Viktor is in the mood to barbeque so it's to be an all American fare. The bar out on the deck will be open in half an hour so slip into whatever minimal costume that makes you comfortable and come on out and strut your stuff. We're expecting our neighbors, Cliff, Brad and Hector to join us."

Cocktail time arrived to find everybody on the deck, draped over the wrap around bench in various poses. Many variations of shorts and tank tops could be seen, stretched tightly over each member of the assembled group. Great quantities of wine and beer were consumed before the burgers and hot dogs started coming off the grille and distributed to the increasingly rowdy group.

Sufficiently sated with food and drink, the hosts suggested an alternative to what would usually be offered for dessert. The guests were to drop their shorts and jock straps into the basket provided and help themselves to condoms set out on the center picnic table in a big glass bowl.

Now a second glass bowl was passed around from which each guest was to pluck out a folded piece of paper with a number and letter on it indicating three groups, 1, 2 and 3 and positions in each group according to the letters A, B and C. The A position in each group called for that member to sit on the picnic table, the B position called for that member to kneel on the backless bench in front of position A. Finally the C position required that group member to stand behind position B.

After learning of their designated group and position within, everyone moved to the big round redwood picnic table and assumed their proper positions. Group 1 consisted of Hector, seated, Gray kneeling, and Viktor standing. Group 2 consisted of Cliff seated, Ivan kneeling and Brad standing at the rear. Lastly, group 3 consisted of Eric seated, Maxim kneeling and Lane pulling up the rear position.

At the sound of the first gong, the kneelers needed to start sucking their seated group member. Thus Gray went down on Hector, Ivan went down on Cliff and Maxim went down on Eric. The wine and beer got the cocksuckers in a party mood and they were off and running before Eric sounded the second gong at which time the kneelers were entered by the standees. Thus Gray was penetrated by Viktor, Ivan was penetrated by Brad and Maxim was fucked by Lane.

An informal competition ensued, ensuring that every ass was thoroughly plowed and every cock voraciously sucked, as the butt boys jerked themselves off. The group climaxed in a crescendo of squeals and shouts of joy. It seemed that Eric and Viktor came up with a dessert treat that was to become traditional for the three house enclave. No one's ass or cock went unserviced; insuring that weekends spent in West Virginia with this group would always be a cherished invitation.

Following the group fuck, the guests went home and everyone else toddled off to bed for the last night of their stay. Most of the household fell into a drugged sleep. Lane awakened in the wee hours of the night and decided to go downstairs to the kitchen for a snack. At the foot of the stairs before turning to enter the kitchen, he noticed a light down the hall, coming from the study. He decided to investigate.

Peering into the study from the darkened hall, he saw Viktor lounging in his leather reclining chair, reading a book. "What are you doing up so late, Viktor. I thought I was the lone insomniac in this household."

"Maybe dessert was just too much stimulation for me. Instead of satisfying me, it made me horny so I decided to reread 'Crossover Spy' that a friend of ours wrote. The book is always good to give vent to one's fantasies."

"Umm, yes Viktor, I can see the evidence in that tent in your shorts. With that banging you gave my Gray, I'd have thought you'd have had quite enough."

"Actually I was in the mood for taking cock up my ass but it was the luck of the draw that my asshole went begging."

"It wasn't my intention of leaving this house without sampling the pleasures in giving you a serious screwing, Viktor, especially now since you've royally fucked me and now my lover. You owe me, babe, and I've come to collect."

Lane removes what little he's wearing. "Get out of those shorts, Viktor and get your legs up in the air." Viktor adjusts the reclining chair to its most horizontal position. Raising his legs so his thighs are pressed into his massive chest, Viktor exposes the great round globes that Lane so wants to experience.

Lane falls into the chair to get up close and personal with the most magnificent ass he's ever likely to see. The muscled mounds hover over the commodious leather chair, demanding reverent attention. Sliding his hands under the hanging cheeks, Lane extends his tongue to meticulously lav every square inch of Viktor's crack before paying particular care to the winking sphincter. Darting his tongue in and out of the softening portal, Lane demonstrates his talent as an emerging booty hound. Viktor is softly moaning, enjoying Lane's ardor.

"The deep screwing you gave me yesterday morning will live in my memory forever, Viktor. I can only hope to give you a small measure of the extreme pleasure you gave me."

"Don't sell yourself short, Lane. I can assure you that I'm anxious to receive every inch of your prick up my ass and to enjoy a long and deep screwing."

"That you shall have, my friend. My only fear is that I'll become addicted to the pleasures to be had in servicing your pussy."

"Actually, your house is not far from our house in Bethesda so you need never go wanting. Eric and I would enjoy entertaining you and Gray often. There are some condoms and lube in the table next to this chair. Help yourself. I'm ready to feel your prick sliding up my ass."

Lane slips on a condom and begins lubing Viktor's ass which requires little preparation. Not a day goes by that Eric doesn't plow his lover which seems only to cause Viktor to want more. "Ok, Viktor, I'm going to slip it in now." Sliding his cock slowly but steadily up Viktor's ass was exquisite pleasure for Lane. The silken shaftway was like a caressing velvet glove. "Oh, Viktor honey, you are such a choice piece of ass. I fear I'm going to lose it too soon."

"Easy does it, babe. Fuck me, fuck me nice and slow so you can enjoy stretching out our mutual enjoyment for a very long time. That's it, honey, slow and easy. Now kiss me like a lover does."

Lane's prick slips into a nice steady pace in screwing Viktor. He kisses Viktor's eyes, nose and mouth. Nibbling on Viktor's ear lobes and inserting his tongue into his ear, hardens Lane's dick even more in the prolonged plowing he's giving Viktor.

Viktor is first to start moaning, reflecting his obvious pleasure in receiving a loving and prolonged fucking. "Oh, Lane honey, you're killing me. I need you to slip into high gear and bang me like a whore."

Slipping his hands up Viktor calves to his ankles, Lane spreads the powerful legs wide apart and begins arching his back and humping the Russian stud in an aggressive pace, punctuated with the loud smacking of groin to buttocks. Lane was unprepared for the delirious high that mounting Viktor was giving him. Grinding his cock deep into Viktor on the down swing of his deeply penetrating thrusts, Lane experienced an amazing high, almost blacking out before emptying pulsating blasts of cum into Viktor who was crying out in ecstasy as his cock spewed rocketing cum over his conqueror's chest.

Collapsing on top of Viktor, Lane savored having his cock securely lodged inside the panting Russian. Viktor wrapped his arms around Lane's neck and kissed him passionately, coaxing another series of blasts out of Lane's throbbing prick. "You answered the call, Lane, and fucked me like a whore. The truth is I'll be your whore whenever you want to slip it to me."

"Right back at you, Viktor. I look forward to the next time you shove your huge dick up my ass. And Gray too enjoyed taking your prick up his young ass. There will be plenty of pussy to go around. But now I better get back upstairs and try to get a couple hours sleep before I have to drive back to Washington in the morning."

CHAPTER 5

The next morning everyone took their leave, returning to their lives in Washington and Durham. Cliff got into the office early the next morning to update his boss, Jason Stone, on developments associated with the Russian connection in the international illegal arms sales.

After finishing his meeting with Jason, Cliff stopped by the office of his best friend and head of cyber security, Debbie Burger, to catch up and exchange confidences in the manner of close friends. Debbie has met Cliff's circle of friends and knew most of the players involved in Cliff's weekend in the country. She was curious about Viktor and Eric's weekend guests.

"Senator Cockerall has got to be the cutest Senator in the Senate!" Debbie gushed. "Glad to hear he's not such a straight stick and has a life outside the stifling boys club in Washington."

"Unfortunately, his private life might prove his undoing if he doesn't handle his present difficulties deftly. The Republicans in the Senate would like nothing better than to savage his reputation just for the sport of it."

"Lane Cockerall is no dummy. I'd put my money on him to negotiate himself through the shoals. You do realize that Marc is writing a sequel to his last book, 'Crossover Spy', which proved to be so successful."

"So I understand, Debbie, your husband is on a roll. He's taken to the new genre in which he's now writing and has mastered it. Mixing a mystery with a love story and gay erotica is a volatile combination. It was a revelation to me that so many women enjoyed reading 'Crossover Spy'."

"The reason I mention it, Cliff, is that Marc is certain to want to interview Lane and Gray as well as Maxim and Ivan. Do you think you could arrange it?"

"It should be easy enough to have Marc and Tommy out to our cabin for the weekend when Viktor and Eric have that group back again for a weekend frolic."

Debbie and Marc keep their marriage viable by each having love interests outside the marriage which they wish to preserve, especially for the sake of their two teenage children. Debbie has a long standing affair going with their boss, Jason Stone. Marc spends weekends with Tommy Brandon who heads up the Washington office of "CYTEK", Cliff and Brad's private security business.

Tommy Brandon is married too, with two small children. His wife, Mary, is a devoted wife and mother but has little interest in sex and is content to remain as Tommy's wife while he consorts with his boyfriend on weekends. Tommy and Marc have been given a room in Cliff and Brad's townhouse, which they use on weekends since Cliff and Brad are often at their West Virginia cabin on weekends.

When Marc started writing 'Crossover Spy', he really didn't have a feel for the genre until Cliff and Brad introduced him to Tommy who took on the task to bring him up to speed, not expecting that they'd become an item. Marc hadn't had sex with another man prior to meeting Tommy who was Brad's squeeze when Tommy wasn't flying for the US Air Force.

Tommy and Marc make themselves available to Cliff and Brad at the townhouse or at the country cabin where they are frequent guests. Sexual favors are a staple shared by everyone in the three house enclave in West Virginia.

"Thanks honey," Debbie said. "Marc will be so excited to have some fresh material to incorporate into his new book. The royalties are still pouring in from the last one. Our finances are finally out of the toilet and we're saving for the kids' education."

"You were due to catch a break, Debbie. You know, with our private security business going great guns, you'd be welcome to come aboard full time rather than just part time as we started you out."

"That's a tempting offer, Cliff, but part time work with your business works best for me right now. Full time would get too consuming, not allowing me enough time for my family. Finally, I seem to have gotten the balance about right and I don't want to rock the boat."

"Well the offer stands should you change your mind. How are you and Jason doing anyway?" Jason Stone sent Cliff on the original mission to Moscow which required Cliff, a straight man, to perform as a gay man so as to ingratiate himself with Igor Petrov, a gay man and suspected illegal arms dealer. While Cliff was a great success in his role, he escaped Russia resenting Jason's throwing him to the wolves. He exacted his revenge by introducing Jason to the joys of gay sex, resulting in Jason's being an avid bi-sexual. Jason had been getting it on with both Debbie and Cliff. Jason's wife is a social climbing Washington matron, only interested in society functions.

"Jason and I manage a tete-a-tete pretty regularly," Debbie answers. "Our relationship has settled into a pleasant and manageable, no strings attached, affair. How about you?"

"Since I introduced Jason to Clarence Sharkey, he's content with only one man in his life." Clarence is the black stud and former army drill sergeant who runs the exercise facility in the basement of the office building where they work.

"Have we become sophisticates in the French manner or are we wanton sexaholics, Cliff?"

"Must we apply labels? Everyone seems content with their lot. Aren't you?"

"For sure but sometimes I feel like we're all — whores."

"Isn't that a good feeling? Would you rather return to climbing the walls in frustration with what was missing in your marriage?"

"You have a point, darling! I guess a little healthy guilt only fuels the fires."

"That's my girl. Well, I'm headed home. We're having Lane over for dinner tonight to bring him up to date on our pursuit of Vince Angotti." They kiss and Cliff leaves for home.

Sometime later, Cliff was busy in the kitchen preparing dinner when the doorbell rang. Going to the door, he found a frantic Lane Cockerall on his doorstep. "Come in Lane. What's got you in such a panic?"

"Cliff, it's Gray! They've kidnapped him!"

"Calm down, Lane, and tell me what happened from the beginning." Lane goes on to explain the call he got from Angotti saying they had Gray and if he didn't call off his dogs, Gray would disappear permanently.

"Angotti obviously is aware of the fact that they were on to him, Cliff, and decided to do something drastic to save himself."

"That appears to be the case, Lane." Just then, Brad arrives home. Cliff explains the terrible development in the illegal arms conspiracy.

"Lane, we've been in the final development stage of some sophisticated spyware that could have national security implications." Brad said. "We could probable utilize these techniques in locating where they've taken Gray. How have they been in touch with you?"

"Mostly by cell phone but sometimes by email," Lane answers. "If they hurt him, I'll never forgive myself! I never should have involved him in the life of a public figure." Lane laments.

"This is no time for soul-searching, Lane. We have to keep our wits about us. Gray's life could depend on it!"

"What must we do, Cliff and Brad, I'm so afraid of making a misstep and putting Gray in grave danger."

"Let me apply some of the newest technology we're about to go public with and apply it to your cell phone and computer so we'll be ready when you're contacted again." Brad said.

Scrapping their dinner plans, the three head to Cliff and Brad's Washington office to get the required devices to hook up to Lane's cell phone and lap top. They phone Debbie Berger to meet them there since she was the one who conceived of the devices. Once outfitted, Lane returns home so as to receive the expected call from Angotti, demanding assurances from Lane that Homeland Security operatives were standing down and would not continue to investigate him.

Unbeknownst to Lane, Vince Angotti occupies a walled estate in Chevy Chase not three miles away from Lane's home. In a secret underground bomb shelter, left over from the days of the cold war with Russia, Gray has been imprisoned. The estate belongs to a Russian expatriate, formerly associated with the Russian embassy that is traveling abroad. Angotti's presence in the estate is nowhere to be found on official records, providing him with the anonymity he requires in his nefarious dealings.

When the call from Angotti came through, Debbie's tracking devices worked as they were designed to, allowing Cliff and Brad to pinpoint Angotti's secret location. Cliff decides that he wants Gray's extraction from captivity to take place under the radar. Thus, he and Brad mount a covert domestic operation to free Gray but to keep Senator Cockerall's name from having any connection to Angotti or the American mafia.

As Cliff and Brad case the walled estate where Angotti bases his operation, it becomes immediately apparent that security is lax. Angotti supposes his cover is so complete that detection is almost impossible. While there is a permanent guard at both the front and rear gates, there's only a single additional guard who circles the house on a regular basis. Cliff and Brad have no trouble scaling the wall with their military gear and timing their invasion when the inner guard was at the far side of the house.

Well trained in matters of stealth entries, Cliff and Brad quickly climb over the balustrade encircling the terrace and slip up to the French doors accessing the dining room.

Once inside the grandiose house, they listen at the double doors of the dining room which lead to the grand two story entrance hall. They can hear faint voices coming from a distance. Entering the grand hall, they steal down a long hallway leading to what is probably a library. At the library doors, they can now discern that there are two men having a heated conversation. One of the voices is familiar to Cliff.

Cliff and Brad burst into the library, guns drawn, to confront the two conspirators. Cliff is stunned to see that, indeed, one voice is a familiar one. It belongs to none other than Grigory Vasiliev. "I didn't suppose you'd be foolish enough to involve yourself in a kidnapping on foreign soil, Grigory. You can't buy your way out of this one." Cliff said.

"Everything may not have a price, Cliff, but it's usually negotiable. Shall we talk for I think we have something you want which we could be persuaded to part with in exchange for your giving us certain — assurances?"

"We don't negotiate with criminals, Grigory. You've made a serious error in judgment in becoming involved with the illegal international arms network. Surely you've made enough profits from your legitimate businesses. Why be so greedy?"

"My lifestyle kept escalating, requiring ever more funds to keep up with burgeoning expenses. Not an unfamiliar scenario for people like me. I admit to being foolish and greedy. It's time to change direction. So you see, Cliff, we may well have some common goals to explore that could net out to being positive for each of us."

"Ok, Grigory, I'm listening but you had better not have harmed a hair on Gray Hillstead's head."

"Rest assured. No harm has come to the young man beyond a little roughing up. What I'm proposing, Cliff, is that in exchange for allowing both Vince Angotti and me to leave the country with a promise to cease our involvement in any illegal arms network, I'm prepared to release Gray and pose no further threat to Senator Cockerall."

"That may be possible, Grigory, but first I want you to dismiss the two guards at the gates of this estate and the one patrolling the exterior of the house."

"Vince will see to that presently but I need you to put away your guns. You will leave your associate here with Vince and I will take you to Gray."

Cliff and Brad put their guns on the fireplace mantel. Vince picks up the phone and arranges for the guards to leave the estate until further notice. Grigory exits the library followed by Cliff. Stopping down the hall, Grigory said, "Cockerall's young friend is quite well concealed, Cliff. If you were to try and find him, he would likely die before you could rescue him."

"What's your point, Grigory? I thought we came to an agreement. Are you reneging on your offer?"

"Not at all, Cliff. There's just one additional condition I didn't want to mention if front of the others."

"And what might that be, Grigory. I'm running short on patience."

"Well, Cliff, you remember that divine fuck you threw me when we first met in my apartment in Moscow? You let me have my way with you so Alexi Volkov wouldn't come to any harm. You seem to be afflicted with what, a Good Samaritan complex? Here we are again, finding ourselves in a similar situation. Give me your ass to insure Gray Hillstead's safety. Very simple really."

"You manipulative pervert! Surely you get enough sex without forcing yourself on me again."

"Come now, Cliff, we both know you enjoyed having my prick stuffed up your ass. You all but purred when I took you. You'll purr again. I must have you one last time."

"All right, Grigory, I'll not risk any harm coming to Gray Hillstead. Do what you must but just do it!"

Ushering Cliff into the maid's room off the immense kitchen, Grigory wasted no time in removing Cliff's clothes. "Get up on the side of the bed on your knees and forearms, Cliff. Yours is a butt etched in my memory as being perfection itself. Years of roaming the world in covert operations have sculpted your cheeks into unparalleled objects of desire." Uttering this, Grigory strips off his finery to match Cliff's nakedness.

"Talk me through it, Cliff. Beg me to eat your ass and fuck you. Make me believe how much you crave being possessed by me!"

Playing along with Grigory, Cliff said, "My favorite fuck buddies are powerful men like you, Grigory, who know what they want and will stop at nothing to get it."

"That's it, Cliff! Like that, yes, tell me more. You're making my cock rise up, knowing what's in store."

"Show me how a rich industrialist, who wants for nothing, craves to eat stud pussy. Eat me, Grigory, stuff you tongue up my ass and feast!"

Falling on his knees, Grigory parts Cliff's creamy smooth glutes and suctions his hole in a frenzied state of need. Cliff moans in spite of himself. Grigory's ardor cannot be denied. "Shit, yeah, Grigory, suck me out, lap my hole!"

Coming up for air, Grigory gasps for breath. "Do you want my dick now, Cliff? Would you like me to pound your pussy?!"

"What are you waiting for, Grigory, jam you cock up my ass and plow me. Let me know who is master and who is a butt slave. Let me hear your groin smack against my butt cheeks as you take your full measure of pleasure, mounting and enslaving me."

Cliff's words had the desired effect and Grigory gets up on his feet to aim his prick at Cliff's hole and proceeds to drive into him with a relentless staccato then slow rhythm, entering and exiting the yawning hole, mindlessly screwing Cliff in complete abandon. Cliff's love mounds well up around Grigory's cock with every thrust enticing Grigory to still higher heights until an eruption is inevitable.

Both men are experiencing a sexual high unrivaled in their experience, causing Grigory's cock to spasm in uncontrollable explosions of cum gushing up Cliff's plundered colon. The assault on Cliff's prostate pushes him over the crest in a free fall, spewing geysers of cum.

Panting, Grigory said, "Christ, Cliff, come back to Moscow with me and I'll set you up like a prince. You'll never want for anything. Whatever you want will be yours."

"We made a bargain, Grigory and now I want you to live up to your end of it. Take me to Gray now!"

"You played your part too well, Cliff, I really believed you wanted me."

"We both know that we have chemistry in the sack, Grigory, but that's the long and short of it. We have incompatible lives as you well know. So please don't let's linger any longer. I must know that Gray is safe." They quickly dress and Grigory shows Cliff to a storage closet off the back hall in which there is a hidden door accessing a stairway to the bomb shelter used to imprison Gray.

Gray is released and brought upstairs. His guard was dismissed and sent home. Cliff makes some calls and arranges to spirit Grigory and Angotti out of the country. Angotti was allowed to exit the house and drive himself to his Gulfstream 450 private jet and escape to the Cayman Islands where he has a home. Grigory was escorted to an Aeroflot flight to Moscow.

Cliff and Brad drive Gray to Lane Cockerall's home and see him safely inside. While the immediate crisis was over, Lane and Gray had some serious thinking to do about their future and whether they wanted to continue living a life in the shadows. Cliff made his case to Jason Stone to justify his actions in the steps he took to rid the country of the menace represented by Grigory Vasiliev and Vince Angotti. Although Jason at first protested at Cliff's taking so much on himself, he finally came around, accepting that the focus had to be on making the country safe.

Some weeks later, with the whole illegal arms affair fading into the past, Cliff was in the mood to resurrect his aborted dinner party. This time he invited not only Lane but Gray too, since he was visiting Lane's Chevy Chase home for the weekend. In addition, he decided to effect an introduction between Lane and Gray with Marc and Tommy. He wanted to fulfill the promise he made to Debbie to help Marc get background for his new book. This evening's meal called for Cliff to prepare his Beef Stroganoff. The dining room was aglow with soft candlelight with a sound track of classical music as background. A nice Cabernet Sauvignon accompanied the meal.

The dessert, a chocolate rum-vanilla cheese cake, was served out on the patio of Cliff and Brad's town house. They'd consumed several bottles of wine by that time but decided that they wanted an after dinner drink as well. Cliff and Brad acceded to their guests' request but with the proviso that Lane and Gray must stay over and not drive home. Marc and Tommy had already moved into their bedroom even though Cliff and Brad hadn't gone to West Virginia for the weekend.

Brad and Lane were elected to go to the wine cellar to select something for the group. Cliff stayed behind to keep the guests entertained when he came up with the idea that they could all do the hot tub/sauna combination that Brad and he liked to do when they had the time to relax.

While everyone repaired to the hot tub room to strip and get into the tub, Brad and Lane entered the wine cellar. Perusing the glass fronted, temperature controlled cabinets; Brad and Lane were viewing the fine selection of liqueurs available. Suddenly Lane embraced Brad and said, "I've never adequately thanked you for saving Gray's life. I'll be eternally in your debt, both you and Cliff. When I think of the risks you took! I'm just — overwhelmed."

Brad kisses Lane on the mouth and answers, "Gray's life was certainly worth defending as would yours, had you been kidnapped. Cliff is hard-wired to be a protector of his country and its citizens. And I'm hard-wired to see that he stays out of harm's way. So you owe us no special thanks."

"You're wrong in saying that. I'm not one to ignore sacrifices others have made in my behalf. You'll find me quite willing to do for you in whatever way I can, whenever you want me to do it."

They enjoy a lingering kiss before realizing their cocks were pressing against each other's trouser fronts. Accepting that they better get back to the awaiting guests, they quickly select a couple of bottles of a brandy cassis and rejoin the group to find them joyously frolicking in the hot tub. After stripping, Brad and Lane serve everyone their drinks in clear plastic cups and get into the six seat hot tub.

While they sip their liqueurs, Cliff uses a hand held remote to activate a drop down movie screen and a ceiling mounted projector. On screen appears some prime examples of stud meat from "Colt Studios". The party slips into high gear. Six stiff cocks can be seen rising above the surface of the water.

"Well, guys, I think it's time to take our act into the sauna," said Cliff. Cliff's timing was impeccable as two Colt studs were just getting it on at the edge of the swimming pool where they'd been engaging in foreplay.

The sauna contains three steps and the guests arrange themselves at will, resulting in Cliff and Brad sitting on the top tier. Below Brad sat Lane and below him sat Marc. Similarly, Gray is seated below Cliff, and Tommy is seated below Gray. Everyone sits quietly for a few minutes, letting the sauna work its magic in relaxing them.

Lane starts the ball rolling with turning himself around, getting up on his knees and going down on Brad. Below him, Marc flips himself around to fall on his knees to start enjoying Lane's proffered asshole. Gray, not to be outdone by Lane, gets into position and starts to feed on Cliff's cock as he feels Tommy's tongue enter his ass.

The two threesomes shift into high gear, outshining the professionals they just viewed on the screen. Lane was looking for an opportunity to express a small measure of his thanks to Brad and Cliff and now he and Gray had their opportunity. Lane and Gray deep throated their hosts with complete abandon while receiving an unrelieved screwing from their newest fuck buddies.

Cliff and Brad were so mellowed out from food and drink that they gave it up quickly as their guests sucked their jumping dicks dry. Watching Lane and Gray's heads bobbing with the professional blow-jobs they were administering, Marc and Tommy unleashed massive loads into Lane and Gray's grasping pussies.

Cliff and Brad, not wanting Lane and Gray's cocks to go unattended, slipped down a step and had their cocksuckers turn and sit on their dicks so that their sodomizers could now suck them off. Marc and Tommy sucked Lane and Gray, respectively, until they suctioned their loads down their gullets.

Viewing the intense servicing Lane and Gray received excited Cliff and Brad anew, surprising themselves with their ability to provide their butt buddies with another powerful screwing. Lane and Gray were beside themselves with joy, having received such a full service fucking. The hosts decided it was time everyone went up to bed. The six went upstairs as directed but broke into different threesomes. Brad and Cliff took Gray to their bed while Marc and Tommy took Lane to their bed.

Brad and Cliff took turns fucking Gray up the ass in many creative positions while Marc and Tommy did the same for Lane. Fortunately, it was a household well stocked with condoms. About 2:00 AM, the screwing stopped and hosts and guests alike fell into a deep sleep to last until mid-morning on Saturday. Miraculously, Lane and Gray were able to walk the next morning and eventually take themselves down to breakfast to be greeted with a round of applause.

"Well, guys," said Tommy, "Marc and I are usually the house whores around here but I can see we have competition. You guys were awesome!!"

"We do feel a little less for wear this morning, gentlemen. Bear with us until we've had some coffee." said Lane.

"No problem, Lane, but how about some breakfast. Pancakes are on the menu this morning. You and Gray look as if you need to recharge your batteries."

"You got that right, Cliff; we have a ways to go to recover from last night. You guys are a force to reckon with. We'll be forewarned in the future." said Gray.

"In your weakened condition, I was hoping I could prevail upon you to submit to an interview for my new book," said Marc.

"As long as we're unidentifiable, Marc, we're game." Lane answered. "Brad gave us a copy of your last book and we enjoyed it very much."

After the interview was over, Lane and Gray returned to Chevy Chase. Lane told Gray that he plans to finish out his term in the Senate but not to seek reelection. He plans to draft legislation which would provide legal protections for lesbian, gay and transgendered people. He plans to open a private practice devoted to providing service for the lesbian, gay and transgendered community. He asked Gray if he'd not only marry him but, on completion of his studies, join him as a partner in their small practice.

Gray was genuinely stunned by both requests and was reduced to tears, unable to respond immediately. "Lane — Lane are you sure this is what you want. Your career! Your career in public office — ?!"

"First of all, I'm sure I want you beside me always, most importantly. My public career has run its course. Now I feel I have more to contribute in the private sector. My biggest fear is that — you don't want me or the life we could have together."

"You can't be serious, Lane! How can you have any doubt that it is you I love? There's nothing I want more than to be married to you. The thought that we could share a law practice is a wonderful bonus. It's all so unexpected and overwhelming, but yes, yes, yes!!!" Gray throws his arms around Lane and they embrace for many minutes.

"You've made me so happy, Gray. But now it's time for you to get back on the road and return to college. My future partner must finish his education. They kiss and Gray departs ending a fateful weekend.

CHAPTER 6

After Grigory Vasiliev is back in Moscow for a short period, he realizes he needs a new challenge. Now that his foray into selling illegal weaponry is over, he needs another business venture to replace it. His lifestyle hasn't gotten any cheaper and he's anxious to start cashing in on a new venture. He decides that his ownership of a sports club, "Global Fitness", presents a golden opportunity to open a related business, i.e., an escort service.

Since the fall of the Iron Curtain and the dissolution of the Soviet Union, American businessmen have been flocking to Russia in search of business opportunities. Grigory sees them as vulnerable targets for his latest scheme. These businessmen are often away from home for extended periods of time and would be in need of — "companionship". Grigory intends to provide them with the best money can buy.

His plan requires that he hire a former Spetsnaz (Special Forces) officer of his acquaintance, Captain Yuri Markov, to head up the new satellite of Global Fitness. A major part of his job will be to recruit former KGB officers who meet the criteria Grigory requires. Yuri knows many of these former officers and knows he'll have no trouble in attracting them to a well-paying job, given that so many of them are desperate for work, any work.

Grigory has developed a stringent list of requirements that these recruits must measure up to. For openers, they must be fluent in English, be between 5'-10" and 6'-2" tall, between the ages of 35 to 45, have a big dick, weigh between 145 and 165 and most important of all, they must be drop dead gorgeous. Those that meet those prerequisites, then must submit to an in depth preliminary interview by Yuri Markov. Yuri must determine if these potential escorts are willing to provide clients with a full range of sexual services. After Yuri has culled down the applicants to a select few, Grigory would conduct the final interview before they will be brought aboard for an initial indoctrination regimen.

Grigory rather enjoys his role, at the conclusion of the interview process, in putting these former officers through their paces. Few candidates make it to the point where Yuri and Grigory join forces to test their metal under pressure. The final interview is with Grigory alone in an office set aside for him at Global Fitness. Given that these men had been in the military, it was assumed that most could give and receive a blow-job since they spent so much time away from home among men. Having established their willingness to accommodate the clients in bed, Grigory put them to the test requiring them to drop their pants and bend over his desk while he evaluated how good a fuck they might be. Mere willingness wasn't enough; they must show enough native talent that could be exploited in making them magnets for repeat business.

Once Grigory and Yuri recruit 25 men to be brought aboard, they must submit to the indoctrination regimen. Grigory hires a former ballet dancer, Anton Balandin, former star of the Kirov Ballet, to be in charge of fitness for the new group. Anton puts the recruits through exercise groups which include warm-up, stretching, abdominal and floor exercises. The goal is to develop very well-toned but not overly muscular bodies. It's expected that each of the 25 recruits will eventually have a magnificent ass with high round glutes which will be super-toned.

During the development stage of this new venture, Grigory returns home to his Moscow apartment to find his son Ivan sitting in his living room. "Ivan! What are you doing home?! You're supposed to be going to college at Duke University."

"Not any more. I quit. College just isn't for me. I've had enough of higher education, so has Maxim. He returned home too."

"Are you two still together? What's going on Ivan?"

"We're very much together and are anxious to go to work. Now that you've returned to your legitimate businesses, we thought you might have something that might interest us."

"Well your timing is rather fortuitous, Ivan, for I'm just in the throes of a start-up that might interest you, now that I know that you and Maxim plan to live an openly gay lifestyle."

"Please tell me about it, father. It sounds intriguing already." Grigory goes on to explain the concept of a high class escort service with a stable of 25 men to provide enough variety to appeal to American businessmen who often stay in Moscow for weeks at a time, leaving wives and family behind.

"That certainly sounds like a new take on an age old profession, father. Do you really think there is enough of a market for such a service? These visiting businessmen can pick up hustlers at their hotels. Why would they want to pay a premium for our services?"

"These gentlemen are used to the best and are willing to pay for it. We can offer them a discreet service that offers them privacy and safety as well as the ability to meet their fantasies. They'll go for it all right, big time."

"What would Maxim and I be expected to do?"

"These former officers are prime examples of Russian manhood but they haven't been exposed to the good life. They need to be schooled in the ways gentlemen act when meeting in social situations such as hotels, clubs, restaurants and the like. Being former military officers, they are often lacking in the social graces. You and Maxim could train them in these skills so they can mix in the best of company."

"How do you propose that we would do that, father?"

"Presumably, Maxim will be living with you in your apartment. We could use his old apartment as a place for you to liaison with these recruits to get them into functioning in an upper class lifestyle. It could have — side benefits — for you as well."

"By that you mean — what?"

"You and Maxim could see who rises above the pack to deliver the goods. At least we need to know that each can measure up to the hype we will have given them. If there are duds, we can eliminate them before they sully our reputation. Do you think you and Maxim can handle the job description?"

"Surely you jest, father. You're actually going to pay us to do this job?!"

"You'll be made partners in the business. If we're successful in Moscow, which I have no doubt that we will, I plan on expanding to other major Russian cities before taking on European cities." What Grigory didn't reveal to Ivan is that his business would have a covert aspect to it. These American businessmen possess knowledge of their corporation's intellectual property which is worth an immense amount of money. Grigory intends to blackmail these unsuspecting pleasure seekers into giving up precious information that Grigory could sell to unscrupulous Russian businessmen.

What Ivan and Maxim will not be privy to is that the hotel where these assignations will be arranged is owned by Grigory. He is having a suite of rooms outfitted with multiple hidden cameras, virtually undetectable. The cameras will produce studio quality pictures, revealing the indiscretions of the targeted businessmen.

While Grigory is happy to have Maxim as a son-in-law, he's sorry to lose his services in bed. In casting around for a replacement, he decides that Anton Balandin, the former principal dancer at the Kirov and now his employee, will do very nicely. Anton was thrilled with Grigory's offer of a nice apartment, rent free, in exchange for his favors. Grigory plans to get his money's worth. Grigory realizes that with this new venture and its satellite business as well as expenses necessitated by keeping Anton that he'd need a discreet accountant, independent of his regular accounting office. He consults Yuri about possible candidates.

Yuri Markov, in managing Global Fitness's satellite business, was keenly aware of Grigory's need to keep the profits of the business secret from government authorities. He proposes that Grigory hire his wife, Olga Kuznetsov, a top flight accountant, to manage the books to insure that the illicit profits from the escort business will go undetected. Yuri knows Olga will be handsomely compensated for her efforts.

Olga Kuznetsov is a comely blue-eyed blonde, 5'-7" tall, 130 pounds, and 34 years old with a full figure. She turns heads on the streets of Moscow with her good looks and stylish western clothes. She's ambitious and has grown weary of the dreary life she leads in Moscow with her husband Yuri. She wants more, much more and begins to imagine a way of getting what she craves, a privileged lifestyle with all the things money can buy. Being Grigory's accountant, while remunerative, won't cut it with the kind of money she'll need to break free. She becomes aware of the covert part of Grigory's business and its obscene profits and conceives of a plan to relieve Grigory of some of his ill-gotten fortune.

The Global Fitness School for male escorts moves swiftly to recruit and train former KGB officers to be top tier escorts. Once the ballet training worked its magic to tone the bodies of these men, Ivan and Maxim's part in bringing these men up to par came into play. Their first trainee was Pavel Jakov, easily the handsomest and most studly member of the initial group of 25. Pavel is 6'-2" tall, 158 pounds, blue-eyed and raven haired. He has high cheek bones, a square jaw, a perfect nose and a wide sensuous mouth.

Part of the early training included grooming. Pavel was sent to a specialty men's salon where a stylist cut his wavy black hair and shaved his privates leaving only a manicured remnant of his pubic hair above his thick dick. His crack and balls were left silky smooth and edible. His chest hair was given a wax treatment, leaving a tailored matte down to his pubes. Pavel was handsome to begin with but now he was quite stunning. Anton's ballet training was enormously effective in shaping and toning his fine body. The crowning glory was his ass, a thing of incredible beauty and a booty hound's wet dream.

Ivan and Maxim knew when Pavel came to them that they would be dealing with the cream of the crop. His only potential flaw was how well he was going to be able to fake his joy when taking it up the ass. If he could act his part convincingly, they'd have a winner.

Arriving at Maxim's old apartment, Pavel was greeted by his instructors, Ivan and Maxim. They'd already met him during his early training at Global Fitness. "Come in, Pavel, welcome to your new home for the next three weeks. Are you ready to take your training up to the next level?" said Ivan.

"It hasn't escaped my notice that you have some reservations about my ability to come up to speed but I plan on winning you over. You'll find me to be a willing student, anxious to please."

"We couldn't wish for more than that, Pavel," said Maxim. "You're sure to be a good student in picking up the social graces we'll expose you to. It's the — rest — that we're uncertain about."

"You're worried that because I'm straight and not bi-sexual that I'll be a dud in bed. That's not a complaint you're likely to have at the end of three weeks. Test me. Subject me to your wildest fantasies. There's nothing that I won't do to satisfy you."

"There's no time like the present, Pavel. The custom suits we've had made for you are hanging in the master bedroom closet. You'll find underwear, shirts and ties, shoes and socks as well. Go in there and get yourself outfitted and return to the living room. We'll go to the guest bedroom and get ourselves appropriately dressed as if we were meeting at a fine hotel."

Sitting on the sofa in suits and ties waiting for Pavel, Ivan and Maxim are entranced when he makes his entrance, wearing the exquisitely tailored finery purchased for him. "What can we say, Pavel, you look amazing."

"Thanks, guys. So what's on the agenda? Who's seducing who here?"

"It would be most likely that, since we're expected to pay, that we would put the moves on you. You just have to come across as someone we must have, whatever the cost. You must have had occasion to observe women doing this. You just must get into reversing the roles," said Ivan.

"For now, we'll imagine that we're in the hotel bar. Just businessmen enjoying a drink together. Nothing too overt should be observable," said Maxim.

"So we're just setting the stage for what comes after," Pavel observes.

"That and getting in the mood, establishing an easy rapport," Ivan agrees. They practice the art of small talk and down several rounds of drinks until Ivan suggests that they have a night-cap up in their suite.

"So now imagine that we've arrived in the suite and we're enjoying our night-cap, sitting together on the sofa. You need to get up to take a bathroom break and remove your jacket to throw it over a chair. Your exit to the bathroom will give us a look at how all that expensive tailoring molds your clothes to your body, revealing your broad shoulders, tapered back, high butt cheeks and muscular legs. We'll be hooked."

"Returning from the bathroom, you'll be stripped down to your Calvin Klein briefs, affirming what you clothes only hinted at, that yours is a body that they'd never see at their clubs. You sit between us again and slouch down and spread your legs, featuring your basket to feed our arousal. Invite us to get — more comfortable, cuing us to remove some clothes."

"Once we're down to underwear and socks, start a little foreplay. Pick one of us and cup his crotch and give him a kiss. When you feel that your first target's dick is hard, move to the other mark. You must work your own dick up to tent the front of your underwear," Ivan instructs as they act out his directions.

Pavel demonstrates that he can control his prick to get it hard when he wants. Maxim gets down on his knees in front of Pavel and slips his undershorts down to his ankles and starts sucking on his knob. Ivan begins pinching Pavel's tits while French kissing him. Pavel moans convincingly.

Maxim gets up off his knees and helps Pavel to his feet, kicking his undershorts aside. "Time to move ourselves into the bedroom." Maxim leads the way. Ivan accompanies Pavel with his middle finger up the hunk's bubble butt, searching for his prostate. Removing the rest of his clothes, Maxim gets up on the bed to prop himself up on the numerous down pillows leaning up against the upholstered headboard.

Pavel releases himself from the three fingers Ivan has up his ass and follows Maxim up on the bed and kneels between Maxim's legs and drops his head to bury it in Maxim's crotch, sucking his stiff cock. Pavel's butt made for an irresistible offering, inciting Ivan's lust. Getting on his knees behind Pavel's spread legs; he was awed with what Anton achieved with his ballet exercises. Pavel's ass mounds were sculpted in great arcs from the small of his back rising in great orbs to frame his shaved crack.

Ivan dove in, wanting Pavel to experience the joy of having his ass eaten out by his new asshole buddy. Ivan indulged himself in an eating frenzy, worshiping Pavel's hole. The obvious pleasure Pavel received was evident in his voracious vacuuming of Maxim's dick. When Ivan came up for air, Pavel stood up to straddle Maxim and demonstrate his mastery of the ballet position called grand plié, slightly modified. Thus, he squatted over Maxim's prick, taking it easily up his ass after Ivan had lovingly prepared his hole in finger fucking him. Squatting and raising himself up alternately, Pavel made short work of Maxim and used his inner ass muscles to coax a massive orgasm out of Maxim, who cried out in ecstasy.

Ivan wondered why he ever doubted Pavel's ability to satisfy another man in bed. Pavel extricated himself from Maxim's slick shaft and fell on his back next to Maxim who was still catching his breath. Raising his legs, Pavel inquired of Ivan, "What are you waiting for, lover; my asshole is ready for more dick." As Pavel tucked his knees behind his ears, Ivan placed his cock at the airborne, freshly fucked hole and drove into him with a crushing thrust, smacking the smooth cheeks and holding fast, savoring his possession of this incredible hunk.

Maxim, recovering himself, moved in to suck on Pavel's big dick. Clearly, Pavel was getting in touch with the pleasures to be had in gay sex. Ivan hunched over Pavel, was intent on giving him a slow and thorough screwing, opening up his asshole wider and wider. In spite of himself, Pavel was moaning in earnest, savoring the servicing he was receiving from his tormentors. "Oh, yeah, Ivan, fuck me! I'm getting off on giving you my pussy. So yeah, fuck me, fuck me good. I'll be your bottom any time you want a good piece of ass."

Pavel knew what buttons to push to drive Ivan over the edge. Ivan proceeded to pound Pavel's floating ass with a driving intensity that couldn't be sustained for long. Ivan's hips swiveled in great swinging arcs, setting Pavel's colon ablaze. In a final collision of his groin against the reddened butt cheeks, Ivan felt his orgasm from his toes, rocketing through his body to explode into Pavel's pulsating pussy. Timing his release with Ivan's, Pavel emptied torrents of cum into Maxim's welcoming throat.

Collapsing in a heap, Ivan and Maxim wrapped their arms around Pavel, acknowledging Pavel's mastery of them in the sack. "Shit, Pavel, you'll never convince us this was a first time for you," said Maxim.

"Hell no, guys, Anton showed me a few moves after ballet classes. I didn't want to come to you a complete novice. Learning to bottom was a challenge but I had no problem functioning as a top. So which of you would like to go first?"

Maxim flipped himself over on his side and backed his ass up against Pavel. "Go for it, babe, stick it to me." Turning towards Maxim, Pavel slipped his prick into Maxim while reaching around to grasp his butt boy's cock. Maxim's asshole easily accommodated Pavel's big dick as he was accustomed to daily servicing from Ivan. There was no denying Pavel's skill. Maxim could easily become addicted to being screwed by such a stud.

Lifting Maxim's free leg, Pavel spread his legs to gain deeper penetration and began to fuck Maxim in earnest and in short order, filled him with hot cum. Pavel withdrew from Maxim and rolled over on his back, his dick still at full mast. Ivan squatted over Pavel's prick, facing away from him and dropped down to be impaled. Leaning back to be supported by his hands and feet, Ivan thrust his body up, and then down to ride Pavel's thick prick. Ivan's experienced colon massaged Pavel's dick to drive him to another high.

Wrapping Ivan in a bear hug, Pavel shoved his dick home to possess Ivan while unleashing volleys of cum deep into his throbbing colon. It seemed everyone was sated at last. This night became a template for the following nights in Pavel's three week stay. Pavel would give as good as he got, establishing him as a prime attraction in their new business venture.

What wasn't known by anyone involved in developing this new satellite business, as part of Global Fitness, was that Pavel had become involved with Greta Kuznetsov, Grigory's accountant and wife of Yuri Markov, the general manager. After leaving Anton Balandin's afternoon dance classes, Pavel would secretly ascend a rear stairway to access Olga's office located in a remote part of the building housing Global Fitness. It was by design that her office was far away from prying eyes and she was encouraged to keep her distance from other staff.

Pavel had met her, previous to her being brought aboard as Grigory's in-house accountant, at a KGB officer's function when she accompanied her husband. There was an immediate chemistry between them which went unpursued until she came to work at Global Fitness. She sought Pavel out and made the initial overtures, indicating her desire for him. Her remote office made frequent assignations possible. She liked to be taken on her desk top, panties ripped off and skirt hiked up for a fast and furious fuck. Pavel liked aggressive women and slaked his lust for her whenever possible.

Olga couldn't get enough of Pavel, given the drought her marriage had been in for years. She decided to invite Pavel into her confidence and reveal her plan to divert an enormous sum of money from Grigory's off-shore account into one she would set up for herself and her lover, Pavel. Grigory felt he had security for his money covered with access codes he had set up. But he had underestimated Olga's ability to circumvent his precautions. She was poised to pull off her scheme, waiting only for the right timing. She would be patient until Grigory's blackmail conspiracy started filling his coffers.

Once the training of the initial 25 recruits of Global Fitness's escort service was completed, Grigory wasted no time in putting his concept into practice. He hired a new bartender for his small upscale hotel that would assist in making introductions between his prey and the handsome escorts. Grigory also installed a new concierge who would facilitate liaisons between lonely businessmen and escorts who were just a telephone call away.

Grigory enjoyed immediate success beyond all expectations and found that word-of-mouth was the best tool in making the availability of these escorts known. While he made substantial amounts of money with the exorbitant fees charged for the company of these escorts, the real money came from blackmailing these businessmen into revealing critical company secrets. Grigory was able to make enormous profits from selling these stolen secrets to corrupt Russian businessmen. His off-shore accounts now contained obscene amounts of money.

Olga became increasingly impatient to implement her plan to abscond with a big chunk of Grigory's newly acquired wealth. She saw her opportunity when Grigory's interest in oil refineries took him to a conference in St. Petersburg at the Oil and Commodities Exchange. He'd be away for a week. She hatched her plot enlisting the aid of her lover, Pavel Jakov. She would cover her absence during the time Grigory was in St. Petersburg by saying she needed to attend a meeting in Kiev of the International Congress of Accountants. Pavel would cover his absence by saying he needed to return to Yekaterinburg for a family funeral. Olga managed to transfer $20,000,000.00 out of Grigory's off-shore accounts into one she set up for herself. Through a complex method of electronically transferring money around the world, she successfully covered her tracks, making her embezzlement virtually untraceable. Obviously Grigory would know who the culprit was as would her cuckolded husband, Yuri.

When Grigory returned to Moscow and discovered Olga and Pavel's treachery, he rather surprisingly didn't hold her jilted husband, Yuri Markov, responsible. Rather he enlisted his help in tracking her down. In the meantime, Grigory continued his illicit business, entrapping American businessmen into betraying their companies and in turn their country as well.

The success of the conspiracy to acquire and sell American intellectual property was potentially its own undoing, in as much as the ill effects on American business interests could not continue to go unnoticed. Soon the problem reached epic proportions and became an issue for Homeland Security in the U.S. Jason Stone, Director of Homeland Security, had been contacted by none other than Senator Lane Cockerall, alerting him to a mysterious problem.

Lane became aware of the problem through a college classmate who belonged to his club in Chevy Chase. It was during a round of golf that Lane was made aware of the concerns that his friend and other corporate executives had in doing business in Russia. Lane later contacted Jason Stone expressing concern for what appeared to be a case of corporate espionage.

In consultations with his agents in Moscow, Jason learned that they were only just receiving information suggesting that there was something going on in business circles there that supported what Senator Cockerall reported. Jason was informed that there may be some connection to former KGB officers.

Jason Stone consulted Cliff Bradshaw on what appeared to be a different type of cold war developing in Russia. What Jason proposed was for Cliff to contact his friend Viktor Sidorov to see if, through his contacts with former officers in the KGB, he could gather any pertinent information which might confirm these suspicions of a KGB connection.

Having developed a close friendship with Viktor, Cliff had no problem asking him to do a favor and see if he could glean anything from seeking out former associates in the Russian military. Viktor contacted several old friends with whom he'd served with no success until he thought to call a Spetsnaz officer he knew but slightly, Captain Yuri Markov.

When Viktor spoke to Yuri on the telephone from his home in Regensburg, Germany, he could tell by Yuri's evasiveness that he wasn't willing to be forthcoming, certainly not on the telephone. Viktor lied and said he needed to come to Moscow on business and would like to take Yuri to dinner while he was there. Yuri was not one to pass up a free meal and agreed to meet with him.

Viktor arranged to meet Yuri at the Hotel Baltschug Kempinski and arranged for a private dinner to be served in his suite. With several vodkas before dinner and much wine with dinner, Viktor got Yuri to open up. Yuri was distraught with the loss of his wife to his rival, loosening his tongue about the work he was doing and his suspicions about a hidden agenda. When Yuri had gotten around to naming his employer at Global Fitness, Viktor ears perked up, knowing that something had to be afoot if Grigory Vasiliev was involved.

Viktor decided that Yuri needed some winning over. Getting up from his chair, he moved to Yuri's chair and pulled it around so that Yuri was facing him. Dropping to his knees, Viktor started unbuckling Yuri's belt.

"What, what are you doing, Viktor?!"

"You know as well as I do, Yuri, that we who have been in the military know how to take care of 'business' when we're away from home. Relax and enjoy it. You obviously haven't had any in a while."

Encountering no further resistance, Viktor pulled down Yuri's trousers, followed by his undershorts, revealing a jumping dick. Yuri was ready. Viktor made love to Yuri's cock, teasing the sensitive underside where the head met the shaft. Yuri was close to losing it already. Viktor proceeded to vacuum suck Yuri's cock, driving him to the brink in seconds. Lacing his hands through Viktor's hair, Yuri plowed his mouth, jamming his prick to the back of Viktor's throat and pouring out his pent up load in seemingly endless waves.

"Viktor, what makes me think you haven't leveled with me as to why you suddenly wanted to see me."

Getting up off his knees and returning to his chair, Viktor decides that the time had come to be honest with Yuri. "Your suspicions that everything is not as it seems at the new Global Fitness venture you're managing is most likely correct, Yuri. We may be able to be of some help to each other. By that I mean if you agree to help find out what Grigory Vasiliev is up to, I can use my considerable resources to locate your missing wife."

"Despite what's she's done, I want her back. Whatever it takes, I'm prepared to do."

"Then let me lay it out for you, Yuri. You must be willing to become a more — integral — part of Grigory's escort business. To be clear, you must become an escort yourself."

"How am I to pull that off, Viktor?! Grigory is so cunning, I'd never fool him."

"You must appeal to his mercenary instincts. Convince him that you can earn more money for him."

"How do you propose I do that?!"

"Simple. Suggest to him that since you've already recruited his initial 25 escorts that you now find yourself with time on your hands. Tell him you wish to go through the training and become available, as necessary.

He'll see that you'd be of increased value to him and he'd be glad to earn more money by increasing his stud stable of whores."

"You know, Viktor, I've given head to another guy on occasion but I've never — taken it up the ass."

"Take off the rest of your clothes, Yuri, and get up on the bed on your stomach. Once I've taken your cherry, you'll soon be taking it up the ass like a pro. Yuri, with some trepidation, did as Viktor requested. Watching him with increasing arousal, Viktor stripped off his clothes, got condoms and lube from the night table and joined Yuri on the bed. "Spread your legs, Yuri. Try to relax while I finger fuck your ass to loosen your sphincter muscle." Viktor greased up and worked a finger up Yuri's tight ass.

Turning his head, Yuri viewed Viktor's huge engorged cock and exclaimed, "Christ, Viktor, you'll split me in two with that big thing!" Viktor worked another finger into Yuri's hole.

"Nonsense, Yuri, you can take it, I assure you. You must relax and trust that I'm going to pleasure you with your first ass screwing."

"You find my Olga for me and you'll own my ass so I'm willing to give you a down payment." Viktor works a third finger up Yuri's hole, revolving all three and achieving the desired effect of opening the aperture for Viktor's enormous prick.

"That's the spirit, Yuri, get into it. Know that you're desirable and that I'm really going to get off in screwing you." Viktor extracted his fingers and lay on top of Yuri, rubbing his stiff prick up and down the deep cleft. "You already have a great set of buns, Yuri, even before the training regimen you'll go through at Global Fitness."

"If I can take your cock, Viktor, I should be able to take on anybody they throw at me."

"Now concentrate on relaxing, Yuri, particularly in the region of your asshole. I'm going to slip the head of my cock in. It's going to hurt at first but try not to react by stiffening up."

Viktor eased in the big purple head of his cock. Yuri squirmed but remained quiet. Viktor slowly pressed forward until his entire shaft disappeared inside Yuri's asshole. "That's not so bad, Viktor. It's starting to feel — good."

Viktor was enjoying being Yuri's first anal lover more than he expected. Yuri's body had lost none of its tone since his days in the military. He still possessed the classic broad shoulders and beautifully tapered back, meeting great muscled mounds giving way to powerful thighs and bulging calves. Yes, Yuri was choice and his potential as a paid bottom would begin to be exploited tonight.

Resting his arms on top of Yuri's and clutching his hands, Viktor gently thrust his ass in the air which slipped his cock partially out of Yuri's ass. Hesitating briefly, Viktor swung his hips forward to slide back slowly into Yuri's shaftway. He continued this gentle screwing until he could feel Yuri's pussy relaxing with being possessed by a big cock. "How is it, Yuri, you ok?"

"God yes, Viktor, it feels so much better than I could have imagined. I actually want to make you come, feeling your prick exploding inside of me. Take me like you would a lover. It's time I knew what it's like to be fucked up the ass, especially by a stud like you."

Yuri's words inflamed Viktor's ardor and he began fucking Yuri in earnest. Yuri excited Viktor even more by thrusting his ass cheeks up to meet Viktor pounding thrusts. Viktor's groin smashed into Yuri's buttocks with a loud thwack, thwack, thwack, adding further to the eroticism of the moment.

Yuri's asshole was stretched wide open, fully welcoming the pistoning prick. Viktor, his heart racing, grabbed fistfuls of Yuri's hair and proceeded to let his hips fly in an unrestrained deep fucking of his howling conquest. As Viktor pounded Yuri's upturned ass, his buns ballooned up fetchingly to drive Viktor into orbit. In a final crushing thrust, Viktor drove his dick into Yuri's pussy to the hilt, his body convulsing in a series of explosive orgasms.

When his dick had expended every drop of cum his balls could produce, Viktor rolled himself and Yuri onto their sides, still firmly implanted, and jerked Yuri's prick until he got him off again. Yuri's rectum convulsed around Viktor prick, pulling still another couple of squirts of cum.

"Now I know what it's like to be had, Viktor, and you can take me anytime you want. In the meantime, I'll become one of Grigory's escorts and find out what his game is. You can be sure of that. It's my fervent hope that you'll be able to find my Olga in exchange."

"You needn't doubt that I will keep a promise, Yuri. What her fate will be once she's found is an unknown."

"Please, Viktor, I'm counting on you to afford her every consideration, given the help I will have given you in nailing Grigory."

"Count on it, Yuri, but I can't speak for Russian authorities. She may face some criminal charges."

"With your help, Viktor, I expect that they will cut her some slack. After all, corruption is rife in business circles in this country. They needn't single out one fairly minor player in a criminal justice system so compromised."

"Very well, Yuri, I'll make sure she doesn't wind up in prison. It will help if I can get her to return what's left of the money she stole from Grigory, who no doubt got it illegally."

CHAPTER 7

Viktor contacted Cliff Bradshaw in Washington, DC and explained that he had enlisted the aid of a friend and former Spetsnaz officer, Yuri Markov, who now managed a facet of a sports club in Moscow called Global Fitness, owned by Grigory Vasiliev. Viktor went on to outline the plan he hatched with Yuri to flush out whatever racket Grigory was now engaged in, involving an escort service featuring former KGB officers.

Cliff asked Viktor if he found any connection between Grigory's new venture and the corporate espionage problem that has Homeland Security in the US so concerned. While Viktor couldn't claim he found a direct connection, his suspicions had been aroused. Viktor requested that Cliff use any expertise he could bring to bear in cyber security to find Olga Kuznetsov whom he considered to be a critical player in the conspiracy. Viktor explained the deal he had to make with Yuri Markov in order to secure his agreement to infiltrate Grigory's escort service.

Cliff reported back to Jason Stone to bring him up to date on developments in Moscow concerning the problem with proprietary information belonging to American corporations falling into the hands of competing Russian businesses. Cliff requested that Debbie Berger, head of Cyber Security for Homeland Security be assigned to track down Olga Kuznetsov who had disappeared, seemingly without a trace. Jason readily agreed and Debbie was put on the case.

While Olga was very resourceful in covering her tracks, she was no match for the skills of Debbie Berger who took but a few days to track her to Grand Cayman Island, a British Overseas Territory in the western Caribbean. Jason wanted Cliff to be the one to go despite his semi-retirement status with Homeland Security. What was at stake was too important not to send the best Homeland Security had in its arsenal of special agents.

Cliff flew to the Owen Roberts International Airport in Grand Cayman and checked into the Ritz-Carlton, Grand Cayman. Debbie traced Olga to an address in George Town on Tropical Gardens Road. In doing reconnaissance of the residence, Cliff learned she was indeed living with her lover, Pavel Jakov. However, it became clear that their relationship has soured and he was frequenting the Reef Grill and Beach Bar on West Bay Road every night, often getting drunk. The bar was considered one of Seven Miles premier beach bars with prices to match. Money was obviously no object for Pavel.

Cliff decided to pay a visit to Pavel's favorite bar and insinuate himself into Pavel's company, using the alias, Anatoly Nevesky, he'd used when previously on assignment in Moscow. Cliff found Pavel sitting alone at the bar and sat a couple of stools away, ordering a drink in English, affecting a Russian accent. Pavel's ears perked up and he swiveled towards Cliff and asked him where he was from. When Cliff answered that he was from Moscow, they became instant drinking buddies. Pavel bought the first round of drinks.

Several rounds of drinks later, Pavel invited Cliff to take a walk on the beach. Cliff followed Pavel's car in his rented convertible to a secluded house that Pavel said was seldom occupied by its American owners. After pulling into the circular driveway in front of the darkened house, Pavel led the way around the house to a rear deck which had a path that wound through the dune grass to the beach beyond.

"So, Anatoly, how about a swim. It's a beautiful night with a full moon so we'll have no trouble finding our way. Don't be shy my friend, take off your clothes," Pavel said with a leer. Tossing their clothes aside on the deck, the two men, a bit unsteady on their feet with all the liquor they'd downed, wove their way to the beautiful sandy beach aglow from the moonlight. The breakers were rolling onto the shore, gently lapping the shoreline. Pavel was first to wade in, displaying his magnificent body and arousing Cliff. Pavel dove into a breaking wave and then returning to the surface of the water, turned to see Cliff standing there about to join him.

Cliff's erection did not escape Pavel's notice. Diving into the water, Cliff came up next to Pavel and pinched his butt cheeks. "Come here, Anatoly, I think your big dick needs some attending to. As Cliff moves up next to Pavel, he rubs his prick against Pavel's groin. Pavel places his hands on Cliff's shoulders and delivers a smoldering kiss. Both dicks are now vertical and pressed together. Pavel grasps Cliff's dick and said, "When my girlfriend's giving me a hard time, it puts me in the mood for some dick. You up for it?"

"With an ass like yours, Pavel, you could have as much dick as you want. Cliff underscores his point by shoving his middle finger up Pavel's hole. "How about we take our act back to the shore." On a rise where the beach meets the dunes is a bench, permanently installed into the ground, facing the water. Cliff sits on the bench with his legs spread and his arms stretched out along the wooden back.

"You look good enough to eat, Anatoly, and I'm starved." Dropping to his knees between Cliff's outstretched legs; Pavel demonstrates why he was a favorite attraction at Grigory's escort service. Lovingly sucking Cliff's balls, Pavel chewed and laved his way up the shaft to wrap his lips around the big head and lick the slit, oozing precum. Stretching his jaws open wide, Pavel swallowed the whole prick until the fat head pushed against the back of his throat. Moving his head forward and back, Pavel serviced Cliff's prick like the experienced cocksucker he'd become. Letting Cliff's cock pop out of his mouth, Pavel said, "What you really want is a little ass pussy. Am I right, Anatoly?"

"When I followed you into the ocean, I couldn't take my eyes off your butt cheeks, highlighted by the moonlight. I knew I'd have to slip my dick between those luscious mounds to pound your hole."

"Yes, talk dirty to me Anatoly. I like to bottom for butch guys like you."

"Get up here on the bench, babe, and spread your legs as you drop that bubble butt down on my cock."

Standing on the bench, feet far apart and holding on to the back of the bench on either side of Cliff's shoulders, Pavel lowers himself until his winking pucker is pressed against Cliff's big knob. Cliff was unwilling to delay entry and bucked his hips so his prick pierced the portal to be lodged inside the hot hole.

"You're a big one, Anatoly. I like a big cock when I'm being fucked. You fill me up."

Digging his fingers into Pavel's luscious buns, Cliff said, "Ride me Pavel, take a nice slow ride. I want to service your pussy until you scream out my name as you pop your load all over my chest."

"Hell, Anatoly, you really turn me on! The head of your dick is kissing my prostate every time my butt hits your groin. You're making me want it like I've never wanted it before."

"Show me what a bitch whore you are, Pavel. Give me a piece of ass that I won't forget." Pavel uses his powerful legs to lever himself up and down on Cliff's turgid shaft when he increases his speed uncontrollably until he's delirious with lust. Cliff begins furiously jacking him off to take advantage of his unbridled lust, culminating in Pavel's screaming Anatoly's name repeatedly as his prick showers cum on Cliff's rippling abs. Sitting on Cliff's groin with his pussy stuffed with cock, Pavel's colon clamps down on the massive invader to cause a cataclysmic eruption to rush up his ass.

"Anatoly, Anatoly — you really fucked me! It's the first time I've gotten screwed where I really wanted it. I'm going to like being your bitch."

Over the next couple of weeks, they get together often at the beach bar, winding up either at the unoccupied house or Cliff's hotel for sex. Pavel trusts Cliff more and more, taking him into his confidence. It's seems Pavel managed to get Olga to give him 20% of the money she stole which he placed in a bank on the island of Little Cayman. He only told Cliff that he had a stash of money but not the amount. Pavel also told Cliff that he had an appointment on Little Cayman with a business associate of his former employer in Moscow. Cliff managed to overhear a conversation Pavel had on his cell phone when the name Vince Angotti was dropped.

Cliff seized the opportunity when Pavel was over on Little Cayman for a few days to finally confront Olga Kuznetsov. He made his case, telling her that she would be captured and returned to Moscow to face prosecution if she didn't agree to his terms in making a deal. She was more than willing to come to terms, having realized the folly of her whole plot to live the good life. She was miserable with Pavel and realized what she had in Yuri, her husband, whom she so foolishly cast aside. The money proved to be no compensation for living on the run with a man she'd come to hate. She readily agreed to return the money, divulging the banks where she'd sequestered the funds.

With the information Pavel divulged about his own account, Cliff was able to convey all the particulars to Debbie Berger who would arrange to transfer the funds to a Homeland Security account. With all that accomplished, Cliff booked a flight for himself and Olga to return to Moscow where she'd be reunited with her grateful husband and be free of criminal charges. It was decided to leave Pavel in Grand Cayman Island penniless as punishment enough for his crimes.

Cliff learned later that Pavel got Vince Angotti to back him in developing an escort business in the Cayman Islands, specializing in servicing wealthy American tourists. Pavel was a star attraction in an upscale yacht club where couples docked their multimillion dollar yachts. Pavel specialized in servicing adventuresome couples. The wives got off on watching Pavel screw their overindulged husbands, seeking new avenues of pleasure. While Pavel bemoaned the loss of the $4,000,000 he got from Olga, he landed on his feet, putting together a nice nest egg from his latest gambit.

While Cliff was away in pursuit of Olga Kuznetsov, her husband, Yuri Markov, became an instant success as an escort and frequented Grigory's small boutique hotel, servicing dozens of sex starved American businessmen. Becoming a fixture at Grigory's hotel gave him many opportunities to observe suspicious activities. Given that he was known to be Grigory's manager of the escort business, no one at the hotel challenged his movements even though he strayed from the suite of rooms where the assignations took place. He soon discovered and subsequently penetrated the room where the videos that were filmed in the specially outfitted rooms were collected. Yuri could immediately see that blackmail figured in whatever game Grigory was playing.

Yuri copied all the data attached to these films, indicating who the businessmen were and what companies they were employed by. Over time he had each film copied, a few at a time so they wouldn't be missed. With this data, he was able to supply Cliff the information so critical for Homeland Security investigators to track down these American businessmen who had returned home to the US. Each of the businessmen involved were discreetly asked to report to regional offices of Homeland Security in their own state. When confronted with the compromising films of them having man on man sex in a Russian hotel, they offered no resistance in confessing to having succumbed to the blackmail scheme requiring them to reveal company secrets.

Debbie Berger flew to Moscow to work with Olga Kuznetsov and Cliff in tracking down all transactions associated with Grigory Vasiliev's blackmailing scheme. They were able not only to trace all the money and recover it but also to identify all the Russian companies that bought the purloined intellectual property. Russian authorities fined the companies involved and contributed the money to a fund set up by Homeland Security to compensate the American companies for their losses. All the money that Grigory had realized from the scheme was added to the fund which helped the American companies to cut their losses.

Grigory, being Grigory, was able again to buy his freedom by greasing the right palms. He continued with his escort business but without the cameras in every room. As part of the deal to allow himself to go unprosecuted, Grigory had to make his escorts available to certain officials when they chose to visit his hotel. His escort business continued to thrive, allowing him to expand by buying a small hotel in St. Petersburg and replicating the formula begun in Moscow. Grigory had his sights set on the cities of Novgorod, Samara and Vladivostok as next in line.

Spending time in Moscow with Yuri Markov and Olga Kuznetsov, who were happily reunited, Cliff became very impressed with their abilities. It occurred to him that the private security business he ran with his lover Brad Ames, called CYTEK, could have a Moscow branch which Yuri and Olga could run. They were, after all, presently unemployed. After running the idea by Debbie who was enthusiastic about the possibility, he called Brad to discuss the idea. Brad loved the idea but wanted to run the numbers by their accountant before making a commitment. While the start-up costs were daunting, they decided to make the leap and open the office, especially after getting assurances from the Kremlin that they'd outsource some business, using their services.

Debbie flew home after giving Olga a crash course on issues associated with cyber security. Cliff stayed on in Moscow to work with Yuri Markov in setting up an office but also to meet with Viktor Sidorov who proved so instrumental in aiding Homeland Security in identifying the culprits in the corporate espionage conspiracy. Viktor invited Cliff to spend the weekend with him and his lover, Eric Holtz, in Regensburg, Germany. In accepting the invitation, Cliff asked if could bring Yuri Markov along. Cliff was just formulating a plan to take Yuri with him back to Washington; Regensburg would then be the first stop on the trip. Viktor was pleased to invite both of them.

Olga proved to be the height of efficiency in setting up the new office for Cliff. It became apparent to Cliff that Yuri could be spared for a couple of weeks if he were to take him to Washington to see the home office of the private security business first hand and meet all the players. Yuri was elated with the prospect of his first trip to America.

Cliff and Yuri would first fly to Germany with Viktor to stay at Holtzhaus for the weekend. Bruno Jahn picked them up at the Munich Airport in a big Audi A8 sedan. Bruno was a 5'-11" tall, sandy haired, brown eyed beauty who ran Eric and Viktor auto parts business when they were away on frequent business trips. He also runs the family mansion, Holtzhaus. While Bruno maneuvered the big sedan through the winding road leading to Holtzhaus, his eyes wandered frequently to the car's rear view mirror to feast his eyes on their weekend guest sitting in the back seat. There was no denying the spark that passed between Bruno and Yuri.

The big sedan drew up in front of the centuries old stucco mansion, belonging to Eric's family for generations. Eric greeted them in the home's gracious two story entrance hall. Viktor introduced their newest guest to Eric. "We're always glad to receive Cliff when he can visit us in Regensburg and we're delighted that this time he brought a friend. Welcome, Yuri, to Holtzhaus. You must be tired form all your traveling so we've planned a light supper, anticipating that we'd all turn in early tonight. Please let Bruno show you up to your room so you can freshen up before dinner."

"Thank you, Eric, for welcoming me into your beautiful home. I could do with a bit of freshening up. Please, Bruno, show me the way."

"Don't be long. We'll be having cocktails in the library before dinner is served." Yuri follows Bruno up the great center staircase leading to the guest rooms upstairs. Having gotten in touch with enjoying man on man sex,

Yuri could appreciate the great set of buns that were bouncing tantalizingly at his eye level as the ascended the grand stair. The conversational banter in the car revealed that Bruno was an avid downhill skier. Entering a guest room, Bruno set Yuri's bags down and turned to find Yuri directly behind him.

Running his hands up Bruno's open collared dress shirt that only hinted at the spectacular torso beneath, Yuri cradled Bruno's face with his hands and planted a soft but passionate kiss on his mouth. Bruno wrapped his arms around Yuri's waist and slid his hands down to feel up Yuri's studly ass. "My lover Denis and I occupy the apartment over the garage. Before the weekend is over, we'll want — to have you — over."

"You've only to ask, Bruno. If your lover is half as cute as you, we're in for a good time."

"Well I'd better get back downstairs before we get ahead of ourselves. See you shortly for cocktails."

The cocktail hour was a festive time for all, enjoying a brief respite before Cliff and Yuri headed for the US to take care of business. Bruno and his lover Denis Girard joined the soiree. Denis was a 5'-8" tall Frenchman with unruly dark hair, piercing blue eyes and a tight skiers body. Being so cute, he always made a nice addition to the group. As luck would have it, Viktor and Eric were also due to go to Washington for meetings with their American suppliers. They arranged to travel on the same flight so that Brad could pick them all up at Dulles International Airport.

Greta, the housekeeper, prepared the meal which was served by a maid in the home's formal dining room, replete with a magnificent oval mahogany table, upholstered Louis XIV chairs and a crystal chandelier. Everyone was in a relaxed mood after the cocktail hour and sat down to enjoy Greta's Weiner Snitzel, served with red cabbage and spatzle. A wonderful Reisling wine accompanied the meal. Greta already received many compliments even before her delicious Black Forest crepes were served. The six diners returned to the library after finishing their desserts and coffee so that Greta and the maid could clean up and go home. They sipped snifters of bourbon in preparation for retiring early.

Bruno and Denis were the first to excuse themselves. They returned to their apartment which was accessible from the house by way of a mud room which contained a stair up to their garage apartment. "Let's go up, guys," said Eric. "Yuri, I want you to take a detour to our room before you turn in."

"Good night everyone, I'm going to crash. See you in the morning for breakfast." said Cliff

The hosts and Yuri bid Cliff a good night. "Sure, Eric, I'd enjoy seeing the master suite in such a fine old house." Arriving at the suite at the end of a long hall, Eric and Viktor stand aside to allow Yuri to pass through the elaborate double doors. Following behind Yuri, Viktor and Eric enter the room, closing the doors behind them.

"Viktor painted a vivid picture for me of your reunion in the Hotel Baltschug Kempinski, Yuri. Perhaps you'll indulge me in a reenactment? Would you agree that it is appropriate for the lover left behind to be afforded the same privileges as his wandering partner?"

"Certainly, Eric, I'm happy to offer you any privileges that you'd choose to avail yourself of."

"Let's begin by you sitting in the chair next to our bed. Yuri sits down in the designated upholstered chair. Now if I remember correctly, Viktor removes your trousers and undershorts. "Do it, Viktor. I want to see if Yuri's prick will be jumping as you described it. Oh I see, Yuri, your dick is responding again! Ok, Viktor honey, let's see you suck cock." Viktor's consumption of liquor has made him horny so that he eagerly fell between Yuri's legs and bobbed his head rapidly as he ravishes Yuri's responsive prick. Again Viktor makes short work of Yuri, suctioning his boner dry.

"Man you're good, Viktor!" said Eric. "You're a receptive audience for Viktor's performance, Yuri. It seems we've come to the point in your hotel tryst where you remove the rest of your clothes and get up on the bed. Do it Yuri!" Yuri is now spread eagled on the bed, naked. "This is where the scene changes slightly from last time, guys. Since you gave up your cherry to Viktor that night, Yuri, it seems you've done the ballet regimen to tone your body so as to please legions of paying American businessmen. I must say the results are spectacular, particularly with what was achieved with your butt. One doesn't expect to see butt mounds like yours except on a principal dancer with the ballet such as Nureyev. This time it will be my pleasure to mount you."

"Viktor opened me up to the pleasures of bottoming. So please fuck me, Eric, because I'd really like to think I could please both partners in a relationship like yours."

"There can be no doubt that I want to experience what my lover described as a singularly spectacular fuck. Let's put a pillow under your middle, Yuri. I want those mounds high and your cleft parted for the maximum in viewing pleasure."

Yuri's butt was now raised high, displaying an incredible feast for the eyes. Eric crawled up between the sinuous legs, parted for maximum access. Eric laved from the base of Yuri's balls all the way up to his asshole and beyond, savoring every square inch. Yuri writhed and squirmed as he purred his response. Running his hands up over the cheeks, Eric kneaded and squeezed the sumptuous mounds. Extending his tongue, Eric darted its point in and out of Yuri's hole, teasing the portal open.

"My god, Eric, this is slow torture! I'm ready for some dick. Shove your cock up my ass. I've got to have it."

Removing his tongue from Yuri's ass, he slides up on top of him to rub the head of his dick along the deep cleft. Eric kisses the back of Yuri's neck and nibbles on his ear lobes, causing Yuri to thrust up his butt, wanting to be penetrated.

"Never fear, Yuri, your about to take it hard and fast as befitting a talented whore." Eric molds his body to Yuri's, enjoying the abundant tactile pleasures to be had. Swiveling his hips so his prick eases forward and back into Yuri's asshole, Eric teases his needy prey. "How does it feel, bitch, am I satisfying your itch?"

"Hell no! Give it to me! Take me like a man. I want it like you give it to Viktor."

"Your asshole would burn for a week if I fucked you the way I do my main man."

"Try me, fucker! Why do you think they pay me $2,000 for the privilege?"

"Thinking you were just a straight guy freelancing, I took it easy on you but no more." Eric lifts his upper body to be supported on his hands and readjusts his feet to get up on his toes, straightening his body and giving himself maximum leverage to properly pound a hungry bottom.

Knowing what's coming, Yuri raises his ass up to encourage the imminent assault. Rapidly pulling his cock out of Yuri's hole completely only to jam it immediately back in with a driving force, Eric plunders Yuri's pussy with a relentless intensity. Viktor sits on the edge of the bed observing while working his big cock.

"Shit yeah, fuck me Eric! No former Stasi officer ever had me. Show me how you treated prisoners."

Driven to the pinnacle of lust, Eric loses all sense of control and hammers Yuri's hole in a punishing pounding. The sound of Yuri's ass being pounded reverberates around the room as Eric slams his dick home flattening Yuri's butt cheeks as his prick releases sperm like an AK-47 assault rifle. Spent, Eric collapses on top of a satisfied Yuri.

"Man you were good, Eric, no wonder Viktor spreads his legs for you every day."

"You were both wonderful!" observes an aroused Viktor. "Now it's my turn to get a piece of the action." Viktor stands to straddle the two prone men, still linked together by Eric's prick. With his finger, he takes the precum leaking from his cock and lubricates his lover's hole, highly charged from watching the rutting pair, Viktor moves quickly to slip it into Eric's open passage, jamming his dick in until his pubes crush against the creamy white globes.

"Ok, Viktor, the feel of your prick never ceases to amaze me. I can never get enough. Go for it, honey! You know how bad I need it."

Viktor's massive cock is housed securely in its favorite lodging place, lovingly caressed along its entire length. Eric's talent as a bottom is unrivaled. Splaying his large hands over each of his lover's perky butt cheeks, Viktor takes his pleasure like a soldier in a foxhole, quick and needy.

While Viktor services his lover's asshole with an almost desperate plundering, Eric's cock is inflamed anew to begin servicing their guest again. Yuri and Eric's colons were ablaze with the friction produced by the jackhammering pricks. Viktor and Eric scream in unison as two rectums are blasted with ropes of ejaculating cum. Viktor's pulsating prick seems to have no limit in pleasuring his lover's pussy before he's able to withdraw, allowing all three men to lie back and savor the moment.

"Wow, do you treat all your guests like this?!" Yuri asks.

"You have unique qualities, Yuri. Surely you've learned from performing as Grigory's highly paid whore that you have universal appeal," Viktor said.

"You don't have to pay me exaggerated compliments to have your way with me whenever you want. I really like you guys."

"Then it's mutual, Yuri. As you know, we're flying to Washington with you and we're going to want to entertain you in our apartment in

Bethesda, MD as well as in our country home in Fletcher, West Virginia. You up for it?"

"Can there be any doubt? Cliff and Brad may have some plans for me too."

"We're all into sharing, Yuri, so have no fear that your services won't be enjoyed by all." Yuri said his good nights, gathered his clothes and stumbled down the hall to his room.

The next morning, Bruno and Denis are invited to have breakfast with Eric and Viktor as well as their guests, Cliff and Yuri. Greta made magic with her homemade Bavarian cream donuts along with her butter crumbled eggs and strong German coffee. After everyone had their fill, Viktor and Eric took Cliff to their auto parts plant to review security issues. Afterwards they were going to go into Regensburg to visit Eric's widowed mother Anna at her condo and all four would then go to dinner at the Eurostar's Park Hotel Maximilian.

Bruno invited Yuri to play tennis with him on the estate's tennis courts located next to the swimming pool. The pool and tennis courts were behind the six car garage and screened from the main house by a tall, manicured hedge. The plan was for Yuri to join Bruno and Denis for dinner in their apartment over the garage. Denis would do food shopping and prepare the meal during the afternoon while Bruno and Yuri played tennis.

Going to the locker room in the pool house, Bruno lends Yuri one of Viktor's tennis outfits consisting of white shirt and shorts as well as sneakers, socks and hat. Bruno stores a matching outfit in his locker. Bruno knew Yuri had a nice body but he was unprepared for the reality of seeing him naked in the locker room, revealing perfect proportions and stunning beauty. Yuri was built like a god. He was forced to turn his back on Yuri to conceal his boner. Turning his back only served to provide Yuri confirmation of what he suspected. Bruno had an extraordinary bubble butt that he longed to fuck.

Playing sets of tennis between such evenly matched players proved arduous and long. They were forced to take frequent breaks in the pool house lounge where there was plenty of Pilsner beer in the refrigerator, helping them to cool off but also making them a bit tipsy and horny. "Do you guys ever play for stakes, Bruno?" Yuri inquired with a rakish smile.

"Traditionally we don't play for money here but other kinds of wagers are possible." said Bruno with an enigmatic smirk pasted on his face.

"Unless I'm misinterpreting your suggestion, Bruno, do you mean to imply that sexual favors may be what's at stake?"

"Bulls eye, Yuri, want to take up the challenge? We'll play three sets to see who wins the match. The loser must give the winner a blow job right here on the court at the conclusion of the match. Then we will continue to play to give the loser another chance to win. If the loser of the first match wins the second match, he gets a blow job. If not, it will cost him his ass. He'll be taken by the winner into the locker room to receive his screwing. So what do you say, Yuri?"

"Yeah, I'll go for it, Bruno. Who do you usually play this game with?"

"We often do doubles. Eric and Viktor against Denis and me."

"Who usually wins? Eric and Viktor look like they'd be a tough pair to beat."

"Actually, it seems to break pretty evenly, allowing everyone to enjoy the joys of victory."

They proceed to engage each other vigorously, both playing well but Yuri's powerful backhand gives him an edge as he wins the first six games to win the first set. Bruno edges him out on the next set to even up the match but Yuri wins the next two sets to win the match.

Jumping over the net to face Bruno, Yuri said, "Looks like you're going to have to get down on your knees and give the guest some head."

"Take off your pants, undershorts and shirt, Yuri, and move over to the chain-link fence."

Now bare-assed, wearing only his hat, socks and sneakers, Yuri moves over against the fence, leans back and raises his arms above his head to link his fingers through the fence openings. His dick is sticking straight out with his ball-sac hanging low. "Let me feel those sweet lips wrapped around my cock, Bruno. Show me how you service Eric and Viktor."

Bruno turns his hat around backwards, strips off his shorts and undershorts and uses them to kneel on when he positions himself between Yuri's parted feet. He grasps his own stiff cock with one hand and uses the other to guide Yuri's pulsating knob past his parted lips. Bruno's tongue proceeds to tease the throbbing prick as it slides in, to be fully lodged in his mouth. Bruno manages not to gag only because he's had long training in swallowing Viktor's huge organ.

"Your mouth is so sweet, Bruno. I want to fuck your mouth!" Splaying his hands on the back of Bruno's head, Yuri thrusts his groin forward and back in a slow exploration of Bruno's suctioning orifice. Bruno works his prick with one hand and with the other, extends a middle finger up Yuri's ass until he feels his prostate.

"Shit, Bruno, you're killing me! I can't last."

With his mouth stuffed, Bruno answers with his eyes, inviting Yuri to go for it. Bruno inserts a second finger up Yuri's ass, then a third, enjoying twisting the three in simulating a fuck.

Now being serviced fore and aft, Yuri's hips begin flying, sending his prick deep into Bruno's mouth, his tongue and cheeks caressing the pistoning shaft. "Uh, uh, ooooh," cries Yuri as his roiling balls pump a choking amount of gism through his convulsing shaft. Bruno guzzles most of it but, inevitably, some cum runs from the corners of his mouth. Bruno pops his load all over the bottom of the chain-link fence.

"After you made me come like that, Bruno, I'll be playing with a handicap. You've drained me of all my strength in an effort to take advantage of me."

"Somehow I think you'll recover, Yuri. From what I hear, you've got great staying power. Let's get dressed and back to the match." They continue the match and as Bruno predicted, Yuri was on his game. This time Yuri won the first two sets but lost the third. Bruno thought he was on a roll only to lose the next set and the match.

"As much as I fantasized about getting into your ass, Bruno, I wouldn't want to do it because you threw the game. You were playing so well. What happened?"

"Don't imagine for a moment that I'd throw the game, Yuri. You just outplayed me this time. Believe me; I wanted to win to see your head buried in my crotch."

"Rather it seems my prick is going to be buried deep up your pretty little ass, boy. I can't wait. Now take off your shirt, shorts and undershorts, I want to see you walking over to the pool house in only your hat, socks and sneakers. Yuri watched Bruno walk to the pool house, displaying a set of buns that rode high and were as round as bowling balls, creating a delectable v-shaped hollow at the small of his back. An ass doesn't get any more fuckable than Bruno's. His penchant for downhill skiing worked wonders on his buns, showing lily white against the tan of his back and legs. Yuri's mouth was watering.

Entering the pool house locker room, Bruno obligingly knelt down on the bench in front of the row of lockers and rested his hands on the face of the lockers. Now, dressed in only his hat, socks and sneakers, Yuri moved behind Bruno. "The minute I set eyes on you at the airport, I knew I wanted you — so bad. It was all I could do not to ravish you on the first night when you showed me to my room here at Holtzhaus. Was I wrong to think you felt the same as I did?"

"Do you really suppose it's possible not to react to a stud like you? Honey, you're gorgeous and I very much doubt you'll be leaving this house before we've all bedded you and you've had your way with each of us."

Yuri rubs his prick, oozing precum, around Bruno's hole and with his fingers, works the natural lubricating gel into Bruno's hole. "That feel good, babe, because I really need to enter you soon."

"Your fingers feel good but I'm ready for your cock. Fuck me, Yuri; I want it too, very badly. Stuff me with your dick."

"You know, Bruno, dressed in what remains of our tennis clothes, can't you imagine being tennis rivals like Andy Roddick and Roger Federer who like to play some games where the prize is sexual favors?"

"That's cool. Why don't you be Andy beating me, i.e., Federer, at Wimbledon. You claim the spoils of your victory in the locker room."

"Ok, Roger, you're on! You've knocked so many guys aside with your powerful serves and backhanded saves that it's time you were brought to account for the devastation you've wrought on so many fine careers."

"You were just one lucky dude to take me out today, Andy, so go ahead. Show me who's top man."

"With pleasure, motherfucker, you better get used to bending over and taking it up the ass because I intend to kick your ass every time we play. I'm going to own your asshole."

"You wish. Rafael Nadal is more likely to have claim to that privilege after beating me in the Madrid Open."

"Well right now your mine, babe." Andy pulls Roger's ass towards him to impale him on his ramrod straight cock. "That probably hurts, Roger, since you're not accustomed to present that pretty ass to rivals since you're used to being #1."

"Yeah it hurts but if I'm to be screwed, I don't want to be fucked by a wimp. Bang me!"

"Ok, slut, you're on for a serious sodomizing." Andy clenched Roger's bulging thighs to steady himself and his prey as he administered a rapid fire penetration of his tight hole. Andy's dick was like a pile driver, pounding Roger's uninitiated pussy into utter submission.

"Oh yes, Yuri, that is Andy, don't stop! I want to feel your dick detonating fireballs of cum bursting in my ass." Roger's shaftway was on fire with molten cum rampaging up his colon.

Working his cock, Bruno, i.e., Roger, jacked himself off, decorating the front of the lockers with splotches of running cum. "Oh Andy, your dick felt amazing! I'd consider throwing a game for you anytime."

"That was a hot fuck, Bruno. The fantasy was nice but your pretty butt is stimulation enough."

"You sure know how to throw a fuck, Yuri, but it's time we returned to the apartment after we clean up this mess and take a quick shower. Denis is probably ready for us to join him for the cocktail hour before we sit down to dinner."

Ascending the stairs up to the garage apartment, Bruno and Yuri find Denis just about to serve wine and cheese before dinner. "Welcome home, guys! So who was the victor on the courts?"

"Our guest proved unbeatable, love. But I hope to avenge myself when we get to play a rematch someday."

"Well you can't always be on top, babe. Relax and have some Camembert cheese. I'll open a bottle of Sauvignon Blanc. Sit! Put your feet up, Yuri. We so rarely entertain a guest. This is a real treat for us."

"Your apartment is such an unexpected surprise. It's every bit as nice as the main house. This large living area with the combined kitchen, dining and living room is magnificent. The beamed cathedral ceiling with the large windows on either end of the room plus the beautiful wood parquet floors is so beyond what I expected. Was the apartment provided with the Persian carpet, comfortable upholstered furniture and the antiques?"

"Yes, Yuri, my parents had lived here for years when my father acted as factotem for the estate. Eric's mother Anna insisted that this apartment not be furnished with cast-offs but rather be treated just as another part of her house."

"What's that marvelous odor wafting over from the kitchen, Denis?"

"It's my Coq au Vin, Yuri, prepared especially for you. With it we'll have mashed potatoes and corn."

"Playing tennis with Bruno all afternoon, I didn't realize how hungry I'd become."

"We'll sit down shortly. Have some more wine. I'll open another bottle for us to have with dinner," said Denis.

By the time dinner was put on the table, everyone was buzzed. For Yuri, playing so many exhausting sets of tennis, culminating in imbibing so much wine made him feel like he was floating. He was sure eating would help to stop the room from spinning. While eating the delicious food helped, the additional glasses of wine he drank only served to make him experience an out-of-body event. However, the chocolate mousse they had for dessert plus the strong German coffee brought him down to earth, but barely.

"Your place here is just great, guys, and dinner was beyond excellent. Eric and Viktor are lucky to have you here to — look out after them."

"Yes we like to take care of them. They are very kind to us in return." Bruno goes on to tell the story of how Denis came to Holtzhaus at Eric and Viktor's invitation so that when they were away on business, Bruno would not find himself without a companion. Denis, he went on to explain, is a Mercedes-Benz representative out of the Stuttgart factory who is responsible for interfacing with outside auto parts suppliers such as with Eric and Viktor's business.

While Denis keeps an apartment in Stuttgart, he spends as much time as possible in Regensburg to be with Bruno. Bruno describes when he first ushered Denis upstairs to inspect the apartment that was to become his home away from home. They'd just finished having dinner in the main house with Eric and Viktor. "Perhaps the story is better told down the hall in our bedroom where the initial tour of the apartment culminated," said Bruno.

Filing down the center hall to the large bedroom at its end, they enter another cathedral ceilinged room with a great antique four poster bed featured in the center of the room against the outside wall. To one side of the bed was an area containing a bath and dressing room surrounded by mirror paneled doors concealing the closets. On the other end of the room was a sitting area with a wraparound window seat under the wall of windows. As it was now dark just as it was on that first night, they could look out to a splendid moon lit view. Snowcapped mountains with a forest in the foreground were highlighted by a full moon just as on that magical first night with Denis. It was on the window seat that Bruno had first taken Denis.

"Since I've been monopolizing you all afternoon, Yuri, I thought it timely to share you with my lover. He caught a glimpse of what transpired on the tennis court this afternoon from the kitchen window while he was preparing dinner. So I thought sharing our first meeting with you could be combined with our first threesome. Are you too sated with food and drink to accommodate us?"

"Hardly, Bruno, you gave me a little taste this afternoon but now I'm ready for the three course meal."

"Take off your clothes, Yuri. It's time you let Denis see what ballet training can do for a former Spetsnaz officer's physique." Yuri complies and stands naked in front of the wall of windows with moonlight streaming through, bathing his body in a warm glow.

Denis drinks in the sight of the apparition gracing his bedroom and began to remove his clothes. "Since you had my ass this afternoon, Yuri, I didn't think you'd mind reciprocating," said Bruno. Bruno positions himself between Yuri and the window seat and proceeds to drop his trousers and undershorts. Sitting on the window seat, Bruno displays his very stiff dick, primed for action. "Sit on it, Yuri; you owe me some good pussy."

Climbing up on the window seat to face and straddle Bruno, Yuri lowers his mounds to hover over the pulsating prick. Bruno came prepared with lube and condoms. He hands one condom to Denis, standing behind Yuri, and puts one on himself and then begins to lube Yuri's asshole suspended in midair.

"Ok, Yuri, let my prick enter your ass for the first time." Yuri lowers himself down, while spreading his cheeks with his hands, until his hole is filled and his buns spread over Bruno's groin. "Shit yes, Yuri, your asshole feels like the softest velvet."

Yuri leans forward to begin French kissing Bruno. Bruno's prick slides partially out of Yuri's ass, leaving only the head inside. Suddenly, Bruno's prick is joined by Denis's cock to stretch Yuri's sphincter to its limit. Bruno and Denis's cocks act in concert and slowly work their way to thoroughly fill Yuri's hole.

"Wow, you boys make a fine tag team. Seems I'm to receive a proper double barreled screwing."

"We knew when Viktor and Eric got through with you last night that you'd have no trouble taking our combined effort. Do you like it?"

"Umm, I'll say. Fuck away boys. I never imagined that two dicks could feel so good. As he continued to explore Bruno's mouth, Bruno and Denis's dicks formed a monster cock that ramrodded into Yuri's gaping orifice and bumped against his joy spot. They serviced their raging stallion whose clenching colon, in turn, drove them to a frenzy of unrestrained fucking, battering Yuri's hole unmercifully.

Collectively, they were sent to sensual nirvana as Yuri was the first to fire sprays of cum all over Bruno's shirt. The initial volley from Yuri was the cue for Bruno and Denis to send answering volleys of cum up Yuri's asshole. There was a cacophony of shouts of joy.

Yuri frees himself from the invading cocks to allow Bruno to go to the bathroom to clean himself up. "After that, Yuri, I intend to lobby Eric and Viktor to extend frequent invitations for you to visit Holtzhaus," Bruno said, dragging himself to the bathroom.

Yuri gathers Denis up in his arms and lays him down on the side of the four poster bed. "I'm not finished with you yet my hot little friend."

"Give me a little of what you gave Bruno in the pool house locker room, Yuri. I won't have it said that we weren't perfect hosts."

"Never fear, Denis, your burning asshole will be testament enough to your excellent hospitality."

Yuri slides Denis's buns beyond the edge of the bed and hauls his legs high into the air as he spears his asshole with his prick, taking no care to proceed gently. "Was I wrong to think this household's favorite butt boy would want to be taken without the usual preliminaries?"

"You got that right, stud. There's no need to feed me a lot of tired lines, just demonstrate your need for me by plowing me senseless."

With his back arched and with an iron grip on Denis's ankles, Yuri was positioned to deliver a deeply penetrating invasion. Denis ran his hands over Yuri's heaving chest and pinched his erect tits to further inflame his attacker. Yuri's prick plunged into Denis's rectum with ferocious speed, reducing Denis to a fawning conquest. "Yuriiii!!!" screamed Denis as his battered prostate forced another orgasm out of his rioting cock.

Viewing his prey in extremis, Yuri rocketed over the edge of control and called out Denis's name. "Denissss!!! Yuri's prick vibrated furiously as he injected great volumes of sperm up Denis's ass. Yuri collapsed on top of Denis as his waist was encircled with Denis's legs.

Returning from the bathroom Bruno said, "Give it a rest, boys. We don't want any casualties!" As they were dressing, they heard the big Audi A8 sedan coming up the driveway, delivering Eric, Viktor and Cliff back to the house. "Thanks for a wonderful evening guys. You're the best," said Yuri as he kissed Bruno and Denis and bade them goodnight.

Yuri descended the stairs leaving the garage apartment to return to the main house to find his hosts and Cliff in the kitchen. "Well, gentlemen, how was your evening in Regensburg with the former mistress of Holtzhaus?" Yuri inquired.

"It was a truly memorable evening," said Viktor. "Anna was in good form and most entertaining. She has charm to spare."

Just then Cliff's cell phone began to ring and he had to excuse himself to take a call from Jason Stone. After concluding the call, Cliff announced, "Looks like I won't be returning to Washington with you guys."

CHAPTER 8

The urgent assignment Jason Stone dropped on Cliff so suddenly required him to fly from Munich International Airport to the St. Thomas Airport in the Virgin Islands. From there, Cliff took a small plane to the British Virgin Islands and ferried to the island of Virgin Gorda. He checked in at the Rosewood Little Dix Bay hotel and took a junior suite. Cliff was to look up a certain Sir Malcolm Howard who was known to keep his yacht at the Bitter End Yacht Club on Virgin Gorda. Sir Malcolm was suspected of being involved in the laundering of money from the sale of illegal narcotics. He started his own bank, located on Grand Cayman Island, several years ago which is believed to have on deposit hundreds of millions of dollars in numbered accounts belonging to drug dealers.

Sir Malcolm, a British aristocrat and former polo champion, comes from a distinguished banking family. However, his dissolute lifestyle caused him to squander much of his inheritance and to alienate himself from his illustrious family. Needing money to continue his extravagant lifestyle, Sir Malcolm turned his skills in banking to a criminal venture. The United States Drug Enforcement Administration (DEA) had him on a watch list for some time. So far he's managed to escape prosecution. Now the department of Homeland Security has taken an interest, given fears that the laundered money is finding its way into Al Qaeda groups in the Middle East.

An intelligence report given to Cliff indicated that Sir Malcolm employed a captain for his yacht named Bartholemew Wimble, who spent what little off time he had at a bar which was located in the Fischer's Cove Beach Hotel. Captain Bart was 38 years old, 5'-11" tall, with brown eyes, dark brown hair and a cleft chin. He was handsome in a roughhewn sort of way and played rugby when he attended public school in England. He went on to a career in the Royal Navy but opted out when lifestyle issues became a problem. The dashing young Commander was gay.

Bart Wimble met Sir Malcolm at the christening of a Royal Naval ship where his mother, Lady Cavendish, did the honors. Bart joined Sir Malcolm in a pub afterwards to enjoy downing a few pints of beer together. They became lovers despite the fact that Sir Malcolm was married. When Bart left the Royal Navy, Malcolm took him on as captain of his 126' yacht called the Miss Uranus. The yacht remains in the waters of the British Virgin Islands most of the year but there are occasional trips to London and New York. Malcolm's wife visits Virgin Gorda maybe twice a year at most.

Despite Captain Bart's status as Malcolm's unofficial lover, Bart enjoys finding bedmates when he's on his own, usually at his favorite hotel bar. Cliff sees the bar as the perfect opportunity for him to seek out Bart's company. Determining that one of the bartenders was gay as well as a former playmate of Bart's, Cliff enlisted his aid, with a substantial gratuity, to affect an introduction. When Bart next came into the bar, the bartender was to present him a drink, complements of the American at the end of the bar. When Bart came in, the drink was offered which he gratefully accepted by raising his glass in thanks. Cliff, after a short interval, joined him by slipping onto an adjacent bar stool.

"Thierry, the bartender, allowed as how you like Beefeater martinis. Hope he didn't steer me wrong."

"Not at all, my friend, and to whom do I owe the honor of being singled out for such generosity?"

"Cliff Bradshaw and who is it I'm talking to?"

"Bartholemew Wimble. Bart to you," he responded with a warm smile.

"Well, Bart, you have the look of a former navy man. You look like you belong around boats and the sea."

"Guilty as charged, Cliff my boy, you have keen instincts. What brings you to these islands?"

"Well I have a private security business that requires me to travel, often in pursuit of philandering husbands. Not the most elevating work at times but it pays the bills." Cliff lied.

"Do you get to take compromising pictures of the wandering spouse?"

"Part of the job I'm afraid. Some of the illicit liaisons are not what the wife expected."

"Now you've tweaked my interest, Cliff, tell me more!"

"Well you know. Some of the guys like variety — as in — man on man stuff."

"That must make your job more interesting, Cliff. Does that sort of thing happen often?"

"Much more often than you'd imagine. Some of these guys really got off on switch hitting, especially when they found themselves on the bottom."

"You must have quite a collection of prurient shots. I'd love to see them sometime."

"No problem. I'm staying over at the Rosewood Little Dix Bay hotel. Why don't you take a run over there with me?"

"Don't mind if I do. But I mustn't stay too late as I must get back to the yacht where I'm employed as captain.

Cliff's junior suite has all the comforts you could ask for. The cathedral ceiling is high with wood beams and decking, the walls stucco, the floors tiled. The large four-poster bed faces a wall of sliding glass doors, flanked by wood shutters, looking out on to a tiled patio surrounded by palm trees with a small pool overlooking the ocean beyond.

Anticipating that he'd lure Captain Bart to his room with the promise of viewing these incriminating photos, Cliff had contacted Debbie Berger to research websites featuring these items and to e-mail pictures she found so he could call them up on his laptop computer when needed. Gay porn sites couldn't boast of more stimulating images.

Sitting together on the wicker couch and sipping their martinis that Cliff mixed in the suite's kitchenette, Bart's eyes were popping out of his head at the array of X-rated photos. His shorts could barely contain his stiff cock. "Christ, Cliff, you're an artist. These photos are professional."

"Placing his hand on Bart's shorts to grip his stiff dick, Cliff said, "Yes I see they're not lost on you, Bart."

Bart placed his hand on Cliff's where it rested on his cock and leaned over to kiss him on the mouth. "I knew you were going to taste good, Cliff."

"Before you have to leave, I want you to enjoy the pool on the terrace. It's big enough for two and the view can't be beat."

They each undress and take their martinis out to the small pool. The moon filters through the cloud cover to dapple the terrace and pool with a soft glow. Bart's body retains the physical fitness from his soccer days, reflected particularly in his muscled legs and ass. Since there's only a minimal crew on Malcolm's boat, Bart gets a daily workout keeping himself shipshape. Cliff's dick rises in appreciation of what his score has to offer.

Bart sits at the edge of the pool facing the view. "This view sure beats the views from the yacht club marina, Cliff."

Sitting next to Bart, Cliff encircles his prick with his hand and said, "The view is perfect now that you're here, Bart." Cliff works Bart's stiff dick. "That feels ok?"

"More than ok but I bet your mouth would be even better." Slipping into the pool to face Bart, Cliff sinks down to suck in Bart's throbbing prick. Bart leans back, supported by his outstretched arms and spreads his legs to give Cliff greater access. Bobbing his head, Cliff gives Bart a thorough servicing of his cock and balls.

"Cliff, Cliff! You're the best. Your mouth is incredible!"

"Get on your back, Bart, and raise your legs. I want a taste of that pink pucker buried in your crack." Bart falls on to his back and with his hands behind his knees, he raised his legs with his thighs against his chest and the lower half of his legs stretched vertically in the air.

"Oh yeah, eat me, Cliff. I'd hoped you were going to be a booty hound. Go for it!"

Using his hands to spread open Bart's crack, Cliff's tongue pierced the pink gateway and entered the pleasure passage. Pausing to gasp for air, Cliff asked, "What would you say to having my prick stuffed up your ass, Bart?"

"I'd say sign me up, Cliff! Let me get my butt up on the chaise lounge so you can plow me proper with enough cushion so you won't have to bank your fires." Getting himself up and positioning himself on the chaise, he said, "Cliff you're such a stud! I knew before the night was over that I couldn't deny you getting your fill of my asshole. Fuck me! I don't get much shore leave and need to be taken when I can find a buck like you. Don't spare me. Screw me like you would one of the beach boys."

"When I enter you, wrap your gorgeous legs around my waist, Bart, and then wrap your arms around my neck and then kiss me like you mean it. You're going to be screwed like a common whore."

Wetting his fingers with saliva, Cliff inserts them into Bart to apply minimal attention to lubricating him before taking him. Then, forcefully bucking his hips, Cliff jams his engorged cock deep into a moaning Bart. Savoring his conquest and possession, Cliff works his hips gently to tease the grasping orifice. There was no question of Bart's complete surrender.

"Shit yeah, Cliff, don't tease me! Screw me until my eyes roll in their sockets. Pulverize my asshole with cock!"

"You kinky English slut!" Cliff's great butt mounds rose up high to drop back down with tremendous force, inserting his dick in and back out in an unabated cadence so as to plunder Bart's colon savagely.

Engaged in a tongue sucking kiss, Cliff and Bart's dicks gave up their copious loads in many ecstatic ejaculations. They stayed locked together for many moments until they regained their senses. "You need to come ashore more often, Bart. I could do with more of that."

"Well the remedy for that is for you to come aboard the Miss Uranus. My friend and employer, Sir Malcolm, would appreciate meeting you." *Bingo,* Cliff thought.

A couple of days later, Cliff received a call from Captain Bart inviting him to come aboard the Miss Uranus to take a trip out to the South Drop of Virgin Gorda where there was excellent fishing. Sir Malcolm, it seemed, was up for catching some blue marlin. Cliff was pleased to accept. The next morning he found his way to the Bitter End Yacht Club to seek out where the Miss Uranus was moored. Approaching the boat, Cliff couldn't help but be impressed. It was a 126' long luxury yacht with a dazzling white fiberglass hull, powered by twin diesel engines. A crew member met him and ushered him aboard.

Upon entering the elegant salon, he was greeted by Captain Bart who introduced him to Sir Malcolm. "Pleased to meet you Sir Malcolm. Captain Bart, while heaping praise on your beautiful yacht, was too restrained. It's quite magnificent."

"Kind of you to say so, Mr. Bradshaw. We're very informal here on the islands. Please call me Malcolm. May I be permitted to call you Cliff?" Sir Malcolm wasn't at all what Cliff expected. He's 6'-2" tall, very fair with chiseled features, long blonde hair and light blue eyes, maybe 42 years old but looking much younger. He's obviously very physically fit although his polo playing days were over. More surprising is that he's quite likeable with an easy grace. But upon further inspection, his eyes revealed a person with certain ruthlessness, disguised by impeccable manners.

"Please call me Cliff, Malcolm. Your invitation to join you on a fishing expedition off of Virgin Gorda is a real treat. At home in the US when I went fishing in the Potomac River, I fished for bass. Fishing for blue marlin will be a welcome challenge."

"Yes, Cliff, you'll find it so. Blue marlin can often be 100 to 200 pounds or more," said Malcolm. "Let Bart show you to your stateroom so you can stow your gear and then we can take you for a tour of the boat before we cast off."

Bart showed Cliff to his luxurious stateroom. It was wood paneled, had built-in storage with plush carpeting and recessed lighting. The en suite bathroom was a study in marble luxury. "With deluxe accommodations like this, you must have trouble with guests wanting to overstay their welcome."

"You'll never wear out your welcome, Cliff. You don't know Malcolm the way I do but let me tell you, he was very taken with you. No question."

"Looks like I'm in for an interesting few days, Bart."

"To be sure, Cliff. You're something of a captive audience on a boat like this. Hope you're up for it. Malcolm is used to having — his way," Bart said with a sly smile.

"Malcolm is easy on the eyes, Bart, much more so than I imagined. I don't feel we'll have any difficulties in finding — common ground."

"Just so you're forewarned. With a couple of scotches, he can be quite aggressive."

"Can you be relied upon to keep me from harm's way, Bart?"

"Hardly, Cliff. Your presence will serve to give me a respite from the nightly visits to my cabin. I could do with a little relief."

"Do I take you to mean that you'll be idle during my stay? I'd hoped to enjoy a reprise of our tete-a-tete at my hotel patio."

"Not to worry. You won't be denied anything you want. But the master of this ship has priority."

"Point taken, Bart. How about a little preview of coming attractions?" Cliff embraces Bart and French kisses him while feeling up his ass through his starched white cotton shorts.

"We mustn't keep Malcolm waiting. He wants to give you the grand tour before we set out for the South Drop."

The tour of the ship terminated at the pilot house so that Captain Bart could begin the procedure to cast off. Crew members were at the ready to cast off when the captain so ordered. They were underway, proceeding out of the marina and into open water. Their destination was not far from the island. When the captain found an agreeable spot, he dropped anchor. The cook was just serving lunch on the aft deck as the twin diesel engines were turned off.

After a lunch of seafood salad, Cliff joined Malcolm and Bart at the stern of the boat to begin fishing. Blue marlins were reported as being in the waters around the South Drop but until you cast off your line, it was impossible to know for sure. Being sport fishermen, the catch was not particularly important but Malcolm wanted to have blue marlin for supper that night.

The great catch of the day was to be Cliff's prize. He landed a 120 pound blue marlin, after a bit of a struggle, with assistance from Bart and advice from Malcolm. They enjoyed many bottles of Blackbeard Ale while trying for another great catch. It wasn't to be but all enjoyed their afternoon out on the ocean before calling it a day. The blue marlin that Cliff caught was given to the cook to prepare for the evening meal.

Cliff returned to his stateroom to shower and dress for dinner. The steward had unpacked his bag and put his clothes away in the built-in cupboard. His dop kit was deposited in the bathroom and towels were laid out for his use. Living in luxury must become a necessity when you've become accustomed to it, Cliff reflects. Sad that Sir Malcolm resorted to a life of crime to support what he obviously considered his birthright, i.e., an absolute right to all the luxuries the world had to offer.

Malcolm and Bart were at the bar in the salon when Cliff joined them. The steward had mixed up some martinis which suited everyone. Dinner was to be served in the adjacent dining room separated from the salon by a glass screen etched with a lovely Art Deco design. Another steward was already setting the table with English bone china, elegant stainless steel flatware and tempered glass goblets on a fine linen tablecloth with matching napkins,

Malcolm was in high spirits entertaining Cliff and Bart with stories of his carefree youth, traveling the polo circuit in the company of royals and aristocrats. The dinner gong was rung and the three men went to the dining room, now sparkling with candlelight. Tchaikovsky's Serenade for Strings in C Major was featured on the sound system.

The chef did wonders with the blue marlin, broiling it in a Marsala cream sauce. The side dishes were long grain wild rice and asparagus. A light rum cake completed the meal. Given that an afternoon out in the hot sun had wearied them, it was decided that they'd take in a movie in the media room. The stewards and the cook would clean up and return to the lower level where their facilities were located. It was understood that they were to remain below unless summoned by either Malcolm or Bart.

The movie 300, featuring the Spartan King Leonidas with a force of 300 men fighting the Persians at Thermopylae in 480 B.C., served to stir their libidinous spirits. Afterwards Malcolm invited Cliff and Bart to the master cabin where he mixed up another batch of martinis. Malcolm's cabin was the full width of the boat with oversized portholes on each side. Built-ins abounded for everything such as clothes, television and sound system. Built under the portholes on one side was a white leather sofa. On the other side was a built-in desk with a laptop computer sitting on top. Malcolm motioned Cliff and Bart to sit on the sofa.

Malcolm, standing, adjusted the recessed lighting to a low setting so that the outside light provided by the many stars in the night sky could be appreciated. "Glad you waited to show me your cabin until night time rather than on my tour. It would be beautiful anytime but it's spectacular at night."

"Admittedly, it was by design that I waited, trusting that you'd be so affected. Why don't you kneel up on the sofa and get a close up view out of the porthole. You'll be able to see the twinkling lights on Virgin Gorda in the distance."

Doing as Malcolm suggested, Cliff got up on his knees on the sofa to face out the porthole, his elbows propped up on the sill. His lightweight linen shorts were stretched tightly across his buns, instantly resulting in Malcolm's cock coming to full attention in his shorts. Setting his martini down on the coffee table, Malcolm drew up to Cliff and pressed himself up against his buns. "I'm feeling a bit like Xerxes the Persian King, Cliff. Would you like to be King Leonidas, the Spartan King whom I'm going to defeat in battle?"

"The movie really sparked your imagination, Malcolm, rather Xerxes. Perhaps if we — negotiate — you'll go easy on my men. You obviously far outnumber us."

"Certainly, Leonidas, if you offer me a manly fuck, I could see my way clear to sparing some of your men by merely enslaving them. They'll be welcome in our camps and used like wives."

"Then I'll do as I must. You would take me here on my knees?"

"Indeed, my commander Hydarnes will strip you and prepare you for entry. Do it Bart!"

Bart gets condoms and lube out of the built-in end table. Handing a condom to Malcolm, he strips Cliff and lubricates his asshole.

"Very well, Leonidas, present your hole to me. Place your hands on your butt cheeks and spread open that crack so I can view your pouting portal." As he glances behind to access the size of the invading equipment, Cliff spreads his cheeks and tries to relax his anus to receive a cock rivaling Viktor Sidorov's. No wonder Bart needed some relief from his nightly screwings.

Bart lathered lube on Malcolm's pole and sat back to watch Cliff's defilement. Malcolm bumped his cock head against Cliff's winking pucker before ramming his dick home, burying his huge cock to the hilt. Cliff, no stranger to big cock, took it without flinching and tried to relax and enjoy it. Truth be told, Malcolm's dick felt good and Cliff wanted it.

"Butch studs who know how to take cock up their ass turn me on, Cliff. Your velvety smooth hole feels sooo fantastic!"

"Shove that big dick into me, Malcolm. You know I love it. Give it to me good, man. Fuck my pussy!!"

"Butch studs who are cock whores excite me even more, Cliff. Hold on while I pound a great set of buns and service your hole." Malcolm proceeds to batter Cliff's quivering mounds while screwing his quaking rectum. "Oh god yes, Cliff!!!" Malcolm screams out as his rioting body releases oceans of swimming cum. Cliff was truly well fucked.

Pulling himself out of Cliff's ass, Malcolm fell on the sofa next to Cliff and grabbed hold of his prey's jumping dick. "So what are we going to do with this, Cliff?"

"Well, Malcolm, you're packing some nice butt cheeks and I'd say it's time you got in touch with spreading your legs for your man. Get over on that king bed on your back. You're about to find out what it's like to put out."

Having drunk four martinis since dinner, Malcolm's usual resolve to remain the dominant male was diminished sufficiently to allow him to relax his macho stance and do as he was bidden. With his head comfortable placed on a down pillow, Malcolm lay on his back with his legs bent at the knees and spread in welcome.

Cliff lay on top of Malcolm, nestled between his thighs with his cock exploring Malcolm's crack. "None of your polo playing buddies managed to get to first base in seeking out your potential as a bottom?"

"They managed to get a finger or two past my derriere into my anus to tease my prostate but that was as far as I allowed them to go."

"So what about now, Malcolm. Do you think you're capable of tossing me a fuck comparable to the one you just gave me?"

"It seems we're about to find out, Cliff. There was no question I was going to give it up to *someone*. You're the only one to come along that I could offer myself to. You see, I couldn't do it until I encountered a man who made me feel — submissive. You'll find me unresistant. In fact I want to be dominated, conquered and deeply sodomized."

After exploring Malcolm's mouth, Cliff said, "Wrap your legs around me. I want to feel the heels of your feet dug into the small of my back. When I begin fucking you, dig them in to increase the depth of my penetration. Your anus will be permanently stretched to offer no further resistance to your many future lovers. For after tonight, you'll be transformed into a bottom with an insatiable appetite for cock."

Malcolm, incredibly turned on by Cliff's words, moves his knees back so as to lift his feet off the mattress and create a cradle to house his deflowerer. "Christ, Cliff, I want you in me. How can it be that I waited so long?"

Bart hands a condom and lube to Cliff. Sheathed in the condom, Cliff slips a lubed middle finger into Malcolm's tight hole and works to loosen the clutching sphincter. Patiently, he waits until he can coax the portal to open further to accept a second finger and then a third. Malcolm is already responding to being finger fucked, writhing and moaning with pleasure.

"You ready for my prick, Malcolm because I've had enough of this preliminary shit."

"Mount me, Cliff. You've made me crave to be taken more than I've ever wanted to take anyone. Screw me! Make me your slave!"

Cliff's dick popped through the loosened entry to begin the inexorable journey up the love chute. Malcolm was toast, realizing he never before felt complete until he was filled with Cliff's cock. Cliff's groin stopped with its first smack against Malcolm's splendid arse. "Ooohhh, Cliff!! Yes, yes, yes please!!!"

Cliff worked his hips like a pendulum, swinging forward and back in a slow tantalizing rhythm, driving a mewling Malcolm to unrestrained cries of joy. When the slow torture became too much to sustain, Cliff introduced Malcolm to the Olympian peaks of passion. No longer sparing the bottom in training, Cliff power fucked Malcolm, grinding his big English fanny deep into the mattress.

Malcolm's screams escalated to high pitched cries of ecstasy as Cliff exploded into his condom, stretching its endurance to the brink. Cliff's cries of ecstasy joined Malcolm's into a discordant cacophony of nonsensical sounds. Malcolm's chest was awash in cum he jet sprayed over his bulging pecs.

Pulling out, Cliff announced, "You're officially a slut now Malcolm. Come, Bart, time for you to relate on an even playing field with your friend and employer. Mount up and take a ride. I can assure you his pussy is ripe for further action." Bart greedily took Cliff's place and mounted Malcolm and took him as if he were a bitch in heat, not sparing his tender tush. Bart and Malcolm sang the same song of ecstasy that Cliff just got finished singing with Malcolm. It seemed that Malcolm really was the needy bottom, as advertised.

After Bart dismounted, he got up and said he needed to call it a night as he was exhausted, but happily so. He returned to the Captain's Quarters. Malcolm entreated Cliff to stay and spend the night in his bed. While Cliff acceded to the request, he excused himself to go to his stateroom to retrieve his tooth brush.

Slipping on his shorts, Cliff returned to his stateroom to gather up not only his tooth brush but also two additional items, knock-out tablets and a flash drive to transfer data from one computer to another. When he arrived back in Malcolm's cabin, his return was timed perfectly to find Malcolm in the bathroom. Cliff dropped the knock-out tablets into Malcolm's martini and took off his shorts to pose himself on the king bed with his martini in hand.

When Malcolm returned from the bathroom, Cliff proposed a toast to their — *friendship.* "Drink up, Malcolm; you're not going to sleep until you give me a little more pussy. Down your drink and take up a position on your stomach because you're going to be fucked repeatedly until you fall asleep, babe." Malcolm was only too eager to comply. When the tablets did their job of knocking Malcolm out, Cliff inserted the flash devise in to Malcolm's laptop computer. Booting up the laptop, Cliff put Debbie Berger's training to work to by-pass the security wall and access code to gain entry. It took a bit of trial and error to hit on the file where Malcolm concealed the special numbered accounts at his bank, belonging to the heavy hitters in the drug trafficking trade.

Once he downloaded the pertinent files, Cliff assiduously followed Debbie's instructions in covering his tracks so his surreptitious visit on the laptop would go undetected. Cliff hastened back to his stateroom to conceal the flash drive containing all the purloined data in a secret compartment in his dop kit. Mission accomplished, he slipped back into Malcolm's cabin to spend the night.

Upon awakening the next morning, Cliff discovered Malcolm's head bobbing over his morning boner. Last night's marathon fuck fest hadn't diminished Malcolm's cravings for Cliff's cock. "Your mouth is every bit as good as your ass, Malcolm."

"Thanks, old boy, but I was merely priming the pump before getting to my real objective." Moving up to straddling Cliff, Malcolm guided his ass down to receive Cliff's towering prick. Fully impaled, Malcolm leaned over to kiss Cliff fully awake. "Now that you're up and running, Cliff, why don't you have another go at my arse."

Reaching around Malcolm's fulsome cheeks, Cliff ran his fingers into the deep cleft to spread the luscious buns apart. Malcolm's ravaged hole, swollen from last night's plundering, opened engagingly to receive another pummeling from Cliff's dick.

Cliff's hips seemed to run riot of their own volition in submitting Malcolm's spasming colon to another punishing screwing. Malcolm was delirious with pleasure, as he rode Cliff's bucking hips while jacking himself off. Quickly coming to climax, the two joined in discordant moans as their cocks erupted with fresh, early morning sperm.

"This is the way I'd like to wake up every morning, Cliff. You've done the impossible in converting me into an insatiable bottom."

"Bart seems poised to take on the task, Malcolm. Your new itch won't go unattended."

"Well there is that of course but I'll expect you to return to us aboard the Miss Uranus for a return engagement. Time to shower and dress! Cook will send you off with a nice American style breakfast."

Breakfast on the aft deck was as promised, scrambled eggs and bacon with English muffins. They were just getting up from breakfast as they sailed into the yacht club marina. A steward had packed up all of Cliff's things and brought them to him so he could disembark from the yacht. Malcolm and Bart stood on deck extending their farewells to Cliff and urging him to come again.

Unobserved by Cliff were the people on the neighboring yacht, moored alongside the Miss Uranus. Sitting around a table on the aft deck was a group of four people having breakfast. Among them was none other than Pavel Jakov, the former Russian KGB officer turned hustler. Pavel couldn't believe his eyes when he observed Anatoly Nevesky, the alleged Muscovite who turned out to be an American spy, leaving the neighboring yacht. Anatoly ensnared him into a brief relationship only as a ploy in a conspiracy to grab the money he and Olga Kuznetsov stole from Grigory Vasiliev. Pavel's stash was removed from his bank account electronically by underhanded means, leaving him penniless. Now he was relegated to servicing affluent American couples who enjoyed sexual experimentation while vacationing in the Caribbean.

Excusing himself to make a call, Pavel went into the salon to make a cell phone call to his financial backer, Vince Angotti. Pavel related to Vince who he just observed leaving Sir Malcolm Howard's yacht at the Bitter End Yacht Club. Alarmed by the implications, Vince immediately phoned his partner in crime, Malcolm Howard.

When Vince spoke to Malcolm on his cell phone, there was immediate confusion as to the identity of this Anatoly Nevesky. Malcolm's first reaction was that it was a case of mistaken identity for his guest was an American named Cliff Bradshaw. Vince decided he'd better make sure that there was no mistake. He determined to check with his former business partner in Moscow, Grigory Vasiliev, who had many government sources for information.

It took a couple of hours but Grigory phoned Vince back to confirm that Anatoly Nevesky and Cliff Bradshaw were one and the same man and a dangerous American agent for Homeland Security. Vince got back in touch with Malcolm to inform him that they indeed had a serious problem on their hands.

That led to the question of what Cliff was about in wrangling an invitation aboard Malcolm's yacht. When Malcolm became candid about last night's activities that made his laptop computer available to Cliff, Vince became alarmed with the possibility that Cliff may have downloaded sensitive information. Malcolm assured Vince that his laptop had sufficient protection to prevent unauthorized access. Vince was not convinced and decided that Cliff would have to be apprehended.

After finding out from Malcolm where Cliff was staying, Vince dispatched two of his best men to capture him and bring him to his yacht which he was in the process of moving to the waters offshore of Cliff's hotel. Their instructions were to not only bring Cliff to the beach but also his luggage, where they'd be picked up by a dingy from the yacht under the cover of darkness. Capturing Cliff was made easy given that he had no inkling that his cover was blown. Angotti's thugs found Cliff asleep on a chaise lounge out on his terrace, recovering from his marathon sexcapades from the night before. A quick injection rendered him harmless so he could be transported to the shore where they'd be picked up.

After being brought aboard Angotti's yacht, Cliff was taken to the lower deck where a cabin was prepared that would serve to imprison him while he was submitted to questioning. In the meantime, his luggage would be thoroughly searched for whatever might be revealed. The secret compartment in Cliff's dop kit was duly discovered revealing the flash drive containing the information on the illicit numbered accounts.

While Cliff was on Virgin Gorda, he had been in constant touch with both his lover Brad Ames and Debbie Berger, head of Cyber Security at Homeland Security. He spoke to Debbie earlier in the day after he relayed the purloined data from Malcolm's laptop to her computers in Washington. She immediately set to work in divesting the funds from the numbered accounts into Homeland Security accounts.

Brad had been trying to rouse Cliff on his cell phone, unsuccessfully, when he began to become worried. The GPS device imbedded under Cliff's skin revealed that he was now offshore in a location opposite his hotel. Cliff had said nothing about going out on a boat, having just returned from his fishing trip with Malcolm Howard. Brad was sure something was wrong.

Deciding that something had to be done immediately, Brad phoned Jason Stone, head of Homeland Security, to volunteer to go to the island of Virgin Gorda to do what was necessary to secure Cliff's safe return. Jason gave the ok and Brad made arrangements to take the next flight.

Meanwhile back aboard Vince Angotti's yacht, Cliff was questioned intensely by Angotti to no avail, despite several beatings. Frustrated, Angotti decided to bring Pavel Jakov into the picture, thinking he might have better success given their brief but intense relationship. Pavel was upset when he came aboard to find Cliff battered and bruised. He was told to get Cliff talking because time was running out before they would take Cliff out to sea and dump him overboard, eliminating any further interference from him.

What Vince hadn't calculated was that Pavel had genuine feelings for Cliff despite the fact that Cliff was responsible for making him $4,000,000 poorer. Also, he hadn't signed up for murder. While he liked money, he was no killer. Pavel decided to assist Cliff in escaping from the yacht, regardless of the consequences.

Once it became known that Cliff was a Homeland Security operative, Malcolm contacted his bank to freeze the numbered accounts shown on his laptop so that the monies contained within would be secured from any transfers. Debbie Berger had already beaten him to the punch. All the numbered accounts in question had been transferred out and were untraceable. Malcolm was beside himself and resorted to binge drinking to escape from thinking about the ramifications.

When Cliff had regained consciousness, Pavel explained what Angotti was planning to do but pledged his support in aiding Cliff's escape. Cliff asked Pavel to retrieve his cell phone from his luggage so he could phone Brad. Willing to risk it, Pavel left Cliff long enough to find out where the luggage was being held and to snatch the cell phone. Once the phone was in Cliff's possession, he phoned Brad to discover he'd just landed at the St. Thomas Airport.

"Christ, Cliff, it's so good to hear your voice. I was so worried!"

"No one's done me in yet but there is a plan about to be enacted to silence me once and for all." Cliff outlines his predicament to Brad. They strategize a plan calling for Brad to get hold of an inflatable yacht tender with a quiet motor so that he can approach the Angotti yacht to pick up Cliff and Pavel.

The yacht's only security at night was the presence of one of Angotti's thugs in the pilothouse. When Pavel sighted Brad's tender approaching, he went topside to check out who was on duty that night to find the designated lookout fast asleep with an empty bottle of gin in his lap. Pavel returned below to assist a still shaky Cliff out on the lower deck where they could disembark at the stern platform. Cliff helped them aboard the tender and they were able to escape undetected.

"We owe you a debt of gratitude for helping to save Cliff's life, Pavel. Why did you take such a risk?" Brad asked.

"While it's true that I've done some things I'm not proud of, I draw the line at murder. It seems I've come full circle but where I go from here is anybody's guess."

"You sure as hell can't stay here, Pavel. After tonight, you'll be a marked man." said Cliff.

"You're telling me. What the hell, I've been in worst spots and have come out on top."

"Brad, we'll have to take Pavel back to Washington with us. There's no way we can leave him here."

"What do you say, Pavel, are you ready to pull up stakes and come to the US with us?" Brad asked.

"Looks like the best option I have if I want to stay alive. Angotti would pull out all the stops in meting out punishment for my betrayal."

"Do you have your passport and ID in your bag?" Cliff asked.

"Don't go anywhere without it. You never know when it's time to bid a hasty retreat."

"Good, we'll head for the airport and get on the next flight to Washington," Cliff said.

They barely made it to get on the last flight to D.C. The plane was maybe one third full with most of the passengers clustered at the front of the plane. The steward, a friendly young man with a French accent, showed them to three seats at the rear of the plane where it was private and quiet.

The three fell into their seats exhausted but exhilarated to have pulled off their escape. Pavel was wired, thinking of the new adventure he was embarking on and wondering when his life would ever settle down.

Cliff sat in the window seat looking out over the Virgin Islands as the plane climbed into the night sky. He couldn't help feeling elated that he cheated death again and was reunited with his lover, Brad. His feelings for Pavel had changed into one of an enduring friendship, tinged with lust. He committed himself then to seeing that Pavel's life didn't continue to unravel.

Brad, sitting in the aisle seat, was breathing a sigh of relief that Cliff was safe and coming home with him. He acknowledged to himself what a debt they owed to Pavel for the risks he'd taken for them. Brad reached over and clasped Pavel's hand in a silent tribute, reflecting all that he was feeling. Cliff, from the other side of Pavel, joined in clasping Pavel's other hand, understanding what Brad's gesture meant.

Hand in hand, they dozed off awakening in time for a late night snack served up by the flight attendant, who they learned hailed from Martinique. "More scotch for you gentlemen? Compliments of the house!"

The three were only too happy to indulge themselves. It had been, after all, a very long day. Henri, the flight attendant, provided blankets and pillows so they would be more comfortable when they chose to doze off again. The armrests were adjusted up so that the seats weren't so confined. Pavel took advantage of this fact to curl up with his head in Brad's lap. Brad's prick took immediate notice and was straining against his fly.

Brad's arousal wasn't lost on Pavel who came to the rescue by unzipping Brad's fly and removing his stiff cock. Once the big thing was out, Pavel had no choice but to make love to it. Big cock always made him crazy. Cliff, seeing the developing situation, decided to join in for a bit of recreational sex. He unbuckled Pavel's belt and pulled his pants down, exposing the lush pair of buns which commanded so much money on the islands. The blankets were deftly arranged to mask the forbidden carnal acts. With a little saliva for lubrication, Cliff slipped his prick between Pavel's cheeks and into the velvet passage.

Henri passed down the aisle signaling his complicity with a wink of an eye and a smile directed at Brad who returned both. Brad was awed by Pavel's obvious talent in servicing his cock. Turning towards Cliff, they exchanged eye contact, communicating the pleasure each was receiving from the ever willing Pavel. Looking lovingly into each other's eyes, Brad and Cliff popped their loads into Pavel whose body racked with the pleasure of being doubly serviced.

When Pavel sat back up in his seat, Brad got up to go to the bathroom while Cliff went down on Pavel, greedily swallowing his shaft to hungrily feed on his prick. Henri passed by their seats moving to the rear of the plane where Brad had gone.

As Brad opened the door to the lavatory, he found Henri right behind him, leaving no doubt as to what his intentions were. Brad moved on into the lavatory, dropped his pants and sat on the toilet with his cock pointed up to the stars. Henri squeezed himself inside and closed the door behind him. Shedding his trousers and red bikini underwear, Henri faced away from Brad and dropped down to sit on his cock. "There was no way you were getting off this plane before I experienced every inch of your dick up my ass."

"Henri, I feel honored that you singled me out for your favors. And honey, it's good, it's way good."

"Your dick is awesome, man. Studs like you are few and far between on my route and I intend to take full advantage when one comes my way."

"Work that ass, babe; show me what a Frenchman from Martinique can do for the American tourist trade." Henri's perfect little globes bobbled on Brad's lap as he rode the arc of lust while working his dick to maximum fullness. Brad slipped his hands under the bouncing flight attendant's T-shirt and pinched his raised nipples, causing him to lose all control; splattering the wall of the lavatory with dripping cum. Brad delivered an answering volley of cum up the young man's rioting asshole.

"Ummm, thanks, man. That ought to hold me for the rest of the flight. Time for me to get back to work before my absence is noted."

Slapping the flight attendant's buns, Brad said, "The pleasure was all mine, babe." Brad returned to his seat just as Pavel was getting up to make a visit to the rest room. Cliff motioned him to sit in the middle seat next to him.

"The flight attendant had a shit eating smile plastered on his face when he walked up the aisle from the rear of the plane, Brad. I don't suppose you had anything to do with it."

"Just giving you a minute to take care of Pavel, hon. Don't tell me you sat there while I was gone to stare out the window."

"Hardly, love. So how was the sexy Frenchman? Was he a pleasant diversion?"

"That's a fair description. So what are we going to do about Pavel?"

"Well you know Yuri and his wife Olga are going great guns with our new office in Moscow. Our private security business has lots of opportunities for growth. How about we see if we can interest Pavel in joining the team. We could train him in our D.C. office and then send him over to Yuri and Olga to expand their reach."

"Sounds like a plan. Why don't we run it by him? We can make room for him in our townhouse if he decides to stay on and learn the ropes."

When Pavel returned from the lavatory, they ran the idea by him. He was at first stunned by the generous offer but recovered quickly to express his very positive reaction. He'd been fighting depression about his descent to the bottom and was thrilled with the prospects opening up for him. He could now take solace in the fact that Cliff and Brad were now his friends and benefactors. They knew that they could always count on his loyalty.

After landing at Dulles International Airport, they passed through customs quickly to exit the terminal to find Tommy Brandon at the curb waiting to usher them away in Brad's SUV. Brad had phoned ahead from the lavatory after his dalliance with the flight attendant, explaining the events leading up to their escape and requesting a ride home from the airport. "Hey, Tommy, great to see a friendly face!" said Brad, grabbing Tommy in a bear hug. "Say hello to our new pal, Pavel Jakov, who will be staying with us in the town house for a few weeks."

"Welcome to Washington, Pavel!" said Tommy, giving him a friendly embrace. "And, Cliffy, get over here you big lug." Tommy wraps his arms around Cliff. "You had us pissing our pants worrying about you. Well come on you sons-of-bitches. Get your sorry asses into the chariot so I can take you home."

Arriving at the townhouse in Bethesda, MD, they were greeted at the door by an ecstatic Marc Berger. "Cliff, Brad, come here!! Group hug!" The three men hug and kiss. Marc drags them into the house as Tommy and Pavel bring in their bags. "And you must be Pavel! You, my friend, are going to be wined and dined and whatever. Come; give your new best friend a hug and a kiss. Whatever you need or want is yours. Do you hear? What you did for our Cliff — well what I can say. We owe you big time!"

"Nice to meet you too, Marc. I hope you will find me worthy of your trust and friendship."

"Honey, you're home free. Now let's get you all to your beds. Time to catch up on your beauty sleep. Tomorrow I'll expect a full report. My book needs a little infusion of excitement."

As they go upstairs, Cliff explains to Pavel that Marc is an author whose last book was based on Cliff's wandering around the world on behalf of Homeland Security. Marc, he explains, is just completing a sequel after enjoying great success with the first book. "He'll no doubt want to interview you too, Pavel."

CHAPTER 9

Pavel took to life in Washington with a spirit of adventure, reveling in new experiences. Knowing his stay was going to be short, he took in all the sights with a vengeance, such as his free time permitted. Most of his stay was spent at the Washington office of Brad and Cliff's security business, learning the requirements of his new job. Yuri Markov was just completing his brief stay in Washington before returning to Moscow. Yuri and Pavel's brief overlap in Washington gave Cliff and Brad the opportunity to smooth over the problems of their past. Pavel and Tommy Brandon became joined at the hip. There was clearly a spark between them that they tacitly acknowledged without acting on it. But that would soon change.

Brad decided that Pavel needed a break from the intense indoctrination he was subjected to in learning the private security business. Pavel was to be treated to a week at the country cabin in West Virginia, belonging to Brad and Cliff. Cliff decided to remain behind because he had a lot of catching up to do, working with Debbie Berger who still worked for Cliff and Brad on a part-time basis. Also, Cliff could then complete Yuri's apprenticeship in private security before sending him back to Moscow. Tommy and Marc would accompany Brad and Pavel so Marc could put the finishing touches on his book while Tommy took advantage of Cliff's being at the office, allowing him to take a break.

Hector Rios, Brad and Cliff's hunky caretaker, had everything in readiness for Brad and his guests. The house was fully prepared including being stocked with food and drink. Tommy was charged with the task of showing Pavel around the property, ending up at Hector's neighboring ranch where they ran into Hector's lover, Cole Strong. Cole is 6'-2" tall with broad shoulders, narrow hips and long legs. His ruggedly handsome face lights up with a winning smile. "Howdy, partners, glad to have a little company in these here parts. Gets pretty lonely when you guys are in the city. Hope y'all will be stayin' a while."

"Hector's cooking for us tonight, Cole. That's always ample encouragement to stay a while to enjoy home cooking. You're joining us of course," said Tommy.

"You bet, dude, wouldn't miss it. Nice you've brought a new face along with you this time. Hi good lookin'. I'm Cole Strong." Cole shakes Pavel's hand, perhaps holding it a bit too long.

"Man, you're a real cowboy!" said Pavel. "I always wanted to meet the real thing." Pavel's eyes unabashedly took in Cole from head to foot, lingering longingly on the bulge in his crotch. "My name is Pavel Jakov. Good to meet you."

"You boys up for a tour of the barn? I was just on my way to feed them four-legged critters."

"That'd be great, Cole. Didn't know you'd be around for our visit. You always seem to be riding in some rodeo somewhere," said Tommy.

"True enough but these bones need a little rest after being tossed to the ground so often. I can't leave Hector too long, the horny little bastard."

Entering the barn, Cole makes short work of feeding the horses in their stalls while Tommy and Pavel view the horse flesh and the stud feeding them. Cole's tight jeans, as he bent over the feed bags, have caused a strong reaction in his two admiring guests. Their hungry glances didn't go unnoticed for Cole had become a quick study on the rodeo circuit as to who was an easy mark.

"The critters are content for now. How about you guys taking a look at the tack room. It's the room in the barn that visitors are always drawn to. Guess it's all the leather shit, harnesses, reins, whips and all. Come on!"

Cole swaggers along to the tack room and swings open the door to motion them inside.

"This room reminds me of the many spaghetti western movies I watched as a kid in Russia," said Pavel. Cole takes three cans of beer out of the fridge and throws one to each of his guests.

"Set yourselves down on that there leather couch while I show you some of the equipment us cowboys use on the rodeo circuit. Cole runs through the various saddles displayed on wood racks. Pavel hangs on his every word, fascinated by a world he's never experienced. When Cole gets around to the wide array of whips hung on the walls, Pavel's attention is riveted. "How would you boys like to try on some of this western drag? Best way to really get into the cowboy way of life. Get out of those city duds and try on some of this leather shit so you know what it feels like to be a real man," Cole said with a penetrating grin.

Doing as they were told, Pavel and Tommy strip naked and put on black buffalo chaps with matching vest and boots, topped with black suede cowboy hats. "Well how do we look, Cole? Would we pass muster on the rodeo circuit?" Tommy asks.

"Well I'd have to toughen you boys up a bit first. Won't do to look too soft. Cowboys get thrown off their horses and tumble around in the mud. Ain't no place for pretty boys ya know? So come over here and bend over on these western saddles we got on display. Those pretty butts you're displayin' need to show some wear and tear." Tommy and Pavel bend over the western saddles, displaying their vulnerable, pristine white asses.

Cole takes a braided nylon riding quirt off the wall and takes a few swings to cut the air and to alert the butt boys to their fate. Soon the forked type whip is whirling through the air in a relentless flogging of the two uninitiated city boys. Cole takes no heed of their cries of pain as he paints a diagonal pattern of red welts across their buttocks. Despite themselves, they're getting off on the tactile sensations of submitting to a whipping.

"You boys are doin' good! You've got the makin's of prime western studs. On the rodeo circuit, it's expected that you put out for a good buddy. They get enough pussy back home with their bitches but on the road, well you know — ."

"Hell, Cole, what's your pleasure? You want to poke us or what?" asked Pavel.

"You got it, babe. I'm into a double header with you two pussies."

"Got a big mouth don't you Cole. Show us some dick, some big dick if ya got it," said Pavel.

"Ok, wise ass, you're gonna have your butt plugged by some American stud cock. Think you can handle it, bitch?"

"Try me big guy! You may be used to banging cowboy butt but I've got experience with Russian military dick. Think you can measure up, fucker?"

Pavel's words have served to inflame Cole with a searing desire. Pavel would have to sacrifice his hole for Cole to begin to quell his need to cornhole male butt. Cole slips on a condom and lavs his fingers to begin lubricating Pavel's pulsating anus.

"You've got rough fingers, cowboy. It feels good but I'd rather you slipped me a little cock. Let's see what you've got," said Pavel. Cole unbuckles his jeans and pulls them down along with his undershorts. Then he nudges his big head against Pavel's sphincter.

"Think you can take this, slut? Guys with the biggest mouths begging for action scream like girls when I finally pound their tight little holes."

"Bang away, dude. I thought you cowboys were supposed to be macho men, not prone to a lot of idle chatter."

Clutching the sides of Pavel's buffalo chaps, Cole drives his big veined prick deep into the velvet channel, flattening the ripe globes to achieve maximum penetration. Pavel emits a satisfied grunt, getting exactly what he wanted. Cole holds fast to his deep engagement with Pavel's hole and swivels his hips to widen the channel before getting into serious fucking.

"Oh yeah, man, like that! Show me how a horny cowboy takes his pleasure with his rodeo buddies." Tommy has fallen on his knees behind Cole to grasp and spread his butt cheeks so he can rim the succulent pink pucker. Cole's prick goes into overdrive as a result of Tommy's darting tongue servicing his anus.

"Your pussy is choice, Pavel. It must have taken hundreds of pistoning pricks to smooth your colon into such a velvety glove. Yeah, clench those ass muscles, babe. Your asshole works my prick better than any blow job I've ever had." Cole is furiously pounding Pavel's pussy, building to a frenzied peak until the point of no return is reached. Pavel's colon clenches down on Cole's deeply planted cock to coax out wave after wave of rocketing orgasms. Tommy holds fast to Cole's quaking body with his tongue extended fully up his fuck channel.

"Tommy, you worked my ass so good. Pavel wouldn't have received as good a screwing without your tongue up my ass. It's only fair that you get a little piece too, babe." Cole slips out of Pavel's ass, grabs a horse blanket and moves over to the leather sofa. Stripping from the waist down, he rolls the blanket into a roll and lies on top of it, face down on the sofa. Now his great muscled cowboy ass is propped up in the air, displayed as an offering. "Come get your reward, Tommy boy!"

Tommy slips on a condom and mounts Cole. Cole's butt needed no further preparation after Tommy's spirited rimming. "Oh Cole, your butt is the best stud pussy available anywhere," said Tommy with his cock fully lodged deep between Cole's proffered butt cheeks and up his ass.

"Well, Tommy, I think the time has come for you to give me a bit of ass pussy too. I've managed to keep my hands off of you until now but no more," said Pavel. Putting on a condom from Cole's packet, he joins the prone pair on the sofa to mount Tommy, creating a daisy chain. With only saliva for lubricant, Pavel easily penetrates Tommy's much used asshole. Tommy and Pavel immediately get into synchronized fucking so that Cole's hole on the bottom of the stack and Tommy's in the middle get a nice steady servicing.

Tommy and Pavel's bodies hunch and crunch, enjoying screwing their fuck buddies. Their combined weight insures that Cole's raised butt gets the deepest penetration and hardest pounding. Cole's prostate is assaulted with every plunge of the stacked bodies, resulting in Cole's thrusting his ass higher for maximum pleasure. The horny cowboy is bucking like a bronco, wanting more and better with each of Tommy's deep penetrations.

Pavel is beside himself with lust, finally getting to first base in fucking an American flyboy's ass. The excitement reaches the pinnacle very fast as the chain of orgasms commences with Cole's and then Tommy's ass receiving volleys of spurting cum, stretching their condoms to the breaking point. Tommy and Pavel scream out with pleasure as their bodies pulsated on top of their buddy's ass.

First Pavel, then Tommy extricate themselves to free Cole on the bottom. Pavel and Tommy sit up on the sofa panting while Cole gets up to stand in front of them. "Well, guys, what are we going to do with this," he said, holding his stiff dick. "You've got me all hot and bothered again" so let's deal with it." Cole stuffs his cock into Pavel's mouth to begin fucking it. Pulling out before he would come prematurely, Cole waits a moment before stuffing his dick into Tommy's mouth. He alternates between their mouths until he stops to jerk himself off, splattering cum into both their faces with their mouths wide open. Wiping their faces clean and lapping up the cum, they settle back and relax.

"Glad you could stop by, boys, but you'd better get your asses back over to Brad's house to help with dinner preparations. Wouldn't want your host to know what sluts you were this afternoon now would we," Cole said smiling. They all get dressed and Cole shows them out. "See you later, guys, come back soon, ya hear!"

Given that the evening was going to be pleasant with cool breezes and a mild temperature, Brad decided to have dinner out on the deck. Hector was just beginning to set the table when Tommy and Pavel returned home from their afternoon tour around the property. "Just in time, guys, to help set the table," said Hector. "Be back out with the ceviche in about ten minutes so pour everyone a glass of guaro which will be the drink for tonight's cocktail hour."

Brad strolled out on the deck with a bowl of tortilla chips to go with the ceviche. "So what did you think, Pavel? Do you like our spread out here in the mountains?"

"It's an ideal place to come on weekends when you need a break from the city. And you've got great neighbors into the bargain. Doesn't get any better than that," said Pavel.

"Do I surmise that you met Cole Strong on your tour? Judging by your satisfied smiles, I'm inclined to think so." Pavel actually blushed, his ears turning bright red.

"Yeah, well, we ran into him and — he well — showed us the tack room — ," said Tommy.

"That's as good a euphemism as any for what obviously went on in the tack room. Don't be embarrassed. Cole is not somebody any of us would say no to. Judging by your high color, I'd say a good time was had by all."

Hector returned with a couple of bowls of ceviche, placing them on the coffee table in the seating area. "Come and get it boys! Nothing like my mother's ceviche to get your appetites going." Everyone consumed several glasses of the guaro cocktail drink while enjoying an animated conversation about the PGA golf tournament that they would be watching on tape after dinner. It seemed everyone had a favorite player, having to do more with how they filled out their slacks than how well they played the game.

Brad invited the group to sit at the oversized redwood picnic table as Hector and Marc were about to serve dinner. First came the wonderful gazpacho soup before the main course. Tonight Hector made a casado dish complete with beef, salad, rice and beans. Marc, also a good cook, assisted in the kitchen but was not versed in Spanish dishes. Imperial Cerveza was served as the beverage best suited to the Spanish cuisine.

The mood was light and the conversation animated. Marc's usual reserve in not wanting to intrude too intensely in matters personal was put aside so that he could ask Pavel to reveal the particulars of his unusual journey through life. Brad had only given Marc a cursory rundown, insufficient to add spice to Marc's book but sufficient to incite Marc's curiosity.

Pavel too was high on guaro and Cerveza which loosened his tongue, allowing him to be uncharacteristically candid. Marc, as well as the other dinner guests, were all ears when he talked about being a male prostitute for American businessmen in an upscale hotel in Moscow. When he got to the part where he and his girlfriend absconded with their employers millions to the Caribbean Islands, they were delighted and appalled.

By the time Hector served the arroz con leche for dessert, the group had become increasingly loud and horny. Capping off the excitement was Pavel's explicit tales about life aboard American millionaires' yachts. After splitting with his girlfriend Olga, he found himself penniless and in need of a source of income. He described how he became a hired 'companion' to these affluent couples in search of new avenues of excitement.

This group was always suggestible when it came to sex but Pavel's exploits put them over the top. It was decided that they'd split into two groups when they got up from dinner. The first group consisting of Brad, Hector and Marc would watch the tape of the golf tournament as planned. The second group consisting of Tommy, Pavel and Cole would immerse themselves in the Jacuzzi below the deck.

Brad led the way for his group to move to the family room. He crawled into the corner of the L-shaped sectional sofa and turned on the television with the remote control. His crotch was still tented with his stiff dick, resulting from Pavel's X-rated stories of life aboard multimillion dollar yachts. He was still hard as a rock thinking about Pavel's claim that several of these hedge fund millionaires loved having Pavel fuck them up the ass while they ate out their jaded wives. These Wall Street cowboys had tried just about everything else and were game to try any new source of pleasure. The wives enjoyed seeing their controlling husbands submit to being dominated and roughly screwed.

Following Brad into the room, Hector could see that his friend and employer's dick was straining for release. Their many experiences together eliminated the need for foreplay. Hector simply went over to Brad and stripped him from the waist down, allowing Brad's oversized dick to pop up into a vertical position. Admiring the stiff prick, Hector stripped off all but his tight black T-shirt.

Getting up on his knees on the sectional sofa, Hector straddled Brad as he went down on him. From behind, Marc watched the action unfolding and stripped off his clothes. Viewing Hector's parted ass cheeks with the winking pucker now visible, Marc sunk to his knees behind Hector to begin enjoying the fruits of his asshole.

Brad was getting off on Hector's sucking his cock while watching the golf game, fantasizing that it was his favorite golfer sucking his prick. Hector worked on Brad's big dick until it was engorged to its maximum length and thickness. He then got up to face away from Brad and drop his buns so as to be impaled on the 10" throbbing cock. Hector's dick was now at full mast enticing Marc to take his fill. While Hector rode Brad's shaft, Marc made love to Hector's jumping dick.

With the windows open, they could hear the mewling cries of ecstasy wafting up from the Jacuzzi below the deck. Cole, Pavel and Tommy were at it again. This background sound only increased the pleasure that the group watching golf were enjoying. While Brad missed Cliff, he never lacked for willing company.

As Brad's favorite player, a 30 year old stud from Germany, leaned over to retrieve his ball from the cup, Brad's balls tightened while viewing the great set of buns as he unleashed copious amounts of hot cum up Hector's clenching ass, imagining that it was the German stud he was fucking. Hector, feeling his rectum filling with rushing cum, gave up his load to Marc's rabid cocksucking.

Hector, feeling that Brad's cock hadn't lost any of its stiffness, got up and switched places with Marc. Marc, while being Debbie Berger's devoted husband, also savored man on man sex, particularly with his boyfriend Tommy. Knowing that Tommy was no doubt getting plowed at this very moment by both Pavel and Cole, Marc wanted his ass filled with cock too. Sitting on Brad's dick, dripping with cum, Marc easily took all 10" without missing a beat.

Marc came to taking it up the ass later in life, well after he was married to Debbie, but he made up for lost time by being an avid bottom. Bouncing on Brad's huge cock while Hector vacuum sucked his prick was sheer ecstasy. Brad's dick blasted off another load to fill Marc's cavity with racing semen. Marc's prostate, bombarded with jets of cum, pushed him over the edge to nearly choke Hector before he could swallow the rush of jism filling his mouth.

Just as the after dinner golf group's sexcapades came to a conclusion, the telephone rang. Picking up the phone, Brad found that it was Cliff calling. "Hi, love! What's been going on in West Virginia during my absence? Everyone happy and contented?" Cliff inquired.

Brad brought Cliff up to date with doings at their country retreat, leaving out the more prurient details. "We've been watching a tape of the PGA golf tournament as we speak. That German golfer, Martin what's-his-name, is sure easy on the eyes."

"You can tell me all the gory details when you get home and I'll expect the unexpurgated version please. We both know you haven't kept it in your pants while you've been away."

"Christ, where's the trust," Brad said with a smile in his voice. "I don't suppose you've been carrying on in my absence."

"Clearly, I haven't had the time. But look, we have another problem on our hands. Maxim just arrived on our doorstep this evening in a very distraught state. I've had to invite him in to cry on my shoulder. He's was disillusioned in working for Grigory Vasiliev and decided to split with Ivan. He came back to the US to finish his education. Problem is that he has no benefactor anymore and he's all but broke."

"What does he suppose we can do about it, Cliff? Unlike his former benefactors, Grigory Vasiliev and then his son Ivan, we're not rich. Even if we were our largess couldn't be extended to alleviate every one's hard luck story. There are limits you know."

"Yes of course there are, Brad, but I would like to do what we can to help him. He's at a very low point in his life and is in need of some guidance. Please don't be angry but I've invited him to stay here for a while until we can sort things out."

"Christ, what are we running a hotel? Where are we going to be able to put him up? We have no more bedrooms in the townhouse."

"Obviously I know that but we do have a convertible sofa in the basement exercise area. There's a bathroom down there too. It will do until a more permanent solution can be worked out."

"What do you have in mind, Cliff? Something tells me you've already cooked up some scheme. Tell me what you have in mind."

"All in good time my love. When are you coming home? While you've been relaxing in the country surrounded by gorgeous and available studs, I've been pining away in celibate solitude. Prepare yourself for a marathon screwing when you get home. Your asshole is going to have to compensate me for my abstinence."

"With pleasure, Cliffy. No one does it better than you do, love. We'll be leaving tomorrow mid-morning and expect to be back in Washington by early afternoon. Pavel will stay for the remainder of the week before we put him on a plane back to Moscow to resume his life in his home country."

"Ok, Brad. I miss you and look forward to seeing you tomorrow." They ring off. The hour is late and all go up to bed after saying good night to Hector and Cole who returned home.

The ride home the next morning through the Blue Ridge Mountains was always a lovely transition back to the city. This day was resplendent in sun with great billowy cumulus clouds lazily gliding overhead. Pavel expressed his appreciation for being afforded such a nice respite in the country.

Arriving back in Washington at the townhouse, they found Cliff out in the garden with Maxim, sipping tea. Everyone, being old friends at this point, hugged and kissed before Tommy, Marc and Pavel excused themselves to go upstairs to unpack. "So, Maxim, Cliff tells me you've experienced some bumps of late in your young life."

"Sorry, Brad, to descend on you like this but I just didn't know who else to turn to. I'm just so confused and I don't know — ," said Maxim very dejectedly.

"That's what friends are for, Maxim. Cliff and I will do what we can to help you get your life back on track. So, Cliff, in what way can we be of service to Maxim? I can see the wheels turning. What have you come up with?"

"Clearly Maxim is going to need a sponsor if he's going to afford finishing law school and achieving his law degree. Who do we know that is both rich and a member of the legal profession? As you have probably already guessed, that would be Lane Cockerall. The question is how are we going to be able to interest Lane in taking Maxim under his wing."

"Indeed, Cliff, how are we going to sell the idea to Lane? This represents no small investment. Rich people are seldom interested in shelling out large amounts of money unless their self-interests are somehow benefited."

"That's where I think we may have an in. Since Lane and his lover, Gray Hillstead, are just starting up a private law practice, they are going to eventually need to hire some lawyers. Enter the soon to be graduated, Maxim Bondar who would be a lowly paid intern, working off his debt. So what do you think, Maxim? If I can persuade Lane and Gray to fund the rest of your education, do you think you could commit to an internship with them in exchange for their financial assistance?"

"If you can convince them to sponsor me, I would be only too happy to commit to an arrangement like that. But would they consider that a sufficient return on their investment?"

"Possibly not, Maxim. Could you countenance extending to them — your 'favors' — as well?"

"As you are well aware, Cliff, we've all gotten it on before during our stay at your country place so it would in no way be a problem. But where would I live? Would they expect me to be close at hand?"

"My guess is yes, Maxim. Lane has a large estate in Durham that he inherited from his deceased parents. That would seem like a place for you to live while completing your studies at Duke University. The house is not far from the campus, fortunately. Living there would put you at their — disposal — for the frequent trips they make to the house when they can get away from Washington."

"Cliff, if you could manage to pull off a proposal like that, I'd be eternally grateful. Do you really think that Lane and Gray would go for it?"

"Maybe, Maxim, just maybe. Brad and I will invite them over for dinner and make our pitch after we've plied them with good food and drink to soften them up. We know they like you so I think we have an even chance. Just keep your fingers crossed, babe."

Cliff and Brad invited Lane and Gray over for dinner the following Wednesday. By that time, Pavel would have returned home to Moscow and Tommy and Marc would be back home with their wives and children. They wanted a quiet setting in which Cliff could present his proposal and be at his most persuasive. Brad, the designated cook, decided to make Beef Wellington, thinking that good food would be another catalyst in convincing Lane to be Maxim's sponsor.

When Lane and Gray arrived at Cliff and Brad's townhouse on the designated evening, they walked into the living room that was soothingly lit with much candlelight and with a marvelous CD of Antonin Dvorak's New World Symphony, providing a background that reflected the brash idealistic enthusiasm attributed to Americans. Lane had his first inkling that something was up but was at a loss to guess what it might be. The guests were shown to the big comfortable sofa so they'd be close to the plates of hors d'oeuvres, consisting of deviled eggs and cheese balls with crackers. Glasses of a nice red wine were served as well.

Cliff and Brad were attempting to subtly build up Maxim in the eyes of their guests in an effort to set the stage for the pitch to come. Lane, used to the political maneuverings on the Senate floor, was obligingly going along with what he could see was a set-up. His fondness for Cliff and Brad allowed him to be gracious and not anticipate them. He knew they'd get around to whatever it was they had on their minds. He was wise to the fact that it had something to do with Maxim being under their roof.

Brad and Maxim excused themselves to return to the kitchen to put the final touches on the meal before bringing everything to the dining room. Cliff continued with a continuous patter of small talk before mentioning that there was something he'd like to discuss with them after dinner. Allowing himself an enigmatic smile in responding to Cliff, Lane said that he and Gray would be happy to discuss whatever it was he had on his mind.

Now seated at the dining room table, Lane and Gray were presented with a very creative Caesar salad. But they were even more impressed when they were served the main course, Beef Wellington along with asparagus in a hollandaise sauce. They weren't expecting gourmet food but were delighted. Cliff poured an Erath Pinot Noir wine which was ideally suited to accompany the Beef Wellington. Gray sent a sidelong smile to Lane, indicating that he too was aware that something unknown was on the agenda.

While Lane and Gray knew they were being primed for whatever Cliff was going to lay on them after dinner, they were fully on board with submitting to the softening up process. Dinner was truly epicurean. While Brad and Maxim cleared the table of the dinner dishes, Cliff showed the guests back to the living room where Cliff had planned to launch into his spiel, aware that both Lane and Gray saw it coming.

"Well, guys, it goes without saying that you are friends that we value dearly and don't want to presume on your friendship. Having said that I can see that my — setting the stage — hasn't gone unnoticed. Forgive the stagecraft but I just wanted to be sure that you'd be in a what — receptive mood — for what I'm going to propose."

"Yes, Cliff, we value your friendship as well and hope that you will honor our mutual trust to just be frank and open with us," Lane said. "It seems likely that this has to do with Maxim or you wouldn't be treading so lightly."

"In a word yes, Lane, it does." Cliff presents his case without further adieu, having the decency to blush when he got to the sexual component of the plan.

"My, my, Cliff, I never imagined that you would come up with such a deliciously outrageous plan," said Gray. "It amounts to something akin to sex trafficking."

"That is something Maxim has had experience in when he was Grigory Vasiliev's kept boy. But this is different. It's about his finishing his education and having a life. There are trade-offs in achieving his goal. You are in a position to help if this level of involvement in Maxim's life interests you."

"Actually it does interest me and I think I can speak for Gray as well. We both come from wealthy families and have inherited vast sums of money. With that comes responsibility. We like to think we can use our fortunes in the service of furthering American ideals, particularly as related to the law. The idea of assisting Maxim in completing his education and bringing him into our new law practice is very appealing. Don't you agree, Gray?"

"Very much so, Lane, but Cliff, Maxim must understand that ours is never going to be a lucrative business, paying high salaries. We are going to be advocates for all the oppressed and forgotten people in the gay community. It won't be a corporate law practice generating big fees."

"Maxim is well aware of that. Coming from a modest background, he doesn't aspire to being rich. He'd just like to make a reasonable living."

"As far as the sexual aspect of this arrangement, Cliff, it actually could help Gray and me with a — rather embarrassing — personal problem we're having — in bed. Not to put too fine a point on it but we've both developed into being dedicated tops — which causes us no little frustration. Given Maxim's background in Grigory Vasiliev's escort business, he could well get us over the hump — as it were."

"Then you'll do it?! You're willing to foot the bill for what remains of his education and will allow him to take up residence in your home in Durham?"

"Yes we will, Cliff, but you must be sure of Maxim's willingness to help us with our — problem. You see, he's going to have to spend a great deal of time in bed with us."

"Not to worry, Lane, he's very interested in making sure that you are pleased with his performance."

Just then, Brad enters the living room to announce that dessert is now ready to be served in the dining room. When everyone is seated back at the table, Maxim and Brad serve the Peach Melba and coffee. Once Maxim is seated at the table, Cliff announces, "It's a done deal, Maxim! Lane and Gray are up for going ahead with everything we talked about."

Stunned, Maxim was at a loss for words until he said, "It will be my fervent hope that you never regret this decision. You will find me anxious to please and willing to work hard to keep up my part of this agreement."

"We have no doubts, Maxim but first we must get you accepted back into the program at Duke in which you had been enrolled. As a major contributor to the school's endowment fund, I feel sure I can make that happen," said Lane. "Actually, we're going down to the house, 'Morehead', the day after tomorrow. So if you can collect yourself, we'll pick you up and take you there. This way we can introduce you to the staff and you can settle in before resuming your studies."

"No problem, I've traveled from Moscow with only two suitcases so there's little to pack."

"We'll be sorry to see you leave us so soon, Maxim, but we know you'll be well served by your new benefactors," said Cliff.

Two days later, Lane's Cadillac SRX pulled up in front of Cliff and Brad's townhouse at 10:30 AM and after warm goodbyes, Maxim was whisked off to his new life in Durham, NC. After the 5 ½ hour drive, they arrive at Morehead. They pass through the gates and up the serpentine drive under the massive overarching shady oaks. Pulling up to the brick-paved circle in front of the columned entrance, they are greeted by Jebediah Stuart, the caretaker. Exiting the front door, Jeb greets his employers and their guest.

Jebediah is a descendant of early settlers who have lived in Durham for generations. Divorced, with an 11 year old daughter who lives with her mother, Jebediah manages the estate, supervises the staff, pays the bills, etc. He's a statuesque man, 6'-3" tall, broad shouldered and sturdily built for all the heavy work he's required to do around the 15 acre estate with its gardens and pathways through the surrounding woods. Jebediah is seemingly unaware of his stunning good looks, being blonde and blue-eyed with flawless features. He has a regular attitude, devoid of any artifice.

"Welcome home, gentlemen, I have prepared the suite of rooms you requested for your guest's extended stay with us."

"Thanks, Jeb, we'd like you to meet Maxim Bondar who we know you're going to help feel at home in this big old house that's so devoid of human company," said Lane.

"Yes, sir, no problem. This house is a grand old dame and hard to resist once you get to know her. Welcome to Morehead, Mr. Bondar."

"We hope Maxim will find her so. Please help him with his luggage and show him to his rooms. What has Abigail planned for dinner?" Abby is Jeb's former wife who now runs her own catering business as well as being Lane and Gray's cook when they're ensconced at Morehead. Lane actually loaned her the money to start her business after she divorced Jebediah. She remains good friends with him despite the failure of their 5 year marriage.

"Abby thought a Southern dish might be appropriate for Maxim's first night here at Morehead. Hope he'll like her Southern, pan-fried quail with country ham."

"Abby never disappoints. I'm sure he'll love it and her," said Gray. Abby was physically so much like Jebediah that they were often taken for brother and sister.

The Southern, pan-fried quail with country ham was a big hit with Maxim but the dessert put him over the moon. Abby made her Humming Bird cake which was a Southern white layer cake made with mashed bananas, crushed pineapples, pecans and spices. Jeb made a fourth at the table. As was customary, Jebediah ate dinner with his employers unless they were entertaining. Maxim was now considered part of the household.

After dinner, Lane and Gray showed Maxim around the house, built in a more gracious period in American history. The center entrance hall featured an impressive central staircase. There were maple floors throughout, 10 original fireplaces, Palladian windows and a vast grand ballroom. Upon seeing the ballroom, Maxim said, "What a great place to have a party!"

"Well actually we're thinking of suggesting to Marc Berger to have a celebration here upon the publication of his next book. We could invite the proprietor of our favorite bookstore at New Hope Commons to be present before featuring Marc's book at his bookstores in several Southern cities. We have plenty of room to put everybody up who comes down from Washington."

"That would make for a great celebration to look forward to," said Maxim.

"Come, Maxim, we want to show you the guest house on the property that we had converted from its former use as a stables. Since we have so few guests, we often use it ourselves when we want to enjoy the pleasures of a smaller, less grand house. We thought it would provide a conducive atmosphere in which you could administer — sex therapy — to us," said Gray.

Finishing the tour through the magnificent little guest house, Maxim concurred that getting themselves away from the formality of the big house would be more conducive to breaking down barriers. "This will be the perfect place for me to ply my trade," he said with an evil smile.

"Let's plan on commencing treatment tomorrow night," said Lane. I have a meeting with the President of Duke University tomorrow afternoon. When I return home I should know if you've been accepted back into the law program, Maxim."

"Anticipating your success, I plan on taking one of your bicycles from the garage, with your permission, and bicycling to the University to try out a route and calculate the time required to make the trip."

"That's fine, Maxim. You're welcome to use a bike anytime you want but you may also use the old Ford Explorer we keep here whenever you need to."

"That's generous of you, Lane, but I prefer to use one of your bikes most of the time. It's one way to make staying in shape part of my daily routine."

While Lane went to Duke University to meet with the President, Gray remained at home to network with various gay organizations to see where the legal services of their new firm could be best put to use. Maxim spent the afternoon bicycling, as planned.

Jebediah worked on the guest house as Lane requested, stocking the kitchen and bar with the necessities and preparing the fireplace for a fire. Abby, responding to Gray's request, prepared a cold supper that she would place in the guest house refrigerator for Lane, Gray and their guest to serve themselves, allowing her to leave the estate earlier than usual.

When evening came, Lane, Gray and Maxim were in a celebratory mood with the news that Maxim was accepted back into the Duke University School of Law. They broke open a bottle of Veuve Clicquot champagne and drank prodigious amounts while enjoying Abby's wonderful shrimp salad. "Well, gentlemen, it's time we all got a bit more comfortable," said Maxim. "I noticed that you have a collection of shorts and T-shirts available to your guests in all three guest bedrooms. While you go to the master bedroom to change into tight T-shirts and skimpy pairs of shorts, I'll do the same in one of the other bedrooms. We'll meet back here where I'll light the fire Jeb laid for us and we can see what gives. Ok?"

"You're on, Maxim. After consuming so much champagne, we should be push-overs, not much challenge at all," said Gray.

"You guys have gone too long without putting out so getting you back in the groove may prove more difficult than you imagine. Submitting yourselves to being dominated is an art not easily mastered, Women are better at it because, despite appearances, they always remain in control even while submitting to their man's carnal lust. Their men only think they're calling the shots."

Looking puzzled, Lane and Gray go off to transform themselves into refugees from a gay beach blanket. Returning in their skin tight, brightly colored ensembles, they see Maxim lying on the hearth rug on his side, silhouetted in front of a crackling fire. On closer inspection, they could see he was wearing only a tight, black tank top and sporting a huge erection. Both their pricks began to dance in their shorts. Falling victims to type, they both imagined how great it would be to slip it to him, fucking his pretty ass. It was not to be.

"Gray, sit on the sofa so you can observe how to perform for your lover when taking it up the ass." With Gray seated, Maxim goes to stand in front of him. Turning to Lane, he said, "Lie down on the hearth rug with your head propped up on a floor pillow." Maxim pulls down Gray's fire-engine red shorts and hikes up his chrome yellow T-shirt. Gray's dick comes to full attention. "Stay put, Gray, work your prick but stay put."

Returning to the prone Lane, Maxim lies on top of him, crotch to crotch, exploring his mouth with his tongue. Lane's dick is testing the strength of his thin cotton shorts in wanting escape. "You see, Gray, you must take it slow. It's like making love to a woman as I'm sure you can recall. Don't rush anything. Wait until you observe signals that you can proceed to the next step in your seduction." While Maxim sucks on Lane's ear lobes and inserts his tongue into his ears, Lane begins to moan softly. "Do you hear that, Gray? Time to take it up a notch."

Maxim pulls down Lane's apple green shorts and hikes up his hot pink T-shirt. Lane's dick jumps with its new found freedom. Laving and sucking each of Lane's tits, Maxim drives Lane to new plateaus of pleasure. With each nip of Maxim's teeth, Lane can feel the effects in his groin and asshole. His sphincter is twitching in a way unfamiliar to Lane. Maxim begins to fondle Lane's balls, slowly and knowingly. Lane responds by wanting to spread his legs, hampered by the shorts clinging to his knees. Reading the signals, Maxim slips the shorts down and off so that Lane can spread his legs in open invitation.

Gray is fascinated to watch the process of Lane's submission. It's clear that Lane is responding to his seduction in ways that Gray thought to be impossible. Gray is jerking on his prick, turned on by the spectacle unfolding in front of him.

With Lane's legs now splayed out, his asshole become accessible to Maxims probing middle finger. Deftly negotiating the tight passage, Maxim's finger seeks and finds the love spot or bulging prostate. Lane's knees bend and his feet begin to lift off the hearth rug, signaling his readiness to be opened further. Maxim inserts a second finger to enlarge the opening as precum drips from Lane's piss slit. Lane begins to crave being filled with Maxim's stiff prick, surprising himself with the intensity of his need.

Gray sees the need painted on his lover's face and begins to understand the pleasures to be derived from being on the bottom. Maxim is indeed a good teacher. Gray, very tuned into his lover, can almost feel what Lane is feeling by just being an observer. Gray's sphincter is twitching in anticipation of what's to happen next.

Lane's legs, seemingly of their own volition, rise up higher encouraging Maxim to insert a third finger into the expanding asshole. Lane throws his arms back, flanking his face, in abject submission, wanting to be mounted, not as a concession but because of a primal need to be penetrated. Twisting his fingers into the welcoming hole, Maxim slowly withdraws them before proceeding with the main event. Lane looked almost abandoned when Maxim withdrew his exploring fingers.

Slipping his hands slowly up the back of Lane's legs, Maxim supported the raised and splayed legs behind the knees as he placed his cock head against the twitching sphincter. "Oh yes, Maxim, take me. I didn't think I'd ever beg for it. But please fuck me!" Lane moans deeply as he feels Maxim's big prick making the slow, inexorable journey up his colon. Fully lodged in Lane's clenching shaftway, Maxim pauses to savor the moment of possession he's earned and to fan up Lane's longing to be taken.

Gray vicariously feels Maxim's prick filling his love chute and experiences the same cravings he sees plastered on his lover's face. Gray realizes he'll be an easy conquest just like Lane and he's glad, knowing that his and Lane's relationship will be more fully realized with their ability to desire bottoming for each other.

Maxim, knowing that he'd worked Lane up into a frenzy to be fucked, begins working his hips to swing himself in and almost out of the floating butt mounds. Lane is almost crazed with longing, wanting to be plowed faster and deeper in a never ending assault. Sensing the need, Maxim increased his speed incrementally until Lane was crying out in unrestrained ecstasy. Maxim drilled Lane's hole like a machine out of control until with a final violent smack into the great butt globes, he unleashed deeply penetrating barrages of cum. Lane's prick exploded with a shower of cum covering his entire chest and the underside of his chin. Lane was shocked with how much he wanted to be screwed and how much he was able to enjoy it. He knew now that he'd eventually be able to be a full service lover to Gray.

"Umm, you have great potential, Lane. You were less resistant than I imagined. With a little more work, we'll have you whipped into shape. Now, Gray, get over here and take Lane's place. And Lane, it's up on the sofa for you to act as observer." Maxim repeats the process with Gray with similar results. Both men seem to be poised to be inspired bottoms, pleasuring the men in their lives who would mount them.

"Maxim you've exceeded our expectations in taking us so far so fast. I'm sorry we'll have to return to Washington tomorrow morning before we can enjoy any more therapy sessions with you. Perhaps it's just as well as you'll be starting back at Duke tomorrow. Fewer distractions may be helpful until you get back into your studies again. Let's get ourselves back together so we can return to the house without looking like — soiled goods," said Lane.

Entering the main house, the three ascended the grand central stair to part at its head. Saying their good nights, Lane and Gray went one way to the master suite and Maxim the other direction to access his rooms. As he passed the rear stair, designed originally for the use of servants, Jeb was just coming up from the kitchen. They exchanged knowing looks. Jeb could easily observe Maxim's reddened cheeks from being bussed by Lane and Gray's beards. His swollen lips were testament to the goings-on in the guest house. Jeb saw it all. Nothing was said as each went his separate way.

Lane and Gray left for Washington the next morning as Maxim bicycled off to his classes at Duke. Life at Morehead slipped into a comfortable routine. With Lane and Gray not expected back for a couple of weeks, Jeb attended to running the house while Abby prepared the evening meals. A local woman came in during the day to make the beds and clean the house. Ever since that night that Maxim and Jeb passed each other at the back stair after Maxim returned from his assignation in the guest house, there was an uncomfortable silence that passed between them. It was tinged with a mutual feeling of something they wouldn't have been able to put a word to. But to anyone who had a chance to observe them, the attraction was palpable.

One afternoon when Maxim chose to return home up the service driveway, he rode his bike around an out building that Jeb used for his big sit down mower and all his necessary tools. Unbeknownst to Maxim, there was also an outside shower that Jeb was accustomed to using every day after his labors on the property. Maxim's timing in coming around the corner of the building coincided with the time Jeb could be seen buck naked under the shower spray, singing "The Man I Want To Be", a Chris Young country song. He croons, "I wanna be a givin' man!" Maxim stops, riveted at the vision under the spray. Jeb's loose clothes only hinted at his physique. He was stacked, looking like a cover model for "Men's Health" magazine.

Sensing Maxim's presence, Jeb stopped singing and opened his eyes to see Maxim boldly taking him in from head to foot. Jeb's traitorous prick rose up, canceling out his urge to protest this invasion of his privacy. Maxim attuned to Jeb's reaction, got off his bike and began stripping off his Ivy League trappings to reveal his toned body and rising cock. Words were superfluous as Jeb turned off the shower and stepped towards Maxim. They fell to the grass in a tangle of arms and legs as they rolled around in the grass, giving expression to the need for each other.

Maxim realized almost immediately that Jeb's ardor was not matched with any experience in being with another man. Intuitively he took over, guiding Jeb into his first experience with man on man sex with sensitivity and care. Jeb was willing to be led and they calmed it down a notch so as to savor a moment to be remembered. There was nothing that Maxim didn't want to do to Jeb but he banked his fires, knowing that if he went too far too soon, Jeb would be turned off forever, after only just getting in touch with his latency.

After much foreplay, Maxim positioned himself between Jeb's legs as Jeb lay prone. Flicking his tongue at Jeb's big cock head, Maxim then wrapped his lips around the engorged knob and laved expertly, inflaming Jeb's latent desires. Looking into Jeb's eyes, Maxim deep throated his cock, reducing Jeb to a quivering conquest, incapable of all thought and focused solely on first-time sensations.

When Maxim brought Jeb to the brink, he released the suctioning hold he had on his rioting cock. Jeb obviously wanted more but Maxim paused, knowing the climax would be increased when it remained tantalizingly out of reach. Maxim shifted his body around so that his cock was available to Jeb's servicing before he returned to his slow torture of Jeb's dick. Now in a 69 position on their sides, both men began sucking cock. What Jeb lacked in experience, he made up for in first-time lust.

Despite his wanting to draw out their mutual pleasure for an extended period of time, Maxim was no match for Jeb's ardor and jammed his cock to the back of Jeb's throat as his orgasm erupted from his toes, producing an overflowing mouthful of cum. As Jeb worked feverishly to swallow every drop, his prick exploded in an unprecedented orgasm, the like of which he'd never experienced in his marriage. Maxim vacuum sucked Jeb's prick, draining the sex starved stud's balls dry.

They lay still, each unwilling to release the cock still lodged in his mouth. When they finally sat up, they were all over each other, falling back on the ground with Maxim lying on top of Jeb. Kissing and rubbing cocks, they came again, bathing each other in cum. Laughing, Maxim helped Jeb up and together they got under the shower to clean up. Standing behind Jeb, Maxim scrubbed his partner's back before working over the magnificent butt mounds and deep crack. Jeb's prick rose up again.

"You're insatiable, Jeb, but we'll have to put off more of your education until later, after Abby leaves for the night."

"What just happened is so — unbelievable — to me, Maxim. How could I have gone so long being unaware of these — tendencies?"

"Seems like there was little opportunity given where you live and your lifestyle. Weren't you ever curious?"

"Curious maybe but nothing I ever imagined acting on until — meeting you."

"Try and relax about it, Jeb. I'll come up to your room tonight after I finish my homework and we'll just wing it."

Maxim's visits to Jebediah's room on the third floor of the house became a nightly routine where Maxim kept pushing the envelope, exploring the depths of Jeb's sexuality. Jeb was always very receptive, eager to get in touch with desires so long suppressed. When the time was right, Maxim decided that he would introduce Jeb to the pleasures of ass fucking. That time came when one night after vigorous oral sex, Jeb flipped himself over on his stomach and spread his legs, not really knowing what he was about but going on instinct.

The sight of Jeb's magnificent butt cheeks offered up for Maxim's pleasure was too much of a feast for Maxim to show any reserve. Running his splayed fingers over the muscled mounds, Maxim parted the cheeks and dove in to maul Jeb's virgin pucker. Their nightly lovemaking accustomed Jeb to accepting Maxim's expanding array of intimacies so that he was more than compliant with the latest probe.

Jeb was delirious with need as Maxim ate out his ass with total abandon. Raising up his butt, Jeb invited what he knew would come next.

With confirmation that the time had come, Maxim rose up on his hands in the push-up position to aim his cock at the virgin gateway. "It will hurt at first, Jeb, but the pain won't last long before you'll begin to enjoy it." Trusting Maxim completely, Jeb relaxed as he was entered, enduring very little pain before his colon was filled with Maxim's turgid prick.

Maxim enjoyed a possession rivaling what he had experienced with his lover, Ivan. Jeb was just a natural bottom with a colon designed for pleasuring cock. Maxim worked his hips so his prick could slowly service the virgin passage, getting Jeb in touch with the joy that he was predisposed to giving and receiving. Jeb took his first screwing as if he'd been bottoming for years, allowing Maxim the freedom to increase his tempo and pound Jeb without constraint.

The moon came up and poured a milky light through the dormer windows of Jeb's 3rd floor room, bathing his writhing body in an ethereal light as he received his first vigorous fucking. The sight of Jeb's muscular body, rendered in such flattering light, moved Maxim to the height of sexual arousal as he screamed in climax, pouring his seed into his conquest. They lay, forged together for some minutes before Maxim rose up still again to repeat the process with the same result. Jeb's asshole was awash in cum.

These nightly couplings continued with Maxim husbanding Jeb through every position in which he could be sodomized. Maxim also assumed the bottom position to round out Jeb's total man on man repertoire. Clearly, Jeb liked taking it up the ass as his preferred means of getting off. Maxim was only too happy to accommodate him.

CHAPTER 10

Back in Washington, Cliff and Brad were experiencing a period of relative calm, enjoying domestic life and expanding their business. That calm was soon to be broken when Cliff received a call from Moscow. It was, of all people, Grigory Vasiliev on the phone. Grigory made the call out of desperation, fearing for his son Ivan's life. It seemed that since Maxim left Ivan to return to his studies in the US, Ivan went into a steady decline. Grigory realized that he'd made a mistake bringing his idealistic son into his business that was not always legitimate.

"Cliff, I know I have no right to ask but I am begging you to come to Moscow to talk to Ivan. He respects you and will listen to you. Nothing I say makes the slightest difference to him. He won't consult with a psychiatrist and all the while he becomes more ill. I'll pay all your expenses and give you a lump sum of $100,000 if you'll do this, please."

"What do you suppose I can do, Grigory? He obviously needs professional help. What I'd have to say to him could actually do him irreparable harm. You know what I am, a tough operative for trouble spots around the world. There must be a kinder, gentler professional shrink around who would serve him better than I ever could."

"No you're wrong, Cliff. You are exactly what he needs. While I haven't been a good father, I'm enough of one to know that. He's always been coddled and indulged. The time has come for him to face reality like a man and get on with his life. He loves Maxim but instead of seeking him out, he's content to pine away in seclusion. I know you can snap him out of it. Cliff, I'm truly desperate. Please accept my request for your services."

"You've made it difficult for me to refuse, Grigory. But understand, I can only give it two weeks or so before I'll need to return to the US. My obligations to Homeland Security and my own private security business require that I be in attendance in Washington. That's not a whole lot of time to accomplish anything."

"Cliff, I'll take what I can get. Plane tickets will be messengered to you tomorrow. The $100,000 check made out to your business will be messengered to your office tomorrow, as well. My car will meet you at the airport and you'll stay at my apartment in Moscow."

"Very well, Grigory, but don't get your expectations up too high. I'm no miracle worker but I'll do my best for you."

"That's all I ask, Cliff. When this crisis is over, I intend to change the direction of my business ventures and eliminate all but my legitimate businesses. The source of much of Ivan's unhappiness can be traced to his distaste for my lack of business ethics."

"That's a good move, Grigory. I hope you mean it because it gives me something to work with in bringing Ivan around."

"Depend on it, Cliff. The seriousness of my problem with Ivan is not lost on me. It's a top priority."

"Ok, Grigory, see you in a couple of days. Brad is going to be pissed at me but it won't be the first time." They ring off and Cliff goes to inform Brad of the assignment for their security business.

"An assignment like this is not what I had in mind when I set up our security business, Cliff. What could you have been thinking?! Anything to do with Grigory Vasiliev is fraught with danger. He's a fucking criminal!"

"He's genuinely repentant for his misdeeds and could very well be an important ally for us in the future. Someone so well connected could be very useful in insuring the success of our Moscow office."

"You're right about that of course, Cliff. I'm just worried about you getting caught up in Grigory's illegal shit and putting yourself in harm's way."

"You know I can take care of myself, Brad. Quit worrying! Our business could use this infusion of capital to aid in its growth."

"Loving you makes me worry, Cliff. There is no way I can avoid it. If anything should happen to you — "

Knowing that Cliff will be away for at least two weeks, Brad and Cliff spend the next two nights having sex rivaling their first experiments in the West Virginia cabin where their relationship began. When the day came for Cliff to board his overnight flight on an Aeroflot, Boeing 767 for Moscow, Brad drove him to the airport in the Jeep Grand Cherokee. "Please call me every night so I know you're all right, Cliff. Otherwise I'll come over there where I can keep an eye on you!"

Smiling at his lover, Cliff said, "You'd think I was a freshman in college the way you're carrying on, babe. You'll be phoned every night without fail." Hugging, they part as Cliff goes through the security queue.

Arriving at the Sheremetyevo International Airport in Moscow, Cliff exits through security to go outside to find Grigory Vasiliev standing next to his chauffeured Maybach limousine. "Cliff, I'm so relieved that you've come," said Grigory, giving Cliff a bear hug. Lev, Grigory's chauffeur, opened the rear door for his employer and his guest.

"So what's on the agenda, Grigory? Where do things stand?"

"Ivan has been a virtual recluse in his apartment, refusing to see anyone. He doesn't answer his phone nor will he let me see him. His despair is total, unmoved by any attempts to offer assistance."

"Then there is no time to waste, Grigory. How can I gain access to Ivan's apartment?"

"Of course I have keys but he keeps the security chain latched, preventing access. We may have to resort to cutting or snapping the chain."

"That would be a poor way to start, Grigory. If I'm to gain his trust, he must let me in voluntarily. Give me the keys so that I can get into the building and go upstairs to unlock his door. From there I'll have to trust to my powers of persuasion to get him to release the security chain and let me in."

Pulling up to Ivan's building in the Patriarchy Ponds neighborhood, Cliff exits the Maybach limousine and asks that Grigory not wait. He doesn't want Ivan's antipathy for his father to rub off on him, making his rescue effort ineffective. The limousine glides away as Cliff lets himself into the upscale building. Climbing the stairs, he finds Ivan's apartment, which he's visited before, and unlocks the door only to have his way barred by the security chain. "Ivan! It's Cliff Bradshaw. Let me in!"

Hearing someone shuffling to the door, Cliff sees Ivan's face wearily peering out from behind the edge of the door. "Go away, Cliff, I'm home to no one."

"Don't give me any bullshit, Ivan. Let me in. I have something to say to you that you need to listen to."

"It's no use. There's nothing anybody can say to me. It's over for me."

"That's just so much crap and you know it, Ivan. Let me spend an hour with you. If you are unpersuaded, then I'll leave you, never to return."

"Did my father put you up to this? You don't have to do his bidding. Nothing has ever really interested him besides money."

"Well you're wrong, Ivan, wrong about a lot of things. You don't know me well, but well enough that you know I'm going to be straight with you. Let me in. Give me an hour. That's all I'm asking."

The door closes and Cliff fears he's lost the battle but he hears the chain being released just before the door is opened revealing a disheveled and despondent Ivan. "For whatever good it will do, come in Cliff."

"You look like hell, Ivan," said Cliff, closing the door behind him. "Come sit with me on the sofa." Ivan flops on the sofa, his head in his hands. "You know, Ivan, when you're really down, it's a good idea to trust in a buddy to help you climb out of the hole you're in. Let me be your buddy."

"My best buddy, lover really, was Maxim and he dumped me and got as far away from me as he could. Why should you give a damn about what happens to me."

"You're too young to be so cynical, Ivan. Trust me; everyone isn't a piece of shit put on this earth to torture you."

"Why do I feel like such a disaster then? Am I so unlovable that my father never had time for me and my lover regards me as toxic?"

"First of all, your father knows he's been less than what's required as a father but he loves you like the best of fathers love their children. He's lousy at showing it, as you know. Since Maxim came to us in Washington, I've spent many hours with him when he needed to unload on someone. His love for you hasn't changed in the least. What he couldn't handle was working for your father, doing things he detested. He's never aspired to being rich, just reasonably successful doing something useful. That's why he returned to the States to resume his studies in the law."

"Without my backing, how can he afford it? I'd have been willing to help him if he asked me. He wouldn't accept money from my father anymore."

Cliff goes on to explain the agreement he was able to broker that Maxim signed on to with Lane and Gray, leaving out the part about sex therapy. "That sounds like something he'd really like doing, being a lawyer for the forgotten and disadvantaged," said Ivan. "If only he trusted me enough to confide in me. I could have been part of the life he sought."

"Maxim didn't want to come between you and your father. He knew you felt betrayed by his former relationship with your father and didn't want to smother any developing closeness you could have had with your father. He thought everyone would be better off if he just got out of the picture. He regarded *himself* as toxic."

"How could he have been so foolish as to suppose that I'd be happier without him? His leaving has damn near killed me. I never felt so low."

"Then it's time you got off your ass and did something about it. The time for feeling sorry for yourself is officially over, Maxim. We need to clean you up and get you back into good health because you're about to accompany me on a trip."

"What do you mean?! I can't go anywhere. I'm too weak to even leave my apartment."

"Didn't you just hear what I said?! We'll spend the next couple of weeks or so getting you up to speed and then you're returning to Washington with me. I'll brook no argument, Ivan. Do you understand?!"

"What are you saying, Cliff?! Do you think Maxim would consider taking me back?"

"Don't be a dumb shit, Ivan! Of course that's what I'm saying! So do your part! Maxim doesn't need to see a burnt out case when he sees you again. I'm going to help you convince him that you're the one."

"Cliff — Cliff please don't lie to me to make me feel better! I couldn't handle it if it turns out that Maxim has moved on."

"Listen up, Ivan, you need to make sure that Maxim understands that you love him and want to be with him always. Can you do that?! Is that what you want?"

"Of course it's what I want! There's nothing I want more!!"

"Fine! Get your sorry ass in the shower because when I come back tomorrow morning, we're going to start your rehabilitation, starting with three good meals a day as well as daily walks building up to a 5 mile run. You're young so you should be able to hack an intense regimen to restore your health and mental well-being. Are you game?!"

"Yes, Cliff, I'm game and thank you. I'm going to apply myself to getting out of this funk, thanks to you. There's no way I'm letting Maxim have cause for complaint when he sees me." Cliff leaves to return to Grigory's posh apartment.

After Cliff is welcomed into Grigory's apartment by Alexi Volker, they embrace and exchange kisses, acknowledging their history with each other. Alexi shows Cliff into the grand salon where Grigory is just rising from the sofa to greet him. "Come in, Cliff! Will you join me in a drink? Vodka ok?"

"Vodka would be perfect, thank you." Cliff joins Grigory on the sofa as Alexi serves him his drink before exiting the room.

"Did you succeed in gaining access to my son's apartment, Cliff?"

"Yes, Grigory, I did. While I found him in a very distressed condition, I feel confident that he's not beyond redemption."

"Then I have cause for hope, Cliff. That alone makes me want to shout with joy."

"He's still in very fragile condition, Grigory. I'm going back there tomorrow morning to begin to work with him in restoring his health. He's demonstrated a willingness to make an effort in turning himself around."

"That's more than I could have hoped you'd accomplish in a first meeting, Cliff. Just stemming the tide of his decline is a major achievement."

"We'll see what tomorrow brings. He seems willing to allow me to assist him in getting himself pulled together but it's hard to say how firm his resolve is."

"You can't imagine, Cliff, what this means to me. I had such fears that he would remain unreachable."

"Suffice it to say, he's not out of the woods yet. This week will be critical in determining if he has the stuff to pull himself out of his tailspin. I'll do everything I can to shore him up."

"Yes, Cliff, I know you can be relied upon to do that. Your coming here like this has been literally a life saver. You've had a long day and I don't want to tax your strength any longer. Alexi has prepared us a light supper. We can eat in a half hour and then you'll be able to retire for what I hope will be a good night's rest. You'll need it for the task ahead."

"Thanks, Grigory, I'll go to my room to freshen up and join you in the dining room in half an hour." Cliff goes to his room and uses his cell phone to check in with Brad, explaining the evolving situation with Ivan.

"That's certainly good news, Cliff, that Ivan is not such a basket case that he's beyond help. But there's the potential problem with the agreement you brokered between Maxim and his benefactors, Lane and Gray. If Ivan and Maxim get back together, that whole arrangement will likely go down the tube."

"That could very well be true, Brad, but let's cross that bridge when we come to it. Right now I have no small task ahead of me in insuring that Ivan doesn't regress into that dark place he was wallowing in."

"My money is on you, babe. Your strength of personality isn't to be denied." After exchanging the usual endearments, they ring off.

Cliff and Grigory sat down to a dinner served by Alexi. Starting with a cabbage salad, they were then served a chicken casserole accompanied by a Russian Chardonnay. Dinner concluded with ice cream, a favorite dessert in Russia. Grigory was in an expansive mood given the news Cliff delivered about Ivan's first step towards recovery. Knowing that Cliff had to be exhausted, Grigory encouraged him to turn in after the dessert course was finished.

After showering, Cliff collapsed into bed naked and fell sound asleep. His dreams were a pastiche of recent events woven into fantastic plots rivaling a film noir movie. About 2:00 AM, he awakened to the presence of someone in his room who was — going down on him. Flipping on the wall switch next to the headboard, the room filled with light revealing, Alexi Volkov's head bobbing over Cliff's boner. "Alexi!"muttered Cliff.

Letting Cliff's stiff cock flop out of his mouth, Alexi said, "Knowing you'll be with us for such a short time, Cliff, I couldn't allow the opportunity of having you again escape my grasp. Ever since I first took you at Grigory's dacha in Zvenigorod, I've craved the pleasures your body offers."

"Don't stop, Alexi. Your mouth is welcome on my cock. Suck it, babe, you really know how to give good head."

"Grigory would be inclined to agree with you, Cliff, but it's a labor of love servicing you." Alexi has developed his cocksucking ability to an art, thrilling Cliff with his tireless devotion in pleasing him. Whenever Cliff came close to cuming, Alexi backed off, causing Cliff to crave the return of his exquisitely intimate attentions. Soon Alexi inserted a finger up Cliff's ass to discover his prostate, massaging it with expert pressure, putting Cliff entirely under his control. Cliff became hungry with need just as Alexi wanted him to be so he'd be his for the taking.

With three of Alexi's fingers now up his ass, torturing his prostate, Cliff's legs raise up and spread in a wide V-formation to allow maximum access. He was ready. Cliff had become a dominant top in his relationship with Brad although he assumed the bottom position with Brad on occasion. With Alex's careful preparation, Cliff was a more than willing bottom, wanting to be entered desperately.

Having carefully planned his seduction, Alexi mounted Cliff to claim his prize, entering Cliff in one smooth and forceful thrust. Cliff's chest heaved in tune with his lust to be lovingly fucked by an ardent admirer. With Cliff's legs wrapped around his trunk, Alexi ravaged his mouth with his tongue, further inflaming a compliant Cliff. Alexi humped and ground himself into Cliff's hole in a carefully orchestrated fucking that had Cliff moaning like a fawning sycophant.

Cliff never wanted release so desperately but he endured an unrelieved screwing, enjoying the slow torture. Alexi wanted to consummate his domination of this American stud but knew that patience would achieve the most heightened results. Sensing when Cliff could no longer be strung out and denied, Alex lifted Cliff's legs higher so his floating ass globes could be plundered with complete abandon. The loud slapping sound of Alexi's groin smashing into Cliff's elevated cheeks reverberated around the room in an endless beat until a crescendo was reached and the two men detonated their loads. Cliff's asshole was filled with searing ropes of penetrating cum as his chest was awash in puddles of his own seed.

Soon after Alexi left to return to his own room, Cliff fell into what seemed like a drugged sleep, not to awaken until his alarm went off at 7:00 AM. As prearranged, Lev, at the wheel of the limousine, was waiting for him outside the entrance to Grigory's building to drive him over and drop him off at Ivan's apartment. Cliff let himself into Ivan's building and bound up the stairs to unlock Ivan's door to step inside. Ivan was already up and sipping his first cup of coffee while seated in the living room. The improvement in Ivan's condition was immediately apparent.

"Good to see you up and about, Ivan! I must say you look a damned sight better than you did yesterday. Are you raring to go?"

"You might say that, Cliff. You have certainly given me cause to hope that things will be different now."

"Hell yes! With a little cooperation from you, we're going to pull this off."

"Cliff, you didn't answer my question yesterday. Why are you doing this? What's in it for you?"

"Ok, Ivan, the truth. Your father asked me to do it. In fact, he practically insisted on it, making me an offer I couldn't refuse."

"Then it's just about money. You wouldn't come near me otherwise."

"Get over yourself, Ivan. The world doesn't revolve around you. Those of us who weren't endowed with a trust fund at birth and who haven't inherited a shit load of money have to pay their own way. Yes your father is paying me. So what! As hard as it may be for you to believe, I do care about Maxim and you. Because I have business interests in Moscow, I need to come here anyway from time to time. Given that, I can manage this assignment for your father as well. It's a twofer. Surely you can see that your father has pulled out all the stops to do whatever he can to help you. In fact, knowing that his involvement in dubious business practices has contributed to the crisis in your life, he's decided to go straight and jettison all his illegal enterprises."

"Do you expect me to believe that, Cliff? His fortune would decline by at least 20% should he act on that. Why would he do it after all the energy he's put in to increase his net worth."

"Why?! Because his priorities have changed. He values having a family and wants to set things right so that he can have one. That's you, Ivan, you and Maxim. He sees now how his singular focus on amassing a fortune has cost him dearly."

"That's truly astounding, Cliff. I never thought him capable of coming around to such a conclusion. What caused it to happen?"

"First, Ivan's leaving you to go back to Duke University and then your decline in the aftermath. It caused him to realize the foolishness of his goal to continue to amass an ever increasing fortune. He saw the damage that was being done to the people closest to him."

"Very well, Cliff, I accept your explanation and I'm placing myself in your hands. Please help me to shake off all my doubts about myself and everything — "

"You've got it, kid. Now slip into T-shirt, shorts, socks and sneakers. We're about to take a vigorous walk. We'll take a little cereal with our coffee and then off we go."

Thus a routine was begun to restore Ivan to his former good health. Cliff insisted on Ivan's eating regular meals with emphasis on good nutrition. Being young, Ivan's recovery happened rapidly, owing primarily to a positive change in his attitude and outlook for the future. Cliff spent many hours counseling him, drawing him closer. After a week of constant contact, Ivan's libido began to stir after being in hibernation for so long. He desired Cliff again, remembering their earlier sexual encounters and wanting a repeat performance.

Cliff spurred Ivan into making a 5 mile run a part of their daily workout. It became obvious to Ivan how horny they'd each become upon the conclusion of these runs. Often they'd pass other studly runners who'd stir their gaydar and make them crave a little action. Ivan decided to seize the opportunity to get it on with Cliff by making his move just as they returned home from a run.

The very next day, as they entered Ivan's apartment and the door closed behind them, Ivan sank to his knees in front of Cliff. Reaching up, Ivan pulled Cliff's nylon running shorts down to reveal his semi-hard prick. Not missing a beat, Ivan sucked in the rising boner to massage it up into its full potential. Cliff splayed his fingers on Ivan's head and began to fuck his mouth, softly moaning.

When he thought Cliff's arousal was sufficient, he let the throbbing cock slip out of his mouth. Standing up, Ivan slipped off his shorts, went to the end table by the sofa and removed a tube of lube which he tossed to Cliff. Kneeling on the sofa, Ivan hiked up his tank top and bent over giving Cliff the go ahead to take his pleasure.

Since Cliff was finding himself on his back every night submitting to Alexi's unquenchable desire to screw his ass repeatedly, Cliff was ready to mount a fuck buddy. "Are you sure you're ready, Ivan. Maybe it's too soon after you've been so ill."

"The opposite is true, Cliff. It's been too long since I've last been with anyone. I need it now. Do you want me?"

"All this week I've wanted you but I feared that coming on to you so soon could ruin the progress we've made in restoring your health if I was seen to be taking advantage of you."

"You say you've wanted me. Show me! Give me a fucking worthy of a stud like you. There's nothing that you could do for me that would better serve to bolster my confidence. Make me feel desirable again!"

Moving to stand behind Ivan, Cliff said, "You know that playing tennis has sculpted your butt cheeks into objects of desire worthy of turning a man's mind to mush. All this week I've wanted to pound your pussy until I filled your hole to overflowing with my seed." Kneading Ivan's buns with one hand, Cliff uses his other hand to finger fuck his needy butt boy.

Ivan drops his trunk to arch his back so as to thrust up his butt and present his asshole for plunder. Grasping the back of the sofa, Ivan throws his head back calling out to Cliff, "Stick it to me, stud!"

With his fingers splayed on the fulsome mounds, Cliff spreads Ivan's cheeks and enters the fuck cavern, slowly but firmly driving his cock deep into his conquest. When the moment of complete possession was achieved, Cliff paused to extend the elation he felt. When his cock stopped pulsating, Cliff began to swing his powerful hips to begin the servicing that would carry Ivan up to thrilling heights of pleasure, so long denied him. Cliff wanted to insure that abstinence would contribute to Ivan's having an orgasm of unsurpassed intensity.

Ivan was emitting unbroken cries of pleasure in having his tender love channel reamed out by an expert. His cries had the effect of ratcheting up Cliff's ardor and the speed with which he was pummeling the clenching colon. Ivan's pretty globes served as pillows to soften the blows of Cliff's now aggressive and unrelieved pounding. Ivan was receiving the treatment he demanded and craved. Threading his fingers through the hair on Ivan's head, Cliff rode him like a stallion until his prick unleashed a penetrating series of orgasms, firing up Ivan's colon.

"Yes, Cliff, yes, you've filled me up!! It feels so unbelievable. What could I have been thinking in waiting so long?"

Rather than dismounting him, Cliff manipulated Ivan's body around so that his back was on the sofa cushions with one leg raised vertically and the other bent and thrust to the side. Still buried to the hilt, inside Ivan, Cliff resumed fucking him. Ivan's prick is jumping wildly as Cliff humped him anew. Looking deep into Cliff's eyes and seeing the desire that the

American stud was demonstrating was all that remained in sending Ivan to the height of arousal. Ivan's prick exploded in a series of soaring jets of cum, soaking into his tank top.

The sight of Ivan's extraordinary orgasm served to renew Cliff's desire to possess him. His prick still lodged in Ivan's rectum, Cliff tuned him on his side and raised his uppermost leg to resume screwing him but this time without the slow torture. Cliff wanted him hard and fast. Cliff's cock rapidly darted in and out of Ivan's hole, making short work of the moaning butt boy. "Aaahhh, aaahhh," screamed Cliff as he shot another series of rushing cum up Ivan's quaking colon. Falling together on the sofa cushions in a spooning position, they fell asleep with Ivan's ravaged asshole still filled with Cliff's cock. Awakening a short time later only served to find Ivan's tender hole falling prey to a fourth insemination.

That session on the sofa characterized the end of their runs after that. What Cliff gave up to Alexi every night, he took with Ivan every day. Soon the day would arrive for Cliff to spirit Ivan back to the US to be reunited with his lover Maxim, if all went as planned. Before they left, Cliff wanted to affect a meeting between Ivan and his father to insure that they would reconcile before Ivan returned to the US to take up with Maxim.

With Ivan convinced that his father had reverted to his honest business practices, Cliff encouraged him to invite his father over for a heart to heart talk so they could clear the air. Ivan's growing excitement about being reunited with Maxim and his improved health contributed to his being willing to be reunited with his father. Grigory was thrilled to receive his son's invitation and a meeting was arranged.

When Grigory returned home to his apartment after an emotional meeting with his son at his apartment, he was a changed man, enjoying a happiness and contentment that for so long had eluded him, despite his wealth. During dinner with Cliff, he waxed ecstatic over the developments with his son and their new found relationship. He gave profuse thanks to Cliff for all he'd done to make this all come to pass. Surprising Cliff, he said he was doubling the fee he'd agreed to pay. The check would be issued the following day. Grigory stifled Cliff's protests with his insistence that it was a done deal.

That night, as Cliff lay naked waiting Alexi's usual arrival, he was surprised to find that his nocturnal visitor for the evening was none other than Grigory himself, dressed in a white terrycloth robe. "What gives, Grigory?"

"You won't be surprised to hear that I know that Alexi has been frequenting your bedroom each night, Cliff. Little escapes me in the goings on within my household. That you've also enjoyed the pleasures of my son's bed is also known to me. My hope is that these fringe benefits were indeed just that. Am I right?"

"You should have been a covert agent yourself, Grigory. Yes, you are correct. I hope you don't in any way think I took advantage of your trust and hospitality."

"Not in the least, Cliff. I'm only glad that this difficult assignment offered you some diversion. Perhaps a little change of pace is in order. Alexi won't be coming to you tonight. Instead, I wish to show you a small measure of my appreciation by giving you a truly memorable blow job and fuck. It's not often that I find myself in the position of satisfying someone else. Since I'm usually paying for it, I'm used to making demands and being accommodated. May I remove my robe and join you in bed?"

"You're more than welcome, Grigory. You must know that virile, take-charge men like you are a turn on. If you were into marrying again, you'd have a 30 something looker on your arm. You are still a fine looking man whose desirability hasn't diminished with age."

Doffing his robe, Grigory flips off the sheet covering Cliff's body and slips into bed with him. "When it comes to desirability, Cliff, you're hard to beat. Ever since I forced myself on you in this very apartment, I've relived the moment I took you with the utmost pleasure. My fondest wish is that when I return the favor that you find it a memory worth preserving." Grigory's words have had the desired effect of stiffening Cliff's cock. Fondling Cliff's balls, Grigory begins going down on him in a carefully orchestrated suck fest. Despite Grigory's claim of always being on the receiving end, he's truly mastered the art of servicing a boner. Cliff couldn't get enough of Grigory's mouth and tongue action.

When Grigory felt Cliff's balls tightening, signaling his readiness to pop his cork, he stopped administering the loving blow job. Instead, he got on his side with his back to Cliff and said, "Come, Cliff, mount your nemesis and plow me the way you would a paid hustler, taking care to satisfy only yourself."

"That would be unwise, Grigory. Your first time should be handled with great delicacy and care."

"You've mistaken me for someone who'd want to be treated with sensitivity and respect. No, Cliff, what I'd prefer is that a former Navy SEAL butch fuck me so I may get in touch with being dominated and discarded. For me to step through the looking glass to experience what it's like on the other side is extremely erotic."

"Strangely enough I do see, having experienced something similar when my lover first fucked me. Being dominated for the first time was enormously exciting. While he didn't discard me afterwards, I never imagined we'd go on to be a couple."

Grigory thrust a leg forward so it was bent at the knee, resting on the mattress. "What are you hesitating for, Cliff? Bringing to heel an arrogant son-of-a-bitch like me ought to kick your libido into overdrive."

"There's still a residue of hostility in me against you, Grigory, for all the harm you've caused so many people. You may find me anything but gentle."

"Go for it, Cliff. Give me a rough screwing. It would only serve to fulfill my fantasies."

Cliff took a condom and some lube from the night table. After slipping on the condom, he lubricated Grigory's tight hole, forcing three fingers inside to stretch open the passage. "Gonna take you at your word, Grigory," said Cliff as he slammed his prick home, grinding his groin into Grigory's butt mounds.

Uttering a small grunt of pain, acknowledging his new status as a compliant bottom, Grigory demonstrated natural talent as he worked his ass back and forth to accommodate the invading prick. His tight virgin hole provided a hot velvet grip on Cliff's raging phallus.

"Oh, Grigory, your pussy is going to become a magnet for cock. You're so good. It's not possible to teach anyone to take cock the way you do, so effortlessly. Now I'm going to really give it to you the way you requested." Cliff moved Grigory around so he was on his stomach with his legs wide apart. Lying on top of him, Cliff appeared to be molded up against Grigory, solidly attached with his prick up his ass. Swiveling his hips, Cliff ground in deeper.

"Christ, Cliff, I never want you to pull out. I never felt so — complete."

While remaining firmly on top of Grigory, Cliff flipped his muscled buns up into the air to then slam himself down into the prone Grigory, building up slowly to an ever increasing butt pounding. Grigory relaxed himself so that his hole offered no resistance to the pistoning intruder, submitting to a relentless invasion.

The hostility to which Cliff referred took hold of him so that he acted on it to lose all control and screwed Grigory as if in a drunken rage. Grigory loudly moaned, not in pain but in ecstasy with being banged like a whore. "Ugggaaahhh!!!" screamed Cliff while mind numbing bursts of sperm rocketed out of his prick into a savaged Grigory.

Both lay stunned as their heaving bodies began to simmer down. Grigory, greedy to prolong his new found pleasure, suctioned in Cliff's softening prick with his intuitive inner ass muscles to cause Cliff's cock to rise again. Still highly agitated, Cliff quickly became aroused anew and began plowing Grigory again. Grigory's ass cheeks were bright red from the battering they were receiving. Pulling out of Grigory's hole completely, Cliff jammed his dick back in with even greater force, repeating the process over and over until Grigory's suctioning hole demanded another blasting orgasm from Cliff's spasming cock.

Grigory managed to roll Cliff and himself over on their sides while Cliff's prick remained implanted into his newly experienced asshole. Thus Grigory could jerk himself off while still being possessed by Cliff. The resulting orgasm was seismic, drenching the sheet covering the mattress. "My god, Cliff, what have you done to me?! Now that I've taken that walk over to the other side, will I ever be able to go back.?"

"It only opens up more possibilities for you, Grigory. Relax; go with the flow, no need to assume a role anymore. When you choose to be with a man, let nature take its course."

"Wise advice, Cliff. Thank you. There are fresh sheets in the closet, help yourself." Putting on his robe, Grigory kisses Cliff goodnight and walks woozily out of the room.

By prearrangement, Cliff leaves the next morning not to spend the day with Ivan but to visit the Moscow office of the private security business, CYTEK, he and Brad own. He's anxious to see how Yuri, Olga and Pavel are getting along given the bizarre circumstances that brought them together. Lev pulls the Maybach limousine up to a commercial building on Tverskaya Street and drops Cliff off. Getting off the elevator, Cliff walks down a carpeted hall to the suite where his Moscow office is located. Upon entering, the secretary/receptionist greets him warmly and ushers him into Olga's office where he's expected.

"Welcome, Cliff. We've been looking forward to your visit. Would you like some coffee? Yuri and Pavel will join us shortly."

"Coffee would be great. How are you, Olga? Have things settled into place with our, shall we say, rather unorthodox staff?"

"Surprisingly well, Cliff. Like you, I had my doubts but we're all working together well and business keeps growing." The secretary/receptionist brings their coffees in and leaves.

"My fear was that Yuri and Pavel would eventually lock horns once the initial show of good will wore off."

"That possibility certainly loomed large, Cliff, but — but — well — quite the opposite turned out to be the case."

"And by that you mean — what — , Olga?"

"You see, their employment at Grigory Vasiliev's 'gentlemen's establishment' awakened them to their taste for — sex with other men. Each displayed considerable talent in entertaining American businessmen. While they've narrowed their range, they haven't lost their taste for — to be blunt — cock."

"What are you saying, Olga? Do you mean to suggest that they've become — involved?"

"Knowing you'd find this hard to believe, I didn't tell them you were coming in this morning although they knew you were due to arrive sometime soon. Come, Cliff, over to the door that connects my office with Yuri's. It's coming on lunch time so you'll be privy to a fringe benefit that keeps this office humming." Olga swings open a panel in the door that conceals a peep hole into Yuri's office. She peers in quickly to check on what she expects to see. "Ok, Cliff, take a look at a scene you'd have to see to believe."

Looking through the peep-hole, Cliff exclaims, "Holy, shit, Olga!" What Cliff sees is a pantless Pavel Jakov lying on Yuri's desk with his legs vertically in the air while Yuri, with his trousers and undershorts around his ankles, is fucking him with wild abandon. "Am I to conclude that you're ok with this, Olga?"

"Who am I to take issue with it? After all, Yuri knows that Pavel enjoyed the same privileges with me when I worked for Grigory."

"Don't you feel betrayed and abandoned, Olga? This must be difficult for you."

"We hope you won't feel offended or wish to censor us, Cliff, but you see we all have participated in the lunch time, desk top sex. We all enjoy our time on our back while being topped by a colleague. It's actually saved my marriage to Yuri. Please don't think ill of us."

"Not in the least, Olga, I'm fascinated and intrigued. You may just have come up with the key to mollify office politics."

"Perhaps, Cliff, you'd like to participate? We owe you our livelihoods and would love to offer you our services."

"Meaning what, Olga? Are you offering yourself to me?"

"Ha, ha no, Cliff. I'm offering you Yuri! Pavel would like to come into my office after Yuri has had his fill. Yuri would then take Pavel's position on the desk so you could top him, as you've done so enjoyably before."

"This is a bit French, Olga. What will the receptionist think?"

"She knows to take her lunch outside during the lunch break. She has no clue what goes on in our offices nor does she care."

"Then you're on, Olga. You're sure you don't mind my banging your husband?"

"Actually I'd mind if you didn't. Pavel is stretched a little thin keeping us both happy. You'll be welcome relief."

With the door left ajar between the offices, the fuck fest commenced with Olga and Yuri taking a prolonged screwing, contributing their whimpering cries of pleasure to the sex charged atmosphere. With the lunch hour nearing a close, Pavel pumped Olga and Cliff humped Yuri for all they were worth to climax simultaneously in shattering orgasms.

Quickly, they righted their clothing and returned to business, all the more attentive for having had a delightful reprieve. Cliff was impressed with their diligence in running the private security business and with the many innovations they'd put in place to increase efficiencies. At the end of the afternoon he left, content that all was well on Tverskaya Street.

The day had finally arrived for Cliff to take his leave of Grigory and to accompany Ivan back to the US where he could start his life afresh with Maxim. Grigory rode out to the airport with them in the Maybach limousine. Father and son, only just reunited, said their good-byes tearfully, not sure when they'd see each other again. Grigory gave Cliff a warm embrace and thanked him for saving his son from his near disastrous decline.

CHAPTER 11

Arriving back at Morehead for an extended visit, Lane and Gray were pleased to find that Maxim had settled into their house so comfortably. It was apparent that Jeb and Maxim coexisted under one roof without conflict. Soon they'd be aware as to why it was so.

Therapy sessions resumed in the guest house with Maxim providing the diversions that Lane and Gray required. In bottoming for them, he was able to school each of them in how to bottom for each other, further cementing their relationship. Lane and Gray were pleased with the bargain they'd struck with Maxim.

One night after Lane, Gray and Maxim returned from their therapy sessions in the guest house and after they'd all gone to bed, Lane couldn't sleep and went down to the kitchen to get a snack. Returning by way of the back stairs, he heard someone coming down from the third floor servant's quarters. Pausing on the steps, Lane saw that it was Maxim crossing the landing above, going back downstairs to his room. Lane was taken aback. Maxim and Jebediah?! Sleeping together?!

The next day while Maxim was at the University attending classes, Lane brought up what he'd seen the night before with Gray as they were having their afternoon tea. "Do you really suppose they're sleeping together, Lane? Jeb never evinced any — sensibilities — in that area that I ever picked up on."

"As hard as it is to get one's mind around it, there really can be no doubt. What do you think about it, Gray? Does this present us with a problem?"

"How do you mean, Lane? Surely we can't impose on them restrictions as to whom they may invite into their beds."

"It's the clandestine nature of it that's troubling. Shouldn't it be all out in the open?"

"Are you prepared for the contingencies, Lane? Where might all this lead if it's an open secret? Have you considered the possibility that Jeb could wind up in our bed?"

"While the thought hadn't crossed my mind, that possibility wouldn't be entirely unwelcome, Gray."

"Why did I know that would be your answer, love? You're not worried that with our list of playmates expanding that we'll begin to lose interest in each other?"

"We're neither of us so insecure in our love for each other to really worry about that happening, Gray."

"So what do you want to do, Lane? Shall we broach the subject with Maxim tonight? Should we ask him if he'd like Jeb to be part of our nightly therapy sessions?"

"Why not? Jeb would be a welcome addition to our bed don't you think?"

"Now that I've allowed for the possibility, yes definitely. It's just that I never allowed myself to think of him in that way. After all, I accepted the fact that he was straight."

After the usual three had sex that night, Lane and Gray brought up the subject of Maxim's having sex with Jeb Stuart. Maxim fessed up and described how it all started one afternoon when he chose to return home up the service driveway on his bicycle to encounter Jeb under the exterior shower. He went on to relate their encounters in Jeb's room on the third floor. "Are you put off by the fact that I'm balling your caretaker, guys?"

"It's more to the point that we're fascinated and intrigued, Maxim. Jebediah is one hunk of a man but we always supposed him to be off limits," said Lane.

"Shall I ask him to join us here in the guest house tomorrow night? My guess is that he'd welcome the invitation."

"Then do by all means invite him, Maxim," said Gray. Thus began expanded nightly sessions in the guest house, providing further delights in imaginative couplings.

Jebediah, being still so close to his former wife Abby, blurted it out one afternoon when she came to prepare the evening meal. He told her that he'd come out and was sleeping with his employers and their student guest. While fearing that she might withdraw from him and forbid him contact with his daughter, he couldn't be less than honest with her about himself.

Surprising him, she said, "Jeb, I've always suspected that you were latent and unable to get in touch with it. In our marriage I always knew there was an impediment to our being a couple in every respect. My love for you hasn't changed. I'm only glad that you can feel free to express that side of yourself."

"You're always full of surprises, Abby. If only I could have been the man for you."

"We had some good years together, Jeb. I have no regrets. Perhaps it's time to tell you that I too have a new boyfriend."

"That's wonderful, Abby. Who's the lucky guy? You deserve the best."

"Well he's actually Lane and Gray's neighbor, the widower Dickson O'Toole at 'Weathersby'. We've only been dating a couple of months but — well — I really like him. I met him through my catering business when he hired me to do a party for his golf buddies and their wives. Since Dicky's wife died four years ago, he hadn't entertained at Weathersby. It was a really elegant dinner party for which I acted as his hostess as well. Things progressed from there. I didn't tell you because you hadn't found anyone and I didn't want to appear to be gloating. Now that your life has taken another tack, I thought you'd like to know that I've moved on too."

"Will you introduce me to Dicky, Abby? I'd love to meet the man in your life."

"Actually I'm catering another luncheon affair for him on Saturday. Why don't you drop by in the late morning, say around 11:00 before I get too busy and I'll introduce you."

"Sounds like a plan. So great! I'll be there. By the way, can I run something else by you?"

"Sure, Jeb, what's on your mind?"

"Like you, I've wanted to have my own business but always got hung up on the means with which to finance it. All the start-up costs are daunting."

"What kind of business did you have in mind, Jeb?"

"Well I'd like to start a garden center. The area has grown enough that it could support a really good one. But the start-up costs for such an enterprise have always presented a roadblock."

"So what's changed that leads you to reconsider taking the plunge, Jeb?"

"Now that I'm on — different — terms with Lane, I thought to prevail upon him to — "

"So what's the problem, Jeb? Do you think he'd turn you down?"

"No not really. Do you think I'd be exploiting the fact that — well — we've gone to bed together?"

"Jeb, don't be naïve about this. If Lane has any qualms about backing you, he won't be shy about refusing you. What you need to do is come up with a viable business plan as I did before he agreed to back me. That's where I can be of some help to you, along with my accountant in town."

"You don't think my asking him would smack of a quid pro quo? In exchange for my favors, I'm demanding money."

"Hey, stud, if it were that easy everyone would try it. No, I think you need to approach this in a businesslike way because that's what it is. You have to convince Lane that your business venture represents an opportunity for him to make money on his investment in you. What happens with your job as Lane and Gray's caretaker if you pull this off?"

"The most time consuming part of my job is the grunt work in maintaining the grounds around here. If I could farm out that part of my job I could still manage the household for them, most of which I can do on my computer."

"Then what you need is an excellent lawn care service. Just so happens that my Dicky uses a local service that's the best in our area. You're in luck because the guy Dicky uses will be working at Weathersby all day tomorrow. His name is Brent Hitchcock but everyone calls him Hitch. I'll make sure that you meet him tomorrow when you stop by in the morning."

"Thanks, Abby. I'll float the idea by Hitch to see if he's interested before I mention it to Lane."

"Do you want me to set something up with my accountant so you can take a stab at putting a business plan together?"

"Yeah, do it Abby. I'm available pretty much anytime next week."

"Ok, then, babe, see you tomorrow. I know you're going to love Dicky. Your daughter thinks he's cool."

Jebediah drove his pick-up truck over to Weathersby the next morning. He found Abby in the enormous kitchen of the large Georgian colonial home, supervising the luncheon preparations. "Good morning, Jeb! Come; let me take you to the study. Dicky is there, expecting to meet you. Be right back, ladies!"

Dickson O'Toole was exactly what Jeb expected, in as much as he was tall, handsome, impeccably groomed and attired with a full head of silver hair and possessing perfect patrician features. He was well mannered and affable and put Jeb at ease immediately. Abby had a winner. The introduction was kept short because Abby had much to do before Dick's guests arrived. "Did you really like him, Jeb? It's important to me that you approve of him. We may — be getting — serious."

"What's not to like, Abby. The man's a prince! You deserve it, hon."

"Oh I'd hoped you'd say that! Abby hugs her former husband. "Come, dear, let me take you outside to the south garden where Hitch is working. But I must fly after introducing you because I'm needed in the kitchen."

Hurrying through the house and then outside to the garden, Abby leads Jeb over to the flower bed that Hitch is working on. Jeb's first view of Hitch is from the rear as he's hunched over a planting bed weeding. Hitch's tight jeans are molded to his ass, revealing a sculptural backside worthy of a classical statue. Hearing visitors, Hitch stands and turns around. The heat of the day and his arduous task had caused him to shed his shirt, revealing his glistening torso, glazed with sweat.

Jeb experienced an electric jolt that damn near knocked him off his feet. In making eye contact with Hitch, it was clear to Jeb that Hitch felt it too. Jeb always thought the idea of love at first sight was a load of bull — until now. As Abby made the introduction, he was barely able to stammer out, "Hello Hitch — pleasure — to meet you."

"The pleasure is all mine, Jeb," Hitch answered while giving Jeb a firm and lingering handshake. Abby immediately excused herself, citing the need to return to her job. Jeb and Hitch stood staring at each other for what seemed like an eternity before Jeb suggested that they sit on a garden bench. Hitch is about 36 years old, stands about 5'-10" tall, has rather long, jet black hair, a roughhewn but handsome face and a body that only hard work could produce. His broad shoulders were naturally muscular as were his pecs and abs. His trim waist topped a set of truly memorable buns over thighs that bulged appealingly, culminating in iron calves and work-booted feet.

Jeb was so overwhelmed with lust that he was tongue-tied and unable to speak. Sensing his problem, Hitch gave him a cue to proceed. "So, Jeb, Abby tells me you had a proposition to put to me."

Jeb knew precisely what the proposition would be if he could allow himself to be so bold. "Yeah, Hitch, it's like this — we may need some help — over to Morehead in maintaining the grounds. That something you'd be interested in taking on?"

"Well maybe, Jeb. Thought you were doing that."

Jeb goes on to explain his plans to Hitch, asking him to keep it confidential until he was ready to move ahead with the plan. "Does it sound like it may be of interest to you?"

"Could be, Jeb, I'd have to walk the property with you and get a feel of what would be entailed." The sound of Hitch's baritone voice was making Jeb's cock rise. He could feel his ears begin to redden.

"How about you coming by tomorrow morning and I can show you around the place. Would say 10:30 work for you?"

"Sure no problem, Jeb. Not to sound like a prima donna, but for me to take on the job the place has to — speak to me. Does that sound too — ?"

"You know, Hitch, I feel that way too, so no I don't think that's far out." Knowing to get up and get out before he makes a fool of himself, Jeb got up and shook Hitch's hand and made his escape.

Hitch arrived promptly the next morning, driving his mint condition, 1954 Ford, F-100 pick-up truck. Jeb was impressed with how meticulously the truck was restored. "Morning, Hitch, welcome to Morehead," said Jeb, shaking Hitch's hand. "Ready to take a stroll around the place?"

"Been looking forward to it, Jeb. Coming up the drive, I could see already how you've taken care of things."

"Coming from you, Hitch, that's much appreciated. In visiting Weathersby yesterday, I could see your handiwork was much in evidence. What say we walk the paths that wind through the property? That way you'll get to see just about everything."

Hitch was genuinely taken with the property. It was handsomely landscaped and scrupulously maintained, as testament to Jeb's commitment to his stewardship. Jeb fell into easy conversation with Hitch, given their common interests in gardening and plant varieties.

However, the sexual tension was simmering just below the surface. Jeb feared he wouldn't be able to restrain himself from laying his hands on Hitch and — do what — he didn't know. Hitch was tuned into Jeb's struggles but was reluctant to make a move for fear of coming across as too aggressive. The stalemate continued all the way around the property until they came back towards the house to the out building where Jeb stored the big sit-down lawn tractor and where he kept his workshop.

As they entered the workshop, Hitch inadvertently brushed against Jeb as he tried to pass by him to go inside. That ignited the spark that set off the conflagration. They were all over each other in seconds, devouring each other's mouths while running their hands over each other's body. The fever pitch ended abruptly when Hitch pushed himself away, gasping for breath.

"Jebediah, you have to understand something about me. I'm not — promiscuous — , a meaningless roll in the hay is not my style."

"Hitch, I haven't been out long enough to be labeled promiscuous but I haven't been celibate either. This is all — fairly new — to me. So far my sexual encounters have been just that. With you I'm feeling something quite different."

"You see, Jeb, I had a lover for 4 years and he couldn't stand this area and ran off to New York City where he could have a more active gay life. That was 2 years ago. I haven't been with anyone since."

"We'll never know what might have been if we don't have the courage to trust our feelings in guiding our choices. All I know is that I want you like I've never wanted anything or anybody."

With that declaration from Jeb, Hitch threw his arms around his waist and resumed kissing him passionately. Jeb responded in kind as they each began undressing the other. Now buck naked, they stumbled towards Jeb's worktable. Jeb stopped abruptly when his back hit the table. Hitch seized the opportunity to drop to his knees and marvel at the perfection of

Jeb's rigid cock. Having done without for so long, he proceeded to service Jeb with urgent intensity.

For all the sex Jeb recently enjoyed in the guest house, this was of a different order. It felt as if electric currents were coursing through his entire body. Watching Hitch gorging on his prick made Jeb want to offer himself up completely to satisfy this man who was staking a claim on him. Standing, Hitch said, "Sit up on the bench, Jeb and then lie down on your back and raise your legs." Jeb's buns were now perched at the edge of the workbench.

"Christ, Jeb, you've got the most incredible ass. Prepare yourself to have your asshole worshiped." Hitch, true to his word, squatted down and ate Jeb's hole like an inveterate pussy hound. For Jeb it was like having sex for the first time because he sensed that the man eating him out was not merely a meaningless lay.

"Please, Hitch, I want you inside me. Let me make up for the years you've gone without."

"Jeb, you can't know how badly I want you. You scare me a little but I must have you now, no matter what comes of it." Standing now, Hitch takes hold of Jeb's long legs and places his mushroom-like knob against the beckoning gateway. "Ok, Jeb, I'm taking you now." Hitch's cock-head slips past the sphincter and glides up the velvet channel. Jeb croons his approval, welcoming the invasion.

Pulling Hitch's face to his, Jeb French kisses him and said, "Make me yours, Hitch. Don't hold anything back. Show me that I'm not just someone to slake your lust. Love me!"

"Oh, Jeb honey, you're killing me! Don't play with me. This feels so right." Hitch is now slamming into Jeb's ass with an unabashed hunger, unafraid to express the burning desire he feels for Jeb. Never having experienced such an uncontrolled and overwhelming screwing, Jeb was fully in the moment, reveling in his domination. Jeb's subjugation culminated with Hitch staring him in the eyes, high with desire, while his prick could be felt rioting in Jeb's colon, saturating him with cum.

When their bodies calmed sufficiently, Hitch slipped out of Jeb's ass and helped him up to a standing position. Hitch then began making love to Jeb's cock again, bringing it to full attention before saying,

"Come, Jeb, over to the lawn tractor. I want you up in the seat of this beast." Jeb, still in a high erotic state, moved to comply as if in a trance. Once seated, Jeb's cock craned up, throbbing for attention.

Hitch took some hand cream that Jeb kept on the workbench and slathered his fingers with a glob before inserting them up his asshole. With that preparation, Hitch climbed up on the big sit-down lawn tractor to straddle Jeb. "You ready for some pussy, Jeb, cause I really want your cock up my ass."

"When I saw your beautiful butt bent over the flower bed yesterday morning, I damn near blacked out. You better believe I want your ass. If you like it any way near as much as I just did, you'll never be free of me again."

Lowering himself on Jeb's more than ample cock, Hitch uttered a contented moan, loving the feel of this big blonde stud's dick, jammed fully up his love canal. Hitch's instincts came back into play despite his long abstinence and he rode Jeb expertly to send them both up to new heights of sexual fulfillment. Jeb grabbed fist-fulls of Hitch's voluptuous ass mounds and kneaded them in tune with their steadily rising excitement.

Jeb never knew it could be like this between two people, total submersion in each other, becoming one. As Hitch's buns kept up their relentless bottoming on Jeb's groin, Jeb's prick erupted in a rolling orgasm that seemed to have no limits, filling Hitch's colon with great swarms of seed.

Now sated, they kissed again before Hitch lifted himself up off of Jeb's cock to get down from the lawn tractor. "Come, Jeb, let's shower together." They stepped outside to the outdoor shower. Each soaped the others body, exploring every part from head to foot. After drying themselves inside the workshop, they began dressing themselves. "So Jeb does this mean I'm hired," Hitch said with an ironic smile.

"Please don't joke about what just happened, Hitch. I need to know that it meant as much to you as it did to me."

"It's just that I'm afraid that we're rushing things, Jeb. You've only just come out. How can you be sure of your feelings?"

"It's not *my* feelings I'm worried about, Hitch. Maybe you're not ready to try again with someone else after being hurt."

"Oh I'm ready, Jeb. Just don't say things to me that may be spur of the moment reactions. You may feel hemmed in later when you've thought it over."

"Ok, Hitch, I guess I'm going to have to convince you that we've started something here that we both want. Please tell me you'll take on the job here at Morehead. That way we'll be able to spend a lot of time together."

"Yes, Jeb, I'll do it. Have no fear that I have reservations about wanting you. It's more that I want you to be sure and not feel any pressure to make a commitment before you're ready."

With that, the bargain was sealed and Jeb and Hitch's relationship began to steadily build into a solid commitment. When Lane, Gray and Maxim were made aware of this development, they understood that Jeb was no longer available for sessions in the guest house or elsewhere.

Sometime later, Lane and Gray received an invitation from Cliff and Brad to join them for another weekend at their West Virginia cabin. The invitation included Maxim as well. Cliff mentioned that there'd be other guests and that they'd have a full house. Lane and Gray accepted with pleasure.

When the day came for Lane and Gray to set out on their long 5 ½ hour drive to Cliff and Brad's cabin, they decided to leave early enough to show Maxim some of Bluestone State Park in West Virginia. They packed a picnic lunch that they planned to have on board a canoe they'd rent so as to enjoy paddling around on Bluestone Lake. The afternoon was perfect, conducive to floating out on the lake while enjoying the marvelous views of the surrounding mountains. Maxim, letting his hair down a little, admitted to being a little — homesick. Lane and Gray knew very well that what he really meant was that he missed Ivan.

"Perhaps you need to reconsider your commitment to staying here in the US after you graduate from Duke, Maxim," said Lane. "We very much want you to join our law firm when your studies are completed but our agreement can be renegotiated if you find that your heart belongs to your native country."

"That's kind of you, Lane, to leave that open as an option but please realize that I'm committed to staying in this country. Doing the work that's involved working in your law firm is ideally suited to my personal interests. It's not an opportunity I should like to miss."

"While Gray and I are happy to hear that, we're just concerned that you've made a choice that's going to make you happy. Obviously we're enjoying our trysts with you, knowing they'll be short lived. Being a very desirable man, Maxim, you're bound to meet someone that you'll want to forge a relationship with."

"So far I haven't shown much aptitude in making that happen. Look how I managed to mess up what I had going with Ivan. He's probably happily involved with someone else as we speak."

"You're not someone easily forgotten, Maxim. Ivan will have to look long and hard to find someone who's anywhere close to your equal. Why don't you put all that out of your mind for now and enjoy the diversions this weekend has to offer."

Finishing up their canoe ride, they get back into Lane's Cadillac SRX and continue their drive through the Appalachian Mountains. They take a detour to pass through Jefferson National Forest before getting back on course in their planned path to Fletcher, West Virginia. Their time for arrival was projected to be late afternoon.

Concluding their leisurely trip, they finally arrived at the long driveway leading up to Cliff and Brad's secluded mountain cabin. Pulling up to the large log cabin, the front door opened, revealing Cliff and Brad who came outside to greet them. "Why it's Senator Cockerall and party!" said Brad. "Welcome to Shangri-La, gentlemen. Glad to have you here. Let's have a kiss!" They do a group hug. "Come on in, we're just gathering out on the deck to have some wine and cheese. So, Maxim, glad Lane and Gray persuaded you to take a break from all those law books for a few days," said Cliff.

"Thanks for having me, guys. Getting away to your cabin is always a treat. Did you bring Tommy and Marc with you?"

"Sure did, Maxim. They're out on the deck stretched out on a couple of lounge chairs catching some rays. Brad will help you take the bags upstairs while I take Lane and Gray outside to wake up our other napping guests."

Brad precedes Maxim upstairs and drops Lane and Gray's bags off in a guest room along the hall. "Come, Maxim, we've put you in the room at the end of the hall that's the best one in the house." Brad holds the door open as Maxim goes inside. This room has a balcony overlooking a spectacular mountain view. Maxim becomes aware that the balcony's sliding door is open and someone is standing outside. As he goes over to check on who could be out there, he hears the bedroom door close behind him.

Just as Maxim approaches the open door to the balcony, he stops short, stunned. "Ivan! How is this possible?!"

Now facing Maxim, Ivan answers, "My life in Moscow was empty without you, Maxim. I had no choice but to come. We were meant to be together. My only doubt was that you may not feel the same way."

Rushing over to embrace Ivan, Maxim said, "There was not a day that's gone by that I haven't regretted my rash decision to leave you without making any attempt to resolve the issues that created obstacles between us."

"If I hadn't been so blind to the trap you found yourself in, I might have been able to offer help in resolving the problems together. It took your leaving for me to come to terms with the fact that I love you and need you."

"Life without you has been no life, Ivan. Please tell me you've come to stay so that we can be together again."

"Why do you suppose I've come? You won't be allowed to escape my clutches again. It's been too long since I've had you, Maxim. I want you naked now so you can be branded forever as my lover and soul-mate."

"We can't insult our hosts by not showing up for cocktails and dinner, Ivan!"

"Not a problem! By mutual agreement, Brad will bring up a dinner tray for us in 2 hours if we don't make it downstairs in time for cocktails and dinner. But we will be expected to join everyone for dessert. Let me undress you. I've been thinking of nothing else since arriving here."

Standing naked before Ivan, Maxim said, "My turn, Ivan, you'll have no need for clothes when we're alone this weekend. We'll have to make up for a lot of lost time." Maxim tosses Ivan's clothes onto a chair as he falls on top of the bed, pulling Ivan with him. Their hands roam freely as they writhe and tumble around on the bed, kissing and nibbling each other. They stopped momentarily to come up for air.

"Cliff explained the bargain you've made with Lane and Gray, Maxim, requiring you to bottom for them in exchange for their financial backing. What say you give your lover a demonstration of your newly acquired talent," said Ivan with a wry grin.

"What a despicable approach to take with your estranged lover, Ivan, you dog! Bottoming for Lane and Gray has given me a taste for topping *you*, babe. It's time you realized what it's like to be somebody's whore, having to perform at their command."

"You make it sound so attractive, Maxim. It seems degradation agrees with you. Can't say you look any the less for wear."

"So you'd joke about the fact that my dire finances have caused me to peddle my ass to the highest bidder."

"No, I'm just awed by your range. The only common denominator seems to be that your quarry must have piles of money."

"Oh you piece of shit, Ivan! Here I was worried that you'd be horrified by what I've had to do and you find it a source of amusement."

"Yes, love, it's nothing more than that. Now stop this idle chatter and show me how much you missed me. Whoever you've been sleeping with is of no consequence to me."

"Oh, Ivan, Ivan, Ivan — -roll over on your stomach and spread your legs. I want to get reacquainted with your asshole." Ivan does him one better by getting up on his knees while resting his forearms on the mattress, providing even greater access.

"Eat me, Maxim! No one does it better than you." Maxim pushes Ivan's buns apart and buries his face in his crack, laving his perineum, darting his tongue into his asshole and sucking on his balls. "Yes, yes, yes, Maxim that's so good but I want you to penetrate me now. I want your cock inside me!"

Moistening his prick with saliva, Maxim straddles Ivan while holding on to his hips. Maxim's engorged cock meets little resistance as it presses through the winking pucker to gain swift entry into the path to pleasure. Ivan is quickly impaled, welcoming the cock most favored. Ivan's butt mounds are raised obligingly, offering a comely target for Maxim's lust. Each time Maxim's groin plowed into Ivan's bouncing glutes, the loud slapping sound served to heighten their shared fever.

"Fuck yes! Screw me Maxim! said Ivan as he worked his prick with one hand while balancing himself on the other. Maxim's prick was now battering his lover's velvet shaftway in an unrelieved staccato rhythm, expanding his prick to the breaking point. Reaching the pinnacle of sexual stimulation together, they each responded with a shattering climax, each emptying his balls of white hot cum. They collapsed on the bed, Maxim on top of Ivan.

"Oh, Ivan, Maxim whispered, I forgot how good it could be when you're with the one you love."

"Don't pull out yet, Maxim, it feels too good." Laying there only a short time, it was apparent that Maxim's prick had come alive again inside his lover's hot hole. "Go for it, Maxim. Give it to me again."

Maxim rolled over on his back, taking Ivan with him. Ivan, on top, supported his upper body on his outstretched hands as he bent his legs to dig his feet into the mattress, allowing him to lever himself up and down on his lover's fully erect dick. "Ivan, that's incredible. Oh yes, don't stop. Give me your ass! Aaaggrrr," screamed Maxim, as Ivan's clenching ass muscles worked another explosive orgasm out of his cock.

Ivan's dick, flapping violently against his belly while submitting to a second screwing, erupted with another wrenching climax, showering his abs with splotches of running cum. "Maxim! You've staked your claim on me. I'm yours."

Maxim and Ivan fell asleep in each other's arms to be awakened some time later by a knock on the door to their bedroom. "Come in," said Maxim, groggily.

"Time for you boys to take a little nourishment. You've probably expended a ton of calories judging from the racket we heard downstairs," said Brad, breezing in with a dinner tray.

"We'll be holding the dessert course until you join us downstairs," said Cliff, carrying a second tray. So eat up! We don't want to be compelled to return to drag you downstairs!" Brad and Cliff place the trays on the bed and make a hasty retreat.

"Guess we're going to have to get our act together, Maxim. This dinner looks really delicious, making me realize how hungry I am."

"You can say that again, Ivan. Brad said they were serving red wine pot roast with porcini mushrooms. It looks every bit as good as it sounds."

After devouring their food, they shower and dress so they can join the dinner party. Approaching the dining room, they can hear much laughter and conversation. As they enter the room Tommy and Marc get up to welcome them. "Maxim! Ivan! At long last, get over here and give us a hug," said Tommy.

"My writer's power of observation is detecting an afterglow," said Marc. "That's something we were all hoping for."

Lane and Gray get up to hug Ivan. "We're so very pleased to see you here Ivan, knowing how much Maxim missed you."

"You've been very kind to Maxim. My hope is that my unexpected arrival won't force you to view me as the fly in the ointment."

"Have no fear of that, Ivan, we're confident that we can come to a mutually agreeable solution," said Lane.

"Everybody sit down!" said Brad. "Dessert is about to be served." Hector and his lover Cole sail into the dining room with dessert trays of Hector's passion fruit cheesecake.

"So there are the missing guests, Hector," said Cole. "Where do you boys get off hiding out in your room when this here cowboy and his mate wanted to say howdy?" Dropping their trays on the sideboard, Cole and Hector give the seated late comers a hug from behind. "Man, you boys look good enough to eat," said Cole, but first things first. Y'all better like my Hector's passion fruit cheesecake or there'll be hell to pay!"

Dessert is served and Cole and Hector sit down at the table with the other guests. A rousing chorus of oohs and aahs travels around the table in response to consuming Hector's amazing cheesecake. "Hell, babycakes, you've really done it this time!" said Cole. "Gonna have to do something special for you when we get home tonight."

"Can't wait, big guy! So what's the verdict from the rest of this crew? Don't talk with your mouths full, guys," said Hector.

"Well I think I can speak for everyone," said Gray. "This is truly phenomenal. My only fear is that there won't be enough for seconds."

"Guess again, sweet-cheeks, don't you think I know by now what I'm dealing with with this crowd."

"Well I for one want another piece, Hector my dear," said Gray. A show of hands indicated that Gray had a lot of company, the rest of the table in fact.

As the feeding frenzy came to a close, Marc said he had an announcement to make. "Before coming out here for the weekend, I got a call from my publisher to say that my latest book was accepted for publication. Without the cooperation and support from everyone at this table, it would never have happened. Many, many thanks, guys!"

"You know, Marc, when I first took Maxim for a tour through our house in Durham, he made the remark that our ballroom would be a great place to have a party. Would you be agreeable to letting us throw a party there to celebrate the publication of your book?"

"That would be awesome, Lane! I'd truly love it."

"Perhaps you wouldn't mind if the party served dual purposes, Marc. You see, Maxim will be graduating from Duke and unless I miss my guess Ivan will be completing his studies there as well. Do you think a graduation party could share the billing with your book publication party?"

"Happily so, Lane, by all means. We'd all be sure to enjoy celebrating together," answered Marc.

"Then it's done. We just have to agree on a suitable date and the arrangements will be made. As you may be aware, Marc, I own the bookstore in town near our home. We'll invite the gentleman who runs it for us to the party and have him feature your book in our store window. His name is Giles Dikau."

"We'll need to get the guest list from you Marc so we can send out invitations," said Gray. "Lane and I think we should be able to put up all the guests at Morehead but if there's an overflow, we'll make suitable arrangements."

"How was it, Lane, that you anticipated me in announcing that I'd probably be completing my studies at Duke?" Ivan asked.

"Being one of the University's major contributors, I'm in constant touch with the President and his staff. It came to my attention that you'd put out feelers recently to determine whether you'd be welcomed back in to the program you had been enrolled in. Rest assured that you won't face any obstacles if you follow through with your intentions."

"That greatly relieves my mind, Lane, thank you," said Ivan. "I plan on calling the University on Monday to make my request."

The party broke up soon after, allowing Hector and Cole to clean up while Lane and Gray as well as Maxim and Ivan went up to bed after a long day. Marc and Tommy stayed up chatting with Cliff and Brad, excited about the prospect of a party at Morehead to celebrate the publication of Marc's latest book. Marc couldn't wait to phone his wife Debbie in the morning to break the news.

"You know, Brad, I'd like to phone Grigory Vasiliev to alert him of our plans for a graduation party for Ivan and Maxim," said Cliff. "I think he could be persuaded to come, assuming he could clear his calendar for the event. What do you think?"

"Brilliant, Cliff, particularly if you could convince him to come on his own plane. This way we could also invite our Moscow office to come as well as Viktor, Eric, Bruno and Denis. Each of them figures in Marc's book. They'd make great additions to a festive affair," said Brad. "Let's not tell Maxim or Ivan of that possibility. Let it be a surprise."

CHAPTER 12

With Lane's support, Ivan had no problem returning to Duke to complete the program he'd started but hadn't finished. He and Maxim rode bicycles, loaned to them by Lane and Gray, to Duke on days when they had classes. Ivan took up residence at Morehead to share Maxim's bedroom. Maxim worked out a new arrangement with Lane and Gray that required him to go to work for them upon graduation at a small initial salary, as originally agreed upon but didn't require him to continue the sex therapy sessions. They were comfortable that they'd already gotten more than their money's worth in that regard.

Ivan's plans after completing his studies at Duke called for him to buy a townhouse in Georgetown in which he'd live with Maxim and where he planned to set up a law practice serving the gay community in the areas of domestic issues such as marriage, divorce, taxes, wills, etc. Maxim planned to stay with Lane and Gray's practice serving the gay community, dealing with litigation issues.

Publication of Marc's book would coincide nicely with graduation time at Duke University, allowing the party at Morehead to go into the planning stages.

During this period, Cliff received a call from Pavel Jakov in the Moscow office of CYTEK about a developing situation involving Sir Malcolm Howard. It seemed that Sir Malcolm had graduated from merely money laundering for drug lords to actually transporting the drugs aboard his yacht, the Miss Uranus. This was of interest to Homeland Security particularly because the outrageous profits involved were often used to support the illegal international arms trade.

Pavel still had friends in the Virgin Islands who kept him current with developments there. It seemed that Sir Malcolm planned on bringing his yacht up from the Caribbean and docking it at The Old Towne Yacht Club in Beaufort, NC, where he'd off load his cache of high grade heroin, supplied by his partner in crime, Vince Angotti. Since Angotti held Sir Malcolm responsible for Cliff's escape from Virgin Gorda, he threatened reprisals if Sir Malcolm didn't use his yacht to run drugs. Angotti counted on Sir Malcolm's supposed respectability to insure the success of the smuggling operation.

Since Pavel knew both a member of Malcolm's crew as well as having an in-depth knowledge of the yacht, Cliff thought it best to bring Pavel to the US to insure that Sir Malcolm would not escape detection and manage to bring drugs into the US. Cliff got Jason Stone to agree to pick up the tab for Pavel's expenses.

Jason Stone made Cliff aware that they had a Homeland Security Operative in the Durham area who had an excellent front as manager of a bookstore. His name is Giles Dikau. Giles had an English mother and a Russian father. He grew up in Moscow but received his education at the University of Oxford in England. He taught a Russian language class at Oxford upon graduation. Having gotten disillusioned with academic life at Oxford, he moved to the US to teach the Russian language at Duke University. He was recruited by Homeland Security to cover the area in which he lived, Durham, NC. He stopped teaching at Duke and took the job managing the local bookstore just as a cover and a place to meet other operatives. He became interested and then concerned with international security which decided him on becoming part of the solution to ever increasing global security issues.

When Cliff heard the name Giles Dikau, he realized that he was the manager of the bookstore Lane Cockerall owned in Durham. It occurred to him that with Pavel coming to the US, Giles would be the ideal person for

Pavel to hook up with. Pavel's cover for being in the US would be as Cliff and Brad's employee on assignment, staying with a Russian expatriate in Durham during a short stay. The fact that both men hailed from Moscow would add credibility to the cover story.

It was nearing the end of the academic year so that plans for the party were in full swing. Cliff picked up Pavel at the Raleigh Durham Airport and brought him to Giles Dikau's apartment, giving further credence to the fiction that Pavel was here on assignment for Cliff and Brad. When Giles opened the door to his apartment, Pavel was taken completely by surprise, expecting to view a dull academic with balding hair and a paunch. Instead Giles looked like a model for "Out" magazine.

"Hello, Giles. I'm Cliff Bradshaw and this is Pavel Jakov."

"Yes, Cliff, I've been expecting you and Pavel. Please come in." They shake hands and Giles precedes them into the living room. Pavel follows right behind Giles and is overwhelmed with the surfeit of riches to be observed. Giles is about 38 years old, 5'-11" tall with curly salt and pepper hair, possessing a swimmers body. While slim, his body is choice given the ample shoulders, narrow waist and buns that swimming honed to perfection. His graceful walk boasted a pair of legs that Pavel wanted to wrap around his neck. He possessed that faraway look that academics often had but when he smiled as he did when greeting them, his face lit up, animating his handsome angular Slavic face.

"Can I offer you something, tea, coffee or a diet soda?" Giles said as he motioned his guests to sit on the sofa.

"Tea would be good, Giles," said Cliff. "For me as well," Pavel chimed in, anxious to be seated to conceal his emerging hard-on.

Shortly thereafter the tea tray came out along with some homemade chocolate chip cookies. "Don't tell me you made these yourself, Giles?!" said Cliff.

"Certainly, Cliff. The cookies available at the local supermarket are inedible. Eating cookies with my afternoon tea is a vice I've become addicted to. Hope both of you will like them."

Pavel took a bite and said, looking directly at Giles, "I'm in love," in Russian. His double meaning was not lost on Giles whose lips turned up at the corners. Cliff agreed on the assessment of the cookies.

"Homeland Security thanks you for providing cover and lodging for Pavel while he's here in Durham, Giles. His assignment is of great importance and your assistance will be very valuable."

"Whatever I can do to contribute to the success of his mission will be done, Cliff."

"We know that very well, Giles, but I really must go now because I have a meeting with Lane Cockerall before heading home. Good luck to you both." Cliff shakes Giles hand before being shown out of the apartment.

"It seems we'll have a bit of a wait until the Miss Uranus makes her way north, Pavel."

"Soon I'll be getting a call. The Coast Guard has been tracking the movement of Sir Malcolm's yacht as it makes its way up the eastern seaboard."

"There's been news reports of a storm brewing in the Caribbean, Pavel. That may require Sir Malcolm to put ashore somewhere on his way here," said Giles.

"So I've been told. It's expected that he would likely head to Bermuda to avoid the worst of the storm. Bermuda, being a British Overseas Territory, is a place where he's known and would be a safe place for him to wait out the storm."

"What do you need to be doing in the meantime, Pavel? Has Homeland Security provided you any assets near the Yacht Club here in North Carolina where Sir Malcolm is planning on tying up his yacht?"

"Cliff is just putting a plan in place. What he hopes to do is get permission from Lane Cockerall's neighbor, Dickson O'Toole, to use his sailboat, docked at The Olde Towne Yacht Club in Beaufort, as a base of operation to pull off the sting. They'd move O'Toole's boat from its usual slip to one more remote. They'd make the adjacent slip available to Sir Malcolm when he puts in at the Yacht Club. I'd conceal myself aboard O'Toole's boat, called the 'Wayfarer II', a 68' custom ketch. This way I can keep an eye on Sir Malcolm's yacht and maybe steal aboard to take a look around when the opportunity presents itself."

"You're not planning to be aboard the Wayfarer alone surely?! You'd never be able to show your face for fear of being recognized."

"Hopefully I can stay concealed so that no one will be aware of my presence."

"That could prove difficult if not impossible if you are there for any length of time. Someone unknown to Malcolm and his crew should be on board with you so that they don't begin to question if someone's on the Wayfarer and become suspicious."

"That may well be but the Homeland Security operatives assigned to this mission have been directed to observe from a safe distance. If I need backup, I'll just have to call it in."

"My job at Lane's bookstore doesn't require me to be there every day. We have several part-time workers who handle the day to day in keeping the store open. So I can be dispensed with for however long it's required of us to be aboard the Wayfarer."

"No way, Giles, you're not a field operative who's used to the dangers involved in a covert operation like this. It's too dangerous!"

"Bull-shit, Pavel! You're stuck with me. I'm not letting you out of my sight."

"Why the sudden concern, Giles. You hardly know me. What's it to you if something happens to me."

"Don't feign ignorance, Pavel. Yes we've only just met but there's something between us that can't be denied. Would you deny it?"

"You must realize, Giles, that I have a past which might give you pause. My conduct has not always been exemplary, to say the least."

"That's of little concern to me, Pavel. Who you are now is what I care about. It has been said that I'm a good judge of character."

"What if I told you that I've sold my body like a common whore?"

"An experience like that must have been very demeaning, Pavel. Is it the lifestyle you'd choose for yourself at this point in time?"

"Hardly, Giles. That phase of my life is over, remaining only as a bad memory, hopefully to be forgotten."

"Then let me help you forget. Let me love you for who you are." Giles moved to embrace Pavel who didn't shy away. Unused to tenderness from anyone, Pavel was surprised to find himself capable of responding and acting in kind. In the past, he'd be headed into the bedroom for a quick romp but this time it was different. He savored being held while Giles poured out his affection. Pavel began to feel emotions he'd long thought were denied to him. "You're scaring me a little, Giles."

"You're feeling exposed and vulnerable, Pavel. That's the price we all pay in allowing ourselves to get involved with someone. Don't fight me, just let it happen." Pavel relaxed and allowed intimacy to begin.

Giles leads Pavel over to the sofa where they sit arm in arm. "You know, Pavel, I'm in the mood to cook now that I have someone I want to please. Why don't you unpack and get yourself comfortable while I get things started in the kitchen."

Wanting to make something that reminded Pavel of home, Giles made his mother's Chicken Ketletki with sour cream, and to go with it he made her Baked Pirohi. For dessert they'd have a Baba Romovaya cake that he'd bought the day before.

When Pavel returned from the guest bedroom, he came into the kitchen, fascinated with domesticity he was so unused to. The aromas reminded him of his youth in Moscow. Coming up behind Giles who was standing at the range, he wrapped his arms around him and gave him a chaste kiss on the neck.

"Umm, that's nice, Pavel. Makes the cook content to slave over a hot stove."

"The cook is lucky not to be ravaged where he stands. The guest is wise enough to bank his fires so not to distract the cook from what's obviously going to be a taste delight."

"That is indeed a compliment to the cook, Pavel, given your revelations involving your — shall we say — sexual prowess."

"It's obvious that with my foolish admission, I've given you ammunition to throw at me whenever we have an argument."

"Quite to the contrary, Pavel, my hope is that your unsavory past will insure that our bed will always be a source of wonder and excitement."

Just then Pavel's cell phone rings. Flipping the phone open, Pavel answers it. "Yes, this is Pavel."

"We're calling to alert you that the storm coming up from the Caribbean has been downgraded to a category 2 but it's still packing a wallop. The Miss Uranus will likely remain there in Bermuda for at least a few more days."

"Good, that will give us a little more time to set things up on this end." They ring off.

"What's up, Pavel?"

"The storm coming up from the Caribbean has been downgraded to a category 2 which would still keep Sir Malcolm's yacht tied up in Bermuda for a few more days, giving us more time to set the stage here for his arrival."

"So what's the plan? When do we leave for The Old Towne Yacht Club?"

"First thing tomorrow morning. Dickson O'Toole had given his permission for his sailboat to be moved to the remote slip we've requested. The move will have taken place this afternoon. The people who need to know at the Yacht Club and our Homeland Security operatives are expecting us to show up tomorrow morning. When I spoke to them from the bedroom, I prepared them for the fact that there'd be two of us staying aboard the Wayfarer."

"Good, then we're all set to go in the morning. We'll go to bed early and get a good night's rest," said Giles.

"Do you think I'm that easy that you can just order me into bed?"

"You, babe, will be sleeping in the guest room alone. What do I look like, a one night stand?" said Giles with a smile.

"Here I was thinking you were plying me with food so you could have your way with me."

"When the time is right, we'll know it, Pavel. The first time should be special."

"Here I am with all the experience and you're teaching me. Don't you see some irony in that?"

"No, you just need a little reprogramming, that's all. It's going to be a little more work, of a different kind, in being with me. Don't suppose it's easy for me to keep my hands off you. But I want the whole of you engaged not just your groin."

"Ok, you're off the hook for now, Giles, but my new found patience can't be depended upon to last long. So beware when the beast is finally released. You'll be responsible for the pent up demand turning me into an animal."

"How you talk, lover! What makes you think you won't get as much in return. No, babe, when it happens, you are going to know what it's like to be bedded by a man who won't be satisfied with anything less than the whole you. There will be no hiding behind a facade of disengaged control."

"Why don't I feel safer being forewarned? Maybe I won't be up to your standards, Giles. This is all very new for me."

"And for me, Pavel, but I'm going on instinct. You are the man I've been waiting for. Now make yourself useful and set the table. The cook must concentrate on his creations."

The dinner was all that could be hoped for. Pavel and Giles fell into easy conversation, filling in more of the blanks in their knowledge of each other. They did indeed go to bed early and slept soundly in separate bedrooms.

Early the next morning, they left in Giles's trusty old Land Rover to make the long drive to the shore. After picking up some provisions on the way, they arrived in Beaufort and found their way to The Olde Towne Yacht Club. Once there, they were directed to the slip where the Wayfarer had been moved. The Wayfarer II was a handsome custom ketch that required deep pockets to own and maintain.

"Since we're going to be stuck here for a few days, at least we won't be relegated to minimal accommodations. The Wayfarer is a beauty," said Giles.

"Guess it will do. Let's stow our gear so we can get familiar with her layout. We'd best know every inch so when the Miss Uranus ties up next to us, we'll be totally aware of where everything is, down to the light switches," said Pavel.

The afternoon passed as they took an in depth tour around the ketch, observing every detail so that if they were observed by anyone aboard Sir Malcolm's yacht, they'd appear to belong on the sailboat. As the sun began to go down, they sat out on the aft deck to enjoy their vodka and tonics. "If we had the requisite bucks, Pavel, this wouldn't be the worst way to pass ones down time."

"With the right crew, we could lay back and relax without a care in the world. Maybe in another lifetime, Giles, because in this one we don't have a pot to pee in."

"Speak for yourself, Pavel. When my parents died in a train crash in a village northwest of Moscow a couple of years ago, I inherited a not insignificant amount of money."

"So, as well as being cute and a potentially good lay, you're a good catch too?! My luck is certainly changing."

"You're lucky I like your fresh mouth, Pavel. Let's go into the salon. We can sit together on that wonderful built-in banquette before I whip up some dinner in the galley kitchen."

"Thought you'd never ask, babe. I was beginning to think you were a cock teaser."

Once inside, they set down their drinks and together fell into the corner of the L-shaped banquette. "All day long I've waited for this moment when we could forget about the waiting game, Pavel. Now it's time I got acquainted with every square inch of your body." Pavel removes his sneakers before Giles is allowed to unbuckle his belt and pull off his jeans. "Ah, Calvin Klein briefs! Nice but they're coming off too."

For Pavel, it's erotic to be pantless while Giles is fully dressed. Giles hands roam over his thighs before brushing over Pavel's rising phallus. "Nice piece of meat, Pavel." Getting on his knees, Giles raises Pavel's legs so they're bent at the knee with his feet resting on the edge of the seat cushions. "Been looking forward to this appetizer before dinner, Pavel."

Nibbling and kissing the inside of Pavel's thighs, Giles works his way to Pavel's crotch to begin sucking on his balls. Pavel's prick begins bouncing against his stomach. Giles slow and deliberate servicing was unlike the frantic sex Pavel was accustomed to. Now moving on to his cock, Giles laved the shaft until his tongue reached the head. Using the tip of his tongue, he darted it in and out of the piss slit and under the head where it met the shaft. Pavel was putty in his hands, not used to being cherished in this way.

When Giles finally took the head into his mouth, sucking on it while grasping the shaft, Pavel almost shot his load. But Giles, attuned to Pavel's every reaction, backed off until Pavel was back under some control. Seizing the opportunity, Giles went down on Pavel, swallowing his entire prick and holding it in his mouth as he gazed into Pavel's eyes, signaling his ownership and possession. Pavel began to understand what it meant to be taken. Giles proceeded to feed on Pavel's cock that he'd, up until then, denied himself. To Pavel, his cock felt like the center of his being.

Again sensing that Pavel was getting too close, Giles backed off. Pavel looked bereft to have Giles's hot mouth removed from his dick. Standing up, Giles slowly shed his clothes in an erotic torture that inflamed Pavel even more. From his jeans pocket, Giles removed a condom and a small tube of lube. In slow motion, he rolled on the condom. Pavel wanted him in a way he never wanted anybody. Giles got back down on his knees to grab Pavel's legs and raised them high so his shapely glutes hung down while separating enough to expose the pink portal.

Having carefully orchestrated Pavel's surrender, Giles restraint was at an end. He dove between Pavel's legs and ate him out in an all-out assault. Pavel was squealing like an uninitiated virgin. Coming up for air, Giles said, "Put your hands behind your knees, Pavel and bring your legs alongside your face." While Pavel complied, Giles lubed up his prick and then Pavel's gaping orifice. "Let me hear you ask me for it, Pavel! I want to know how badly you want it."

"It's you I want, Giles. What I've had before was just sex. When you enter me, we'll no longer be free agents. Is that what you want?!"

"You finally got the picture, babe. Yes of course it's what I want and now, knowing it's what you want, get ready to take your first fucking by your lover." Falling on the seat cushions with his hands outstretched and thrusting back his legs, Giles mounts his lover and enters him forcefully for the first time. "Oh, Christ, Pavel, that's beyond anything — "

Pavel grabs his lover's bubble butt and holds him fast, feeling one with him. "Your prick feels so amazing, Giles. I'm never going to get enough of it."

"Hang on, babe; I want you so much that I feel like a monk coming out of the closet." Giles arches his back and begins bumping and grinding Pavel's raised mounds, plundering his asshole as if he were a virgin novice in a monastic order. "Oh, honey, oh Pavel! Your pussy is the best — "

"Fuck me, Giles! Yes, screw me! Look into my eyes. I want to see your eyes when you lose all control and come inside me. Then I'll know there's no one else for you but me."

Seized by a desire unknown to him, Giles ravages his lover in a totally out of control ramming of his inflamed buttocks. The mind numbing fuck culminated when Giles's cock fired volley after volley of hot cum into Pavel as Giles screamed his lover's name. "Pavelllllllllllll!!!"

Pavel's battered prostate caused his pulsating cock to ignite, sending arching sprays of cum splattering over both of them. Ignoring the mess, Giles fell on top of his lover as they both came down from a life altering high. When their breath approached something like normal, Pavel said, "We need to take a quick shower, babe. And before you start dinner, I have something else in mind."

After showering, Pavel drags Giles into the Master Cabin where the tables are turned. Giles buried his face in the pillows on the bed while Pavel proceeded to demonstrate his skills as a dominant top. Giles spread his legs and popped his luscious buns in the air making clear that his ass was available for plunder anytime Pavel wanted it. Pavel took full advantage. Compatibility in bed with this couple would never be an issue. "Pavel sweetheart that was too good. Before we go to sleep tonight, I want to get on my back for you while you let loose and screw my ass again."

"You've got it babe. And I want to fall asleep tonight with your prick up my ass after you've pumped me full of your cum again."

The next morning, Pavel received another call from the Coast Guard to say that the Miss Uranus was on the way and would arrive the next day by late afternoon. The added time they now would have alone on the sailboat gave them the opportunity to have what amounted to a honeymoon, leaving the Master Cabin only for food, drink and bathroom visits. There were few positions that went unexplored while having sex with each other. To have called them insatiable would have been an understatement.

———————————

Back in Durham, Maxim and Ivan received their degrees from Duke. Maxim graduated magna cum laude and Ivan cum laude. Both were moved by the fact that Ivan's father, Grigory Vasiliev, had made the trip from Moscow on his Gulfstream jet to be present at the ceremony. It was only after receiving their diplomas that Grigory made his presence known, taking them totally by surprise. Grigory had already been received at Morehead by Lane and Gray who invited him to stay in the main house with them. They attended the graduation with Grigory. Viktor Sidorov and Eric Holtz came over on Grigory's plane along with Bruno Jahn and Denis Giraud. Also on board the plane was Yuri Markov and Olga Kuznetsov. Everyone who flew over on Grigory's plane was put up in Lane and Gray's guest house except Grigory.

Cliff and Brad were driving down from their cabin with Tommy Brandon, Hector Rios and Cole Strong. Marc Berger and his wife Debbie drove down with Jason Stone, Director of Homeland Security and Clarence Sharkey, the physical fitness guru at the Homeland Security offices. They too would stay in the main house at Morehead.

Jebediah Stuart and Brent Hitchcock would stay together on the third floor of Morehead on the night of the party. Abby Stuart, Jeb's former wife, would also attend the party with her fiancée, Dickson O'Toole, Lane and Gray's neighbor. It was Thursday night when Cliff and Brad arrived at Morehead. The party was to take place Saturday afternoon. It wasn't long after Cliff and his party settled into their rooms that Cliff got a call on his cell phone from the Commander of the Coast Guard Cutter, the Bayberry. Commander Ted Kirk informed Cliff of an evolving situation in the covert operation taking place at The Olde Towne Yacht Club.

It seemed that a Giles Dikau had called the Fort Macon Coast Guard Station to request a pursuit of the yacht called the Miss Uranus. Pavel Jakov and Giles Dikau were known to be aboard the Wayfarer, tied up alongside the Miss Uranus at the yacht club. According to Giles's panicked phone call that Commander Kirk received, Giles had left the Wayfarer and the marina briefly to buy some food items only to find that the Miss Uranus was no longer at the dock when he returned. After a thorough search of the Wayfarer, Giles realized that Pavel Jakov was missing. Giles felt certain that Pavel's disappearance coincided with the Miss Uranus's departure. It all happened so quickly that the Homeland Security operatives who were observing the dock from a safe distance hadn't realized what was happening.

Commander Kirk was about to put his cutter out to sea in pursuit of Sir Malcolm's yacht. Cliff said he'd be down to the Fort Macon Coast Guard area as soon as he could get a military helicopter from Fort Bragg to overfly the area in which the search for the Miss Uranus was to take place. Cliff immediately phoned an old navy buddy of his who was now a helicopter pilot at Fort Bragg, a Sergeant Major Tim Spencer. Cliff explains the situation to Tim and calls in a favor to enlist Tim's support in going on this special mission.

"For you buddy, no problem, said Tim, "But I'd ask you to have your boss, Jason Stone, call my boss in order for me to get immediate clearance."

"Consider it done, Timmy. How soon can you get here? I'm in Durham on an estate called Morehead." Cliff gives all the particulars.

"You get Mr. Stone to make that call; I could be ready for takeoff inside an hour. Won't take me long to pick you up. Is there a good place for me to land on the grounds?"

"Yes my host was a former Senator and had a helipad installed for when he needed to get back to Washington in a hurry. You can't miss it on the grounds west of the house, next to the swimming pool."

"Ok, buddy, if all goes well I'll be there in about an hour to an hour and a half."

"Great, I owe you, Timmy! I'll be waiting for you by the helipad." They ring off.

Sergeant Major Tim Spencer made it to the helipad at Morehead in just over an hour, landing his Super Cobra helicopter quickly, picking up his old buddy, Cliff Bradshaw and taking off immediately to rendezvous with the Coast Guard cutter, Bayberry, in pursuit of Sir Malcolm's yacht. Sergeant Major Spencer is in his late thirties, 6'-1" tall with light brown hair and has the look of a football hero, once having played that game in college. "Great seeing you, Cliff. It's been too long. How the hell are you?"

"Doin' good, real good. Only working part-time for Homeland Security now. Got my own business with a partner. We've got a private security business going called CYTEK."

"Hell, you paid your dues taking on so many dangerous missions all over the place. Time you settled down."

"Ya, you said it. How about you? How's Angie and the kids?"

"Well, not so good. We split up about six months ago. The divorce will be final in a couple of weeks."

"That's tough, Tim. I'm sorry."

"Don't be. It's probably the best thing for both of us. We're still friends but you know — that's it."

Cliff's cell phone rings. When Cliff answers it, he finds Commander Kirk of the Bayberry on the line. "Hey, Cliff, Ted Kirk here. We've picked up the location of the Miss Uranus on our GPS and will be boarding her in about 15 minutes. Let me give you her approximate position so you can head directly there. Where are you now?"

"We're aboard a helicopter heading your way. Should arrive at the rendezvous point just after you."

"We have intelligence that the Miss Uranus has a helipad on its uppermost deck. Seems the owner, Sir Malcolm Howard, had it installed in case he experienced a medical emergency."

"Very foresighted of Sir Malcolm, Ted, and most convenient for us. I didn't relish being lowered down to the deck from a hovering helicopter."

"Once we've boarded her, we'll take a quick look around in an effort to find this Pavel Jakov who has gone missing."

"There are a lot of places to hide someone on a boat, Ted, so don't be surprised if you come up dry."

"We'll give it our best shot and then you can do an in-depth search."

"Fair enough, see you shortly." They ring off.

"So what do you think, Cliff, we gonna find this Pavel guy or what?"

"My guess is that he's well hidden but what Sir Malcolm doesn't know is that one of the crew is a pal of Jakov's. And guess what. I know who he is. So we've got an edge."

Soon the Super Cobra is hovering over the Miss Uranus and Sergeant Major Tim Spencer expertly lands the small helicopter on the yacht's uppermost deck. Commander Kirk and his men have rounded up everyone aboard in the ship's salon. No one would admit that they had any knowledge of a kidnapped prisoner aboard the yacht. When Cliff exited the helicopter and joined the group in the salon, he sought out the individual that Pavel had described to him.

"We questioned everyone aboard, Cliff. It appears that no one saw a man being forced aboard this yacht. A quick look around produced no results."

"Frankly, Ted, I'm not surprised. Please take Sir Malcolm and Captain Bart to the Master Cabin so I can speak to the crew without their presence." Cliff reads the riot act to the crew, threatening them with being accessories to kidnapping and complicit in smuggling drugs. They gave it up without any pretense of a struggle.

While several of Commander Kirk's crew accompanied members of the yacht's crew to the ingenious hiding places where the drugs were sequestered, Cliff got Pavel's pal aside to get him to divulge where Pavel might have been taken. "All I know is someone was brought aboard when we were tied up at The Olde Towne Yacht Club. I didn't see who it was"

"Are you sure it wasn't Pavel Jakov?" Cliff asked.

"No way of telling. From what I could find out, he was brought aboard and taken below immediately. A buddy of mine was working in the engine room at the time and said that Sir Malcolm and Captain Bart sent him up to the Master Cabin to fix the toilet. When he returned to the engine room, they were gone. He thought something was funny but he couldn't figure out what it was."

"Are you familiar with the engine room?!" Cliff asked.

"Yeah, sort of. I help out with the maintenance there sometimes."

"Come on then. I need you to help me look around to see if anything looks amiss." They go down to the engine room. Nothing jumps out as suggesting a hiding place until Cliff asks about a small door at the end of the engine room. "What the hell is this door?!"

"That's just a workshop for the yacht engineer. I've never been in there."

"What the fuck! This door is locked," said Cliff exasperated. Look, guy, go up to the salon and get the key from the engineer pronto!"

While waiting for the crew member to get back, Cliff listens at the door to see if he can hear anything. He thinks he can hear something clanging like metal banging against a pipe. Key in hand, the crew member returns. Cliff directs him to unlock the door. When entering the tiny room, Cliff finds Pavel bound and gagged, lying on the floor. Cliff rips the tape from Pavel's mouth to ask, "Are you ok, Pavel?!"

"Could be better but I'm grateful to be alive. Untie me please. I thought no one would ever hear me banging my belt buckle against that pipe. It's fucking claustrophobic down here and hot as hell." Once untied, he gives his pal Mishka a big hug and a kiss, not altogether chaste. Cliff received the same, as well as having his ass cheeks cupped.

"Does even being tied up make you horny, Pavel? Give it a rest," said Cliff smiling.

"Come on, babes. Give me a break! Thought it was over for me. How would you feel?!"

"About the same I expect. But save it for Giles. He's been beside himself since you disappeared. He feared the worst."

"Can't wait to see him, Cliff. He's the one you know. When Malcolm and Captain Bart dumped me down here, I thought my luck had run out."

"We have a helicopter waiting on the uppermost deck of this yacht to take you to Camp Lejeune where a Marine Corps doctor will look you over."

"Hell, Cliff, I just want to get back together with Giles."

"Not to worry, Pavel, Giles is headed to the party at Morehead where we'll be going right after you get the ok from the doctor." They hurry upstairs to board the helicopter. Cliff leaves them long enough to report Pavel's discovery to Commander Kirk. "We'll be on our way, Ted. Will you be headed to Fort Macon now?"

"Yes, Cliff, we've seized this yacht and it will be impounded at Fort Macon. Sir Malcolm Howard and Captain Bartholemew Wimble will be detained until we can arrange to have them extradited."

"Many thanks to you and your crew for making this a successful mission. Jason Stone will be very pleased. Good-bye, Ted."

"So long, Cliff. Next time I'm in Washington, I'll give you a call. Maybe we could take in a Redskins game together."

"Be great, Ted! Look forward to it."

CHAPTER 13

Cliff goes up to the waiting helicopter. Once aboard, Sergeant Major Tim Spencer powers up the helicopter and they take off. "How are you doing, Pavel?"

"Not so bad. Just got a bit of a pain in my arm when I hit the deck after being tossed into that maintenance room."

"That's why we want the doctor at Camp Lejeune to give you the once over. Won't take that long. He's expecting us."

After landing at Camp Lejeune, a Humvee ambulance came to collect Pavel and take him to the infirmary, leaving Cliff and Sergeant Major Spencer to wait in the helicopter. "So, Tim, you and Angie split. What have you been doing about finding yourself a new lady?"

"Not a hell of a lot. Been too bummed out to think much about it."

"When we were training to be SEALs together, out in Coronado, California, we used to spend some great weekends in San Diego."

"Yeah, I remember it well. When we couldn't find any willing dates, we'd head back to our motel and — "

"Did each other. Think maybe a buddy could give you a little lift right about now." Cliff proceeds to unzip Tim's pants and pulls out his cock and balls.

"Jesus, Cliff, someone might walk up to the helicopter!"

"We'll see them coming. Relax! You need a blow-job and I'm going to give you one to remember." Cliff suctions in Tim's cock head and lavs all around it. Tim's abstinence was obvious as he grabbed on to Cliff's head and worked his prick in and out of his mouth. "Easy, man, don't want to pop your cork too soon! Your dick needs some loving."

"Ok, Cliff, I'm so fucking horny it's killing me!"

"Sit back and relax. Let me service you slowly. Pavel won't be back anytime soon." Cliff sucks on each of Tim's balls, as Tim moans his pleasure. Precum pearls at the piss slit which Cliff laps up before inhaling Tim's rigid dick. Cliff knows Tim's prick well, having had him many times while in training for the SEALs.

"If Angie could suck cock half as well as you, Cliff, we'd still be together."

"What about all the times I slipped my dick up your ass, Timmy. You toss a mean fuck, man."

"Guess I am a little rusty, Cliff. Just been out of practice after getting married. And you're one of a very few men that ever appealed to me in that way."

Cliff masturbates Tim while he explores his mouth with his tongue. "You taste good, Timmy. I forgot how good you taste. But now I want some more of your prick." Cliff drops his head down to start seriously sucking Tim's engorged cock. Tim's head falls back and his eyes roll up in their sockets.

"Cliff, oh Cliff, your mouth feels incredible. Suck me, yes, suck me!! Tim's cock rams the back of Cliff's throat as Cliff suctions the pulsing shaft with expert precision. With his hands laced through Cliff's hair, Tim arches his back and plows Cliff's mouth feverishly as his orgasm builds to an explosive force. Screaming at the top of his lungs in the enclosed cabin of the helicopter, Tim unleashes a mind numbing orgasm, filling Cliff's mouth and throat with copious amounts of roiling cum. Cliff manages to swallow every drop, saving Tim the embarrassment of having his uniform soiled around his fly.

"Umm good, Timmy. Nice to suck off a guy who's gone without for so long. That was one hell of a load."

"Wow, Cliffy, you sucked me dry, I swear!"

"No, I suspect you've got more reserves, given how long you were willing to keep it in your pants. But it will have to wait because the Humvee is returning with Pavel." Tim hastily puts his privates back into his pants and zips up. Pavel clambers aboard as the Humvee drives off.

"So, Pavel, seems like you had something broken after all," said Cliff, observing the sling on Pavel's arm.

"Yeah, damn! Seems I broke my arm when I hit the deck in the maintenance room. Not a serious fracture. Should heal up soon enough."

"Well that's not too bad considering what they probably had in mind for you. Time to get away from here. What do you say, Tim. Let's head for Morehead! We could do with a party."

"Can only stay for a short time, Cliff, and I won't be able to drink anything while still on duty." Tim powers up the helicopter and they're aloft shortly after.

It's only a relatively short flight to Morehead. Cliff phoned ahead to let Brad know when they'd be touching down. As Tim landed the helicopter on the helipad next to the swimming pool, Brad and Giles came running out of the pool house even before the rotor blades stopped spinning.

Cliff hopped out of the helicopter first so as to help Pavel down to the pad, just as Giles came up to embrace him and lead him away from the helicopter. They walked arm in arm back towards the house. Giles saluted a thanks to Cliff as they moved away.

Tim shut down the helicopter and exited to find Cliff and Brad in an intimate embrace. Cliff released himself from Brad's grip to introduce Tim to Brad. "Timmy, Brad and I are partners in business and — in life." Tim and Brad shake hands first before Brad gives Tim a bear hug.

"Thanks for bringing Cliff home to me." Come on in the pool house, guys, we brought out a few party refreshments we scrounged out of the kitchen."

In the pool house's sitting/dining room area, Brad had set out a selection of hors d'oeuvres and some soft drinks. "Help yourselves, guys; you must be hungry from all that air/sea rescue stuff." Tim and Cliff realize that they're ravenously hungry and devour the exquisite hors d'oeuvres that

Abby Stuart prepared. "So, Tim, bet you could use a shower before you return to base," said Brad.

"Yeah and it would help to revive me for the flight back to Fort Bragg."

"Let me show you the massage room. I'll give you a rubdown that will be sure to get your juices flowing." Brad opens the door to the massage room only to see a pair of bodies in a 69 position on the massage table. Quickly recovering from the shock of seeing the two thus engaged, Brad realized that he was viewing Grigory Vasiliev and Clarence Sharkey getting it on. Closing the door quickly, Brad said, "Seems the room is otherwise occupied but we can go over to the women's massage room instead."

"This looks as good as any health club's facilities I've ever seen, Brad," said Tim.

"Lane and Gray, our hosts, spared no expense when they built this place. Let's go on through to the shower room. There won't be any women using these facilities today." Brad throws Tim and Cliff towels as they enter the locker room to undress before showering. The women's shower room features large individual showers, complete with opaque glass doors.

Tim, eyes closed, was enjoying the gentle spray from the oversized shower head as well as the numerous body sprays when he thought he heard the glass door to the shower open.

"You enjoying that body spray up your ass, Timmy? Because I think I have something you'd consider an improvement." Cliff moves up against Tim with his fully erect cock exploring Tim's crack.

"It's been a long time, Cliff. As I remember, your big dick isn't for beginners."

"It's like riding a bicycle again, Timmy. You can take me, no problem. You just have to get into the mood." That said, Cliff begins kissing the back of Tim's neck while squeezing his dime size nipples. Tim's cock springs to life. Taking the shampoo in hand, Cliff moistens his fingers to start lubing his and Tim's cock. "That feel good, Timmy?"

"Hell yes, Cliff. You always knew how to push my buttons."

"How would you like my big cock stuffed up your ass, Timmy?" said Cliff, as he began jerking him off.

Tim bent over and grabbed his ankles. "Eat me, Cliff. I want to feel your tongue up my ass again."

Falling to his knees, Cliff grabbed fistfuls of Tim's high round butt cheeks and spread them apart to gain access to the tight knot of pleasure. Being asshole buddies from way back, Cliff unerringly laved and lapped the reluctant gateway to gain entrance to the succulent channel. Cliff then darted his tongue in and out before suctioning the hole to loosen the sphincter. Tim's anus was now winking in open invitation to its defilement.

Raising himself up to a standing position, Cliff grabbed the shampoo again so as to liberally lubricate Tim's dormant pussy. "Well, Timmy, time for the main event. You ready?"

"Hell yeah, Cliffy, bang your old boyfriend like you bang Brad. Screw me like you do your lover. Show me no mercy!"

"Timmy, remember you asked for it because I want you real bad. This won't be like in the motels in San Diego. You're going to take a deep screwing like a Hollywood hustler getting paid big bucks."

"Shit yeah! Do it Cliff! I need to feel — desirable — again."

Restraining himself from driving his prick to the hilt as he can do with Brad, Cliff eases his cock inside Tim and slowly works his shaft forward until his groin is pressed against Tim's buns. "Yours is as tight a hole as I've had in a while, Tim, but you feel sooo good."

"It doesn't hurt at all, Cliff, so — please — fuck the shit out of me!!"

"Put your hands against the shower wall, Tim, to brace yourself because you're about to be plowed like a whore." True to his word, Cliff bucks his muscular ass backwards and forwards in a driving plunder of Tim's asshole. Tim's head bobs in concert with every thrust from Cliff's rioting dick.

"Yes, oh yes, Cliff, bang me! Make me feel like there's nobody else you want more."

As Cliff's groin smacks into Tim's creamy butt cheeks, his buns ripple with the violent impact. Tim's ass muscles intuitively clamp down on Cliff's ravaging cock, massaging it to respond with a fierce orgasm.

"Uuuggghhhrrr!!!" shouts Cliff as his prick fires intense storms of cum up his old boy friend's hungry ass. Pulling Tim to his feet while remaining inside him, Cliff jerks him off.

"Oh, Cliffffff!!!!" screams Tim, as he splatters cum all over the tiled walls of the shower. Tim's inner ass muscles clench down on Cliff's prick again, demanding a couple more squirts of cum.

"Man, Timmy, you really could give a whore a run for his money. You are one great piece of ass, guy!"

"Wow, I really needed that, Cliff. Is Brad going to be pissed that we were — in here so long?"

"Finish showering. We're about to find out. But to give you a clue, Brad is more likely to want equal time in banging your ass. Can you handle that?"

"After you've reacquainted me with the pleasures of getting it on with another man, I'm horny for more of the same."

Once out of the shower, they dry off and wrap their towels around their waists before joining Brad in the women's massage room. He's now wearing a tank top and shorts. "So, guys, feeling a little better? From the sounds I heard coming from the shower, I'd have to think so."

"Guilty as charged, honey. Tim has been — out of commission — for a little while what with the impending divorce. He just needed a little diversion. Think it might take both of us to satisfy his — itch."

"No shit, Tim! Well slip that towel off and get up on this table. You're about to get a SEAL style rubdown, babe." Tim complies, displaying, in the process, his finely honed physique that he's worked on since his split with his wife Angie.

"For an old married man, you're looking mighty fine, Tim. What's your secret?" asked Brad.

"Working off my misery at the gym I guess. Had gotten a little soft while I was married." Tim was now stretched out on the table.

Brad's eyes roved over the prone body and took in the feast that was about to be consumed. "Let's loosen up those tight muscles a little more, Tim." Brad's hands worked their magic in kneading, poking and prodding Tim's magnificent body. Tim was literally purring his approval.

"Well, buddy, something tells me you owe me one after spending time in the shower with my Cliff."

"Hope you didn't mind my borrowing him. It had been a while since I was — taken."

"So what do you say? Did you get the taste for it back?"

"Big time, Brad. Cliff said you might like to have a go. If so, slip it to me. I'd like to be stud fucked again."

"You got it, guy! Now that Cliff has opened you up, you should be able to take me." Brad sheds his shorts, climbs up on the table and lies down on top of Tim, rubbing his prick along his crack.

"You know, Timmy, you used to do a fine job sucking my cock. How about it?" said Cliff as he stepped to the head of the massage table and dropped his towel.

Brad levered himself up so Tim could inch forward on the table to access Cliff's stiff jumping dick. In one swift move, Tim sucked in the whole cock. "Glad to see that your aptitude hasn't diminished, Tim. Suck it, babe!" Tim obviously enjoyed the task and fed greedily on Cliff's prick.

Brad rolled up a towel and raising Tim up, propped it under him, raising his ass mounds in preparation for their further plunder. After Cliff's servicing of Tim's asshole, Brad needed only a little saliva to enter the willing butt slave. Tim was now impaled from both ends and loving it.

Brad pounded Tim's ass, flattening the raised peaks with every crushing blow, allowing for the deepest penetration. Tim's hunger for Cliff's prick was increased every time he felt Brad's immense tool forced deep inside him. Like a finely tuned orchestra, they reached their climax simultaneously. As Cliff's copious orgasm ripped down Tim's throat, Brad's jism joined Cliff's earlier orgasm to flood Tim's colon with a great sea of cum.

When Cliff withdrew his prick from Tim's mouth, Tim said, "You two really know how to double team a guy. Wow! That makes up for so many months of abstinence."

"You're not done yet my friend," said Brad. "Turn over. Seems I'm in the mood to suck a little cock too." Casting aside the rolled towel, Brad goes to work on Tim's throbbing cock. Cliff leans over and French kisses Tim. Tim is toast in record time as Brad's head, pistoning down on Tim's vertical cock, sucks a massive load out of the helicopter pilot, seduced still again. "Will that hold you for a while my good buddy?" asked Brad.

"You've left me with barely enough strength to get dressed and fly that helicopter back to the base. When next I get up to Washington, I'm going to be sure to give you guys a call."

"You'll do more than give us a call," said Cliff. "We'll expect to see you at our townhouse where we'll put you up and put you through your paces again. Until you meet your next lady, you might as well not be celibate."

After Tim gets dressed, Cliff and Brad usher him back to the helicopter pad and bid him farewell until their next encounter in Washington. As Cliff and Brad head back to the house, they run into Grigory and Clarence coming out of the pool-house.

"Oh, Brad, I'm glad I caught you! Could I ask you please not to mention to Ivan or Maxim — what you — witnessed in the massage room."

"Mum's the word, Grigory! So how did you like a little American dark meat?" Grigory and Clarence glanced at each other, embarrassed.

"Actually, Brad, I liked it a lot. Clarence is going to spend his next vacation in Moscow with me, although we're not letting that be known just now. Jason Stone can be a bit — possessive."

"Your secret is safe with us. Come; let's get back to the house. We've been gone a long time. The party must be about to get started." Grigory and Clarence precede Cliff and Brad down the path towards the ballroom which comprises a whole wing of the large house.

Taking up the rear, Cliff and Brad amble slowly down the bluestone path, lined with privet hedges. "So, Brad, it seemed you really liked hitting on my old buddy Tim Spencer."

"He was ok but you're the only one for me, babe," Brad answered, with a sheepish smile.

"You'll get to prove it to me again tonight, Brad," Cliff said, as he ran his hands over Brad's buns, kneading them sensuously.

"Oh, baby, you fucking turn-on! You're always at your best when you return from one of your dangerous capers."

"After watching you bang my buddy Tim, my need to get into your ass increased tenfold, Brad. Don't know if I can last through this party before I reassert my claim on these butt mounds."

"This party isn't to be missed, Cliff, but never fear, you're going to get all you can handle when we climb into that four poster in our room tonight. Getting screwed in a four poster adds a little kink factor to our love making. Don't you think?"

Reaching the ballroom's exterior entrance, they go inside to see that the guests had already arrived and were milling around the opulent room, resplendent in gilded antique French paneling and a half dozen crystal chandeliers in a space that was easily 25 feet high. Pairs of French doors punctuated the long walls and accessed a balustraded bluestone terrace.

A rectangular table was set up, in front of the immense marble fireplace at the end of the room, overlooking the ballroom in which 4 large round tables were set up for groups of 6 people. The tables were draped in fine linen and each had a floral centerpiece with individual colors for each table.

There was a large ornate, double door entrance into the ballroom with a delicate fan window above. After guests passed through the entrance, they descended several white marble steps into the sunken ballroom which was richly surfaced in a walnut parquet floor. Centered on the large room just beyond the foot of the stairs was a bar set-up and a hors d'oeuvres table. The guests sipped wine and consumed hors d'oeuvres while mingling and seeking their names on place cards at the tables.

Abby Stuart, Debbie Berger and Olga Kuznetsov acted as hostesses, welcoming guests and making introductions. Abby was radiant in a cream silk gown, wearing her new diamond engagement ring. Her fiancée, Dicky O'Toole was chatting it up with Jason Stone. Dicky, a wealthy developer of shopping malls in the southeast was known to Jason Stone because of his generous donations to the Democratic Party. Also, being around a group of gay men didn't faze Dicky because, as it turns out, Dicky has a twin brother who is gay and a well-respected performer on Broadway.

Olga, being a consummate professional, had learned everyone's name in advance as well as a little bit about each of them. She moved around the room with ease making everyone feel at home. She looked splendid in a tulle gown in hot pink by Kira Plastinina.

Debbie Berger swished around in a daring sapphire blue, Donna Karan plunge dress with belt. Her voluptuous figure was displayed to advantage. She took particular pains to make the Moscow contingent feel welcome, especially enjoying the company of Olga's husband Yuri Markov who looked particularly handsome in a midnight blue, tailored, double breasted suit from Gottschalks in Moscow.

With a signal from Lane and Gray, the women asked the guests to be seated at their tables. Debbie and her husband Marc joined Lane and Gray at the head table, sitting to their right. Ivan and Maxim round out the group at the head table, sitting to Lane and Gray's left. Bearing trays aloft, 6 gorgeous waiters, dressed in tight black pants with matching vests, blue oxford, button-down shirts and paisley ties, ambled around. Champagne flutes were served to toast the honored guests at the head table.

Lane stood up and with a clink on his glass brought quiet to the room. "Gray and I are honored to be able to host this party to celebrate the accomplishments of our very dear friends seated here with us. To my left are Ivan Vasiliev and Maxim Bondar who have just graduated from Duke University with honors. Ivan will be starting his own law practice in Washington this fall. Maxim, I'm delighted to announce, will be joining the law firm that my partner Gray and I have begun, also in Washington. Please join us in giving them a round of applause." Lane sat down.

Gray got up and said, "It's now my great pleasure to announce that Marc Berger has had published his latest book, 'Crossover Spy II'. Please join us in giving him a round of applause." After the applause subsided, he said, "Now please raise your glasses in a toast to our honored guests." With a tinkling of glasses touching at each table, the happy couples drank the magnificent Dom Perignon champagne from Morehead's wine cellar. As Gray sat down, Marc Berger stood up to give his thanks to everyone, particularly Cliff Bradshaw who inspired the book, for coming and to say that he would be signing freshly printed copies that would be available at the entrance to the ballroom. Just then the 6 gorgeous waiters swept into the ballroom to serve the guests their fillet mignon steak dinners.

ABOUT THE AUTHOR

After enjoying a successful career in New York City at his chosen field, Buck Roberts turned his attention to what has given him so much pleasure over the years: books. Mysteries and spy novels are among his favorites but the men featured in them seem needlessly constrained by heterosexual sex. In this book, Buck suggests that by broadening their once limited sexual appetites, they can accomplish much more for their country. Buck writes his novels from his home in the Chelsea neighborhood of Manhattan.

CROSSOVER SPY
BUCK ROBERTS

ROBERTS

CROSSOVER SPY

A
BONER
BOOK